DENIAL

BY STUART M. KAMINSKY

Lew Fonesca Mysteries

Vengeance
Retribution
Midnight Pass
Denial

Abe Lieberman Mysteries

Lieberman's Folly
Lieberman's Choice
Lieberman's Day
Lieberman's Thief
Lieberman's Law
The Big Silence
Not Quite Kosher
The Last Dark Place

Toby Peters Mysteries

Bullet for a Star
Murder on the Yellow Brick Road
You Bet Your Life
The Howard Hughes Affair
Never Cross a Vampire
High Midnight
Catch a Falling Clown
He Done Her Wrong
The Fala Factor
Down for the Count
The Man Who Shot Lewis Vance
Smart Moves
Think Fast, Mr. Peters
Buried Caesars
Poor Butterfly
The Melting Clock
The Devil Met a Lady
Tomorrow Is Another Day
Dancing in the Dark
A Fatal Glass of Beer
A Few Minutes Past Midnight
To Catch a Spy
Mildred Pierced
Now You See It

Porfiry Rostnikov Novels

Death of a Dissident
Black Knight in Red Square
Red Chameleon
A Cold, Red Sunrise
A Fine Red Rain
Rostnikov's Vacation
The Man Who Walked Like a
     Bear
Death of a Russian Priest
Hard Currency
Blood and Rubles
Tarnished Icons
The Dog Who Bit a Policeman
Fall of a Cosmonaut
Murder on the Trans-Siberian
     Express

Nonseries Novels

When the Dark Man Calls
Exercise in Terror

Short Story Collections

Opening Shots
Hidden and Other Stories

Biographies

Don Siegel: Director
Clint Eastwood
John Huston, Maker of Magic
Coop: The Life and Legend of
     Gary Cooper

Other Nonfiction

American Film Genres
American Television Genres
     (with Jeffrey Mahan)
Basic Filmmaking
     (with Dana Hodgdon)
Writing for Television
     (with Mark Walker)

Stuart M. Kaminsky

DENIAL

A Lew Fonesca Mystery

A Tom Doherty Associates Book

NEW YORK

DENIAL

Copyright © 2005 by Stuart M. Kaminsky

This book is printed on acid-free paper.

A Forge Book
Published by Tom Doherty Associates, LLC
175 Fifth Avenue
New York, NY 10010

www.tor.com

Forge® is a registered trademark of Tom Doherty Associates, LLC.

ISBN 0-765-31165-8
EAN 978-0765-31165-8

First Edition: June 2005

Printed in the United States of America

0   9   8   7   6   5   4   3   2   1

To the memory of my cousin
Mark Kaminsky
with love

DENIAL

1

N⁰ A single word. No period. No exclamation mark needed. I wrote the word on the back of a yellow three-folded sheet with a black fine-point Sharpie pen.

The sheet had come to me in the mail, an invitation in a flood of typefaces, an invitation to take the Scotch tape off the attached key, hurry down to the Toyota dealer on Bee Ridge Road and drive home a new Tacoma if the key worked.

I took the Scotch tape off, dropped the key into the partly filled wastebasket next to my desk and slipped the sheet with that single word under the door of my office onto the sunlit landing outside.

Someone knocked. I didn't answer. My *No* answered any questions he or she might ask.

I turned, barefoot, looked around my office. Desk. A thick black-covered notebook the size of an old *Life* magazine on top of it. Two chairs. Walls empty now except for the book-cover size dark painting of a thick patch of Amazon jungle swirled in mist, with shadow, black mountain in the background with a single tiny dab of color, of a bird in flight above the trees.

I shuffled into the small room behind my office, the space in which I did what others referred to as living. Cot with blankets, a couple of pillows. Closet with few clothes neatly folded. Chair, wooden, with arms. Sitting on the chair was my slightly soiled Cubs baseball cap. At the foot of my cot were a dented portable dorm-size refrigerator piled not too high with things that could be eaten—protein bars, cereal, something made of tofu guaranteed to last a century without spoiling and promising no taste. Inside the refrigerator were three gallons of tap water in recycled plastic milk cartons. Next to the refrigerator, on a table with a tender leg, sat my television and VCR. My stacks of VHS tapes were piled neatly on the floor.

Thus was all my space taken.

Another knock. The visitor on my doorstep had taken his or her time to absorb the single word I had written. Or maybe he or she had been puzzling over the missing automobile key?

There was no mirror in the room, but if the blinds were open, which they were not, and the light was right, I could look at what I appeared to be, a slightly-less-than-average-size, thin, balding man with a two-day growth of beard. I was wearing an extra-large wrinkled gray T-shirt with the word VENICE in black written across the front. The left side of the bottom of the N in *Venice* was almost peeled off. I didn't feel like pulling it all the way. Let it hang.

I didn't know which Venice the shirt referred to, the one in Italy, where the sea will soon swoon over gondolas and

Stuart M. Kaminsky

turn the city into an Atlantis of the mind, a city less than a thousand miles from where my grandparents had been born; or maybe it was the Venice in California, where the curious tourists and teens and twenties and thirties go to look at the muscle builders, the transvestite roller skaters, the frantic badminton players, the fortune-tellers, the tattoo artists, the leftover flower children, no longer children, promising to tell their futures or pasts with cards, stones, leaves, bumps on the head. It was more likely the Venice less than twenty-five miles south of where I stood in my second-floor refuge in Sarasota, Florida.

I didn't really know. I had never been to any of the Venices, had only read about them. I had bought the shirt in the Women's Exchange Thrift Shop a few blocks away.

Let it rain. Let it pour. I didn't care anymore. I had those deep river blues. Doc Watson sang that. Catherine and I had an old album recorded at a bluegrass night at the University of Chicago. I had told my cousin Frank Cimaglia, who wore cowboy hats and boots and played the mandolin, to take all the albums.

Another knock at the door. No harder. There was persistence in the caller. He or she had my *No* and chose to ignore it.

I was wearing my blue sweatpants, frayed at the bottom. They weren't purchased at the Women's Exchange. I'd had them before I left Chicago more than four years ago. They had been among the clothes I had thrown together and into two suitcases, suitcases I dropped into the trunk of my car, which I then got into and drove heading south, moving away as far as highways would take me from the death of my wife in a hit-and-run accident.

She had been thirty-five. She had been a prosecuting attorney in the Cook County District Attorney's Office. I had been an investigator. Her name was Catherine. Until a year ago I couldn't speak her name aloud. I had driven till my car gave out in the driveway of a Dairy Queen on 301 Washington Street, in Sarasota. I had been vaguely on my way to Key West.

There had been a FOR RENT sign on the cracked-concrete two-story office building at the back of the parking lot. The metal outdoor railing of the building was rusting. The offices, dingy white doors in need of paint, faced onto the narrow landing.

I rented the two-room office, moved into it with my two suitcases, sold the car for two hundred dollars, and never got to Key West, at least not yet, probably never.

When the money began to run out, I drew on whatever remaining willpower I had and with references in hand got a process server's license and called on some law firms within walking distance.

I made enough to live on, to buy videotapes, eat at the DQ or Gwen's diner on the corner or the Crisp Dollar Bill, a bar across the street where it was always dark and the music was unpredictable.

If nirvana came up and held out its hand, I'd shake it and say I had been waiting for him or it or her. Until then I wanted to husband my grief, savor my depression. I had a right to it. Misery is not reserved for the righteous alone.

Another knock at the door. I sat on my cot and touched my scratchy face. Catherine liked to make Sunday-morning love when I hadn't shaved the night before.

It shouldn't be so bright and sunny and seventy degrees today. It was winter. On this day, I wanted, craved, gloom, cold or rain and solitude and was besieged by sun and visitors.

Another knock.

I had unplugged my phone.

"Lewis," came a voice from the other room, beyond the closed outer door.

Others had come. I hadn't bothered with the *No*. I had sat silently in darkness and dusty sunlight through the closed blinds. I had come to Sarasota to escape from intimacy, friendship and connection. But they had found me.

People had slowly come into my life.

Sally Porovsky, the social worker whose heart broke daily for the children she tried to help and the system too often failed; Flo Zink, the foul-mouthed recovering alcoholic with a pile of money left to her by her departed Gus; Flo, who had taken in Adele, the teenaged mother with an unerring ability to find but not sift troubled sands; Ames McKinney, the laconic lanky seventy-year-old motor-scooter-riding fugitive from a Wild West that had probably never existed; Dave, who owned the DQ franchise and spent as many hours as he could on his boat in the Gulf of Mexico welcoming the sun that turned him a mahogany nut wrinkled brown. They had all come to my door in the last few days. They had all given up when I didn't answer.

But the knocker this morning had been at it for almost fifteen minutes.

The first knock had awakened me from a sleep that had started in darkness. I thought it had come from the television set, which was quiet but running on AMC. Edward Everett Horton was looking at me with startled eyes. Or was he looking at Helen Broderick? Horton wasn't knocking on a door.

I had stumbled from bed, found the yellow sheet, pulled the Sharpie pen from my muddled desk drawer and made my only communication with the outside world in the last seventy-two hours.

I needed another few years of sleep. I needed to watch

Mark Stevens and Lucille Ball in *The Dark Corner* again. I needed to see anything before 1967 with Joan Crawford in it.

Knock.

"Lewis, open the door."

It was Ann Horowitz, my therapist. I had stumbled onto her a few years ago while serving papers. She had been called to testify about a patient who had tried, with less than half a heart, to kill himself. For some reason, Ann had thought me an interesting case and had taken me on for ten dollars a session. Ann and her husband had officially retired to Sarasota from New York a decade earlier, but at the age of eighty, Ann, a small, solid, always neatly dressed woman, was full of energy, curiosity, a love of history and an unending enthusiasm. She was my opposite. We were made for each other. She had a small office off Main Street across from Sarasota Bay.

Ann had gotten me to admit that I didn't want to give up my depression, that giving up my depression meant giving up my grief, my grief over Catherine. I guarded my grief. I had paid a high price for it. I wasn't ready to give it up, but I was willing to address it. Ann had gotten me to finally speak Catherine's name, to admit to small links to people in the present, links I resented but couldn't deny. I didn't want to invest in someone else who might be taken from me by age or accident or intent.

"Lewis," Ann said outside the door. "I've got coffee, biscotti, an open day till a late lunch with my visiting but not welcome cousin Rachel."

I didn't answer.

"I read your note," she said. "No does not always mean no. And sometimes, but not often, when you put that plastic key in the ignition, the car actually starts. Somewhere we are tickled with the fancy that the car might start this time."

Not me, I thought. Putting the key in the ignition meant you thought there existed a glimmer of hope. Putting the key in the trash basket meant you weren't going to be drawn into the game.

I paddled back into the office and opened the door. Sunlight and cool air closed my eyes. When I squinted at her, Ann held out a large paper cup with a plastic top. I took it and stepped back so she could come in.

When she was inside, I closed the door and she handed me a small white paper bag. I carried the coffee and the bag to my desk and sat. Ann sat across from me. She opened the lid of her coffee.

"You have a joke for me?" she asked, taking a sip of her coffee.

I owed her a joke, my assignment from our last session. I was collecting them, telling them to her, part of my therapy. I had not yet found any of the jokes funny.

I drank some coffee. It was warm. I pulled an almond biscotti out of the bag. It was crisp and firm. I shrugged.

"No joke? All right. I'll tell one. How many psychologists does it take to change a lightbulb?" she asked.

I shrugged again and considered dipping my biscotti. I had a vision of my grandfather doing this with biscotti made by my grandmother. I imagined crumbs wet from coffee dropping onto my grandparents' mottled Formica kitchen table.

"Just one," answered Ann, "but the lightbulb really has to be ready," she said. "Your turn."

"A new patient comes into the psychologist's office," I said. "The psychologist says, 'Tell me your problem, start at the beginning.' And the patient says, 'In the beginning, I created the heavens and the earth.'"

"It's hazelnut," Ann said. "The coffee."

I nodded and drank.

"You think we create our own heaven and earth?" she asked.

"It's a joke," I said.

"A joke is never just a joke," she said, pointing her biscotti at me.

"Freud," I said.

"Truth," she answered.

"Three people are dead."

I drank coffee, hesitated and dunked the biscotti. I knew I looked like my grandfather at that Formica table, beard and all.

"Can you be more specific or do you wish to talk about mortality in general and, if so, why focus on so small a number?"

"I don't want to talk," I said, working on my soggy biscotti.

"You let me in," she said.

"I let you in," I confirmed.

"Progress," she said with a smile of satisfaction.

"Look at me," I said.

She did.

"What do you see?"

"A man concerned with how he appears to someone else," she said. "Progress."

"Setback," I said. "Withdrawal."

I finished my biscotti, wiped my mouth with the sleeve of my Venice shirt and swirled the coffee, creamy brown, sugared.

"How long will it take?" she asked.

"Take?"

"To tell me about the three dead people."

"I don't know," I said. "It depends on where I start."

"In the beginning you created the heavens and the earth," she said.

Stuart M. Kaminsky

She reached into her canvas purse, pulled out her cell phone and punched in some numbers.

"Rachel," she said. "Can't make lunch unless you can hold out till three. . . . You will not be starving. You will probably not even be hungry. Find something in the fridge to tide you over. I'll call back when I'm ready."

She flipped the phone closed and returned it to her purse.

"You have my attention and a bonus," she said, removing another, smaller white paper bag and handing it to me.

I opened it. A chocolate chip cookie. A big one.

"Tell me about dead people," she said, folding her hands around her coffee cup.

So, I did . . .

2

IN THE BEGINNING I was an Episcopalian. At least that's what my family claimed to be though my mother was the only one I knew who ever went to church services. All our other relatives were Catholics. Some were good Italian Catholics, meaning not that they were necessarily good people but that they made the right moves, attended Mass, went to confession and crossed themselves.

I start my story this way because of how Dorothy Cgnozic, who called me that morning five days ago as I was headed toward the door, began the conversation.

"Mr. Fonseca?"

"Fonesca," I corrected her, as I had patiently corrected people over the slightly more than forty years of my life.

"Are you a Catholic?"

"No," I said.

There was a long pause on the line, a raspy breathing sound and then, "It can't be helped."

"Guess not," I said.

"You've been recommended. By Sterling Sparkman."

I had no idea who Sterling Sparkman might be.

"You met him here. Gave him some papers saying he had to go to court."

"Here?"

"Seaside Assisted Living," she said. "He said you were polite, talked to him for a while about Chicago, baseball, treated him as if he were alive."

"I remember," I said.

Sterling Sparkman's favorite Cubs of all time were Andy Pafko and Hank Sauer. My favorites had been Ernie Banks and Andre Dawson till the dawn of Sammy Sosa.

"He said I should call you," she said. "So I'm calling you."

"You want me to serve papers on someone?"

"No, I want you to find out who's been murdered," she said.

Her voice was definitely old, not strong but matter-of-fact, determined.

"Murdered?"

"That's right. Last night I saw one of the residents being murdered."

"Who?"

"Don't know. Didn't get a good look, but I'm sure. I was walking past the room, couldn't sleep, pushing my walker. Mine has the yellow tennis balls attached on the feet so they slide better, you know?"

"Yes."

"She was getting killed."

"Did you tell someone?"

"Went to the nursing station. Night nurse wasn't there."

"Maybe she was murdering the woman," I said.

"It's a thought, but the night nurse is Emmie, a small Negro woman with a gold tooth right over here and grandchildren though she is only forty-four years old. Yesterday was her first day here."

"Such people can commit murder," I said.

"She's too small."

"The killer was big?"

"Big," Dorothy Cgnozic said. "She, the new nurse, looked in the room where I told her the woman had been murdered, said there was no one in it. She didn't believe me."

"I'm sorry. . . ."

"I told the desk nurses in the morning," Dorothy went on. "They said no one had been murdered during the night. They are wrong."

"Who's missing?"

"I don't know everyone here. It's too big."

"I'll give you the name of a policeman you can talk to," I said. "You have a pencil and paper?"

"I have several pens and a pad, but I don't need them. The police will think I'm an old nut with a fuzzy brain. Come talk to me."

"I really don't—"

"I can pay," she said.

"It's not the money," I said.

"Sterling said you find people," she said.

"Yes. I'm a process server."

"Well, find the woman who was murdered," she said.

"And find whoever killed her?" I added.

"If you wish," she said. "I'm not crusading. I'm simply trying to prove that I am not a demented old woman. And

Stuart M. Kaminsky

I want to do something besides watching game shows and re-reading books from the library here that I've already read three times. Besides, murder is wrong."

"I'll try to stop by before noon."

"Come any time," she said. "I'm always here."

I hung up. The sky was clear with a few pillow-drifting clouds. The air was cool. I could bike to the Seaside Assisted Living Facility on Beneva south of Clark in about half an hour but I wouldn't have to.

I had been called the day before and asked to be at the office of Tycinker, Oliver and Schwartz, a law firm just off Palm Avenue. I regularly served papers for the partners. I assumed they had a job for me, maybe a summons or two. Two would be fine. I had some cash in a video box mixed in with my stack. I didn't need the money, but I couldn't turn down the request.

When I got to the office, parked my bike and chained it to the drainpipe next to the gray wooden sign that carried the name of the law firm, I thought I smelled gardenias. Catherine liked the smell of gardenias. Sometimes, like this moment, I smelled gardenias and wasn't even sure they were really there.

I had told Ann about smelling things that weren't there when I thought about Catherine. Ann thought it was either a healing compensatory delusion or I was getting migraine auras. I don't get headaches. My teeth are fluoride protected. I've never had surgery and the worst illness I've had was the flu. I was cursed with almost perfect health.

I was expected, nodded to by the secretaries, told to go into Richard Tycinker's office. Tycinker, solid, fifties, gray suit and colorful tie, sat behind his desk and shook his head as he looked at me. I was wearing my jeans, a washed-out white short-sleeved pullover with a collar and a little embossed koala bear on the pocket. Sitting in the chair across from Tycinker looking back over her shoulder at me was a woman who did not look impressed. I took off my Cubs cap.

"Miss Root, this is Mr. Fonesca," Tycinker said.

She nodded and smiled, a sad smile. I had the feeling that I was supposed to recognize her. She was lean, almost skinny, pretty face, not much makeup. Her eyes met and held mine.

"You know about Miss Root's son?" Tycinker asked solemnly. "Kyle?"

I remembered. Page three or four of the *Herald-Tribune* about a week ago. The article had said the boy was Nancy Root's son, but his name hadn't been Root.

"Kyle McClory," Tycinker said. "His father and Nancy are divorced."

Nancy Root was an actress. She appeared regularly at the Asolo Theater and Florida Studio Theater in St. Pete, around the state and from time to time in regional productions around the country. Her name popped into bold type frequently in Marjorie North's column. Once in a while she did a cabaret act, show tunes, ballads at the Ritz-Carlton. She had even had some small speaking roles in television shows like *Law & Order, Profiler, Without a Trace* and *Just Shoot Me.*

I had never seen her act or heard her sing. I had never gone to a play or a movie in Sarasota, seldom watched television and never been inside the Ritz-Carlton. The reviews always said she was good. It was a local given.

A hit-and-run driver on Eighth Street had killed Kyle McClory, fourteen, a student at Sarasota High School, half a block from Gillespie Park. Gillespie Park is a heavily Hispanic neighborhood just north of Fruitville, the street that marks the northern border of downtown Sarasota. The driver had driven away. One witness. I didn't remember who. I didn't have to ask if the driver had been found. I knew from the look on Nancy Root's face that he or she hadn't.

I could now place the look on the woman's face. It was the look of pain and no answers that I had seen in any mirror I looked into. I knew what was coming. I was the right person for it. I was the wrong person for it. I didn't want it, but I knew before the question was asked that I would do it.

"You want me to look for the person who killed your son?" I said.

"I want you to *find* the person who killed Kyle and drove away."

"The police," I said.

She shook her head and said firmly, "It's a case. On a list. In a file. They're 'looking.' That's what they tell me," she said. "Looking. I think they are. I just don't know how hard. I don't know what else they have to do. I don't know if they really care. I've spoken to the detective in charge of the investigation, a Detective Ransom. He expressed his sympathy, promised he would give Kyle's death the highest priority. He gave a very unconvincing performance. I want someone finding, looking full-time and finding. I want to know."

"I understand," I said.

"Nancy, Miss Root has been told that you've done an amazing job finding people for us," Tycinker said, brushing a hint of nothing from his lapel.

"I have a job I'm working on," I said, thinking about Dorothy Cgnozic and her night vision of murder.

"But you will do this?" she said.

"Coffee, Lewis?" Tycinker asked.

He wanted to catch my eye. He wanted his smile to remind me that I was on a small monthly retainer from his office and that I had access to the computer-hacking skills of Harvey, whose room was just down the hall. Tycinker and

Company were my bread-and-butter clients. I looked at him and shook my head yes, acknowledging the offer of both the coffee and the job.

"I'll get it," he said, moving toward the door.

He could have picked up the phone and had someone bring the coffee but either he or Nancy Root wanted Tycinker out of the room and so Tycinker was gone.

I sat in the chair next to Nancy Root. She looked at my face. I was uncomfortable and looked away, placing my cap on my lap.

"What can you tell me?" I asked.

"That my son is dead," she said. "That someone ran him down in the street, that there's a witness who thinks it was intentional, that the driver wanted to kill Kyle. I don't think the police believe him."

I asked more questions. She answered. Tycinker came back with coffee, which reminded me that I hadn't had anything to eat. He went back behind his desk, sat and listened, hands folded, lips pursed, head moving, turning toward whoever was talking.

Traffic whooshed gently by on Palm and I was aware of the passage of colors, yellow, red, black, blue, from people who had someplace to go.

We started with Nancy Root handing me an eight-by-ten color photograph of her son. It looked like it had been taken in his bedroom. There was a poster behind him on the wall of a dreadlocked black man in a soccer uniform about to kick a ball directly at the camera. His teeth were bared. The ball, the camera or whoever was looking at the photograph was his enemy.

Kyle looked like many teens, a little scrawny, mop of reddish hair, face like his mother's, teeth a little large. Good-looking kid. I turned my cap over and laid the photograph gently inside, face-up, so I could look down at it.

Stuart M. Kaminsky

Kyle had been a good student at Sarasota High. Not a great student, but a good one, his mother said. Played soccer, hoped to be a starter the next season, had there been another season for him. Liked science.

I could also tell he liked video games, the new kind with people scoring points for how many prostitutes and men in turbans they kill. She didn't tell me that. I could see the boxes on the table behind the kid in the photograph in my lap.

She told me Kyle had a few friends. He had been out the night he was killed with his best friend, Andrew Goines. According to Nancy Root, they had gone to a movie at the Hollywood 20 on Main Street. Andrew was fifteen, couldn't drive. His mother had picked him up.

When Kyle's father, Richard McClory, had gone to the theater to pick up his son, Kyle wasn't there. Kyle had a cell phone. His father called him. No answer.

McClory called his ex-wife and left a message. She was doing a George Bernard Shaw play, *Man and Superman*, at the Asolo that night. She and McClory had been divorced for six years. Kyle was staying that week with his father, a radiologist. The father had a small house on Siesta Key a block from Siesta Key Village, a one-block walk to the beach.

The night McClory had gone to pick up his son at the movie, he waited, wandered, drove, got the Goines's number from Information, talked to Andrew, who said he had no idea where Kyle was.

"He ever run away?" I asked.

"Kyle?" she said.

"Yes."

She shook her head no, once.

"Nothing like that. Never," she said. "No problems. No drugs. No smoking. No drinking. No girls. Straight arrow. Straighter than his mother, God knows."

I guess I made a sound that prompted her to add, "I didn't wear tinted glasses around Kyle," she said. "He knew he could tell me anything he did. He knew I had done it all. And even if he had decided not to tell me, I'd have known."

"You would?"

"The telltale signs of corruption," she said with that sad smile. "Nicotine stains on his fingers. Knickerbockers rolled down."

I looked at Tycinker.

"Music Man," he said. "It's from *The Music Man.* 'Trouble in River City,' right?"

Nancy Root nodded to show he was right.

"I played Marian the librarian in rep in Portland," she said. "Long time ago."

"Kyle," I reminded her.

"Richard and my . . . our only child."

I drank the coffee. It was straight, black, hot, no real flavor besides coffee. I burned my upper palate.

"Richard was waiting for me after the show," she said, eyes moist, mouth open, taking in air. "They'd found Kyle's body, his wallet, couldn't reach me, called Richard. Kyle had four dollars and sixty-two cents in his pockets. He also had a Susan B. Anthony dollar he kept for good luck. His keys. His . . ."

She stopped, breathed deeply.

"His cell phone?" I asked.

"They couldn't find it, the police," said Tycinker.

"And there was a witness?" I asked.

"Mexican," said Tycinker. "Ruiz or Rubles. It's in the police report. Said the boy was . . . Nancy, is it . . . ?"

"Go ahead," she said, pulling herself together.

"Witness was walking home from work," Tycinker went on. "Assistant cook at some restaurant. Didn't see much.

Came from behind. Car was moving fast. Dark car. Kyle was in the middle of the street. Car caught him in the headlights. Kyle was frozen and . . ."

"Ruiz or Robles see the driver?"

"Says no," said Tycinker. "No license number, even partial. You'll have to look at the report to get any more."

"Anything else?" I asked.

"No," Nancy Root said. "Find him."

"You have a standard fee for this sort of thing?" asked Tycinker.

"Just reimburse me for what it costs," I said. "I'll keep receipts."

"I'd rather just give you a check for professional services," she said. "What's fair?"

Not much, I thought. Not in my life and it looks like not in yours either.

"Three hundred," I said. "Pay me if I find the driver."

"*When*," she said with intensity. "When you find the driver."

"Done," said Tycinker, rising behind his desk before I could respond. He held out his right hand.

I put down my coffee, reached over the desk and shook it. Firm grip. Nancy Root put out her hand too. I took it. It was cold.

When she let go, she opened the small purse next to the chair she had been sitting on, came out with a wallet and handed me five twenty-dollar bills.

"Not necessary," I said.

"Oh yes," she said. "It is. Call it an advance on the three hundred dollars. You'll have expenses."

I understood. I had to be retained for her to feel I had made the commitment.

I folded the bills and put them in my pocket.

"My card," she said, handing me a small white card.

The card simply gave her name, address and phone number. Nothing fancy. No border curls, touches of light. No *Actress* in the lower left-hand corner.

I pocketed the card and told her I'd get back to her when and if I found anything.

"Find something, Mr. Fonesca," she said.

I left the half-finished coffee on a coaster Tycinker had provided. I had no more questions and I was sure none of us wanted to sit in silence or engage in conversation about the economy and tax cuts.

Cap in hand I went to the office door. Nancy Root lingered. As I stepped out I caught a glimpse of Tycinker in front of his desk holding both of her cold hands in his large firm ones. There was nothing covert in the hand holding, but I couldn't tell if he was playing comforting attorney, good friend or something closer.

I'd need a car. I made a decision and biked back to Washington Street, took my bike up to my office, went back out past the DQ and a small line of storefronts on the west side of the street and walked to the driveway of the car rental agency I did business with when I needed four wheels.

EZ Economy Car Rental is a half block north of the DQ. Once, long ago, it was a gas station. That was before I came to Sarasota. It still looked like a gas station without the pumps. The lot was small but there was space behind the whitewashed office for a dozen cars in addition to the four parked beyond the two open sliding doors where once oil was changed, tires repaired, engines overhauled and grease-covered hands cut with the lids of opened cans.

Inside the small office, Alan, a big, bulky man in his late forties, drank two-handed from a pink cup that had the word

MOCHA running in large letters facing me. He was leaning back against one of the two desks.

His partner, Fred, in his sixties, big belly, wasn't in sight.

"Fonesca," Alan said with a sigh. "I'm not sure I'm up to the challenge. I'd ask you to try smiling a little, but I don't think I could take it."

He pushed away from the desk and looked down at whatever was in his cup. Alan was known, as Fred put it once, to "tipple" from time to time. "Nothing serious," Fred had said. "Takes the edge off."

"Edge of what?" I had asked.

"Edge of the weary life we all bear," Fred had said. "Weighs heavier on him than most with the possible exception of Lewis Fonesca, whose very presence proclaims the end of days."

"Where's Fred?" I asked Alan.

"Where's Fred?" Alan repeated. "I'll tell you where Fred is. He's in his third day at Sarasota Memorial Hospital. Third day. Third heart attack. Man's had three wives, three kids. Now he's had three heart attacks. What he needs is three wishes."

"I'm sorry," I said.

Alan shrugged.

"Makes the days long. Coffee?"

"No thanks."

"Transportation then?" said Alan, taking a slow sip from his cup.

"Yes."

"Take the Saturn," he said, tilting his head toward the window. "Gray one, ninety-eight, right out in front."

"How much?" I asked.

"Whatever you want to pay Lewis, bringer of light and

joy, bearer of good spirits," he said, toasting me with his coffee.

It was a little after ten in the morning. Alan wasn't smashed, but he was sloshing down the road to oblivion.

"Same as last time?" I asked.

"Whatever. You caught me depressive," he said with a shrug. "I try to stay manic. Right now, I don't think these walls can hold the power of depression you and I can generate."

"Keys?" I said.

"On the board," he said, nodding his head at the Peg-Board on the wall to his right. "Help yourself."

I found the right keys.

"You all right?" I asked.

"Absolutely not," he said. "I'm hoping the manic stage will kick in, but I don't think it will, not for a while. When I'm manic, I can rent an oil-leaking ninety Honda that shits rust and farts oil to Mr. Goodwrench. Can't stop, but this . . ."

"I know," I said.

"Fred keeps me above the line," he said. "Costello was no good without Abbott. Hardy wasn't much without Laurel. Jerry Lewis . . . you get it. I need a straight man."

I reached for my wallet. Alan, cup to his lips, saw me and held up his right hand.

"No," he said. "I don't feel like doing the paperwork, writing a receipt. Just take the car. Belonged to a secretary in the biology department at the University of South Florida. Standard shift."

"Fine," I said.

The door opened. A couple, Mexican, maybe in their late thirties, both plump, both serious, with a boy about twelve at their side, came in. They didn't quite look frightened, but they didn't look confident either.

"That little car outside for sale?" the man said. "Sign says eight hundred dollars?"

Alan sighed.

"The Focus? Six hundred," he said. "Gala sale day."

I went outside and got into the Saturn. It was clean, smelled a little musty, and the window at my left rattled as I pulled onto 301.

3

I TOOK A CHANCE. It wasn't a big one. I drove past downtown a few blocks away and turned onto Sixth Street past city hall and parked across from the Texas Bar & Grille.

The lunchtime regulars at the Texas, lawyers, cops, construction workers, shop owners on Main Street, lost tourists and snow birds, were about an hour from coming through the door.

A lone guy with three chins and a business shirt with a morning beer and *The Wall Street Journal* sat at a table by the window. Ed Fairing, white shirt, black vest, flowing dark mustache, hair parted down the middle, sat at a table to the right, a book in his hand. Ed was from Jersey, living out his dream of being an old-fashioned barkeep and saying, "What'll it be?" a few hundred times a day.

The Texas was known for its one-pound burgers and beer on tap. Ed was known for his esoteric knowledge of bars of the Old West. The walls of the Texas were covered with old weapons kept in working condition by Ames McKinney, and photographs and drawings of some bars, including the Jersey Lilly with Judge Roy Bean, lean and glinty-eyed, one hand on the bar behind him, the other clutching a thick book that Ed said contained the laws of Texas. Another showed the Suicide Table in Virginia City, Nevada. Ed had been to Virginia City, a pilgrimage, had seen the Suicide Table, where three men were reported to have killed themselves after losing small fortunes.

"Lewis," Ed said, looking up over the top of his rimless glasses.

"Ed," I said.

"If you've come to collect for the United Jewish Appeal, I gave at the blood bank," he said.

I'm not Jewish. Neither is Ed. Ed thinks he has a sense of humor. I wouldn't know. He had given me a joke to tell Ann Horowitz. It had something to do with aardvarks walking into a bar. I had forgotten the punch line.

"Ames is out back," Ed said. "Garbage pickup this afternoon."

I walked past the bar at the rear, down the narrow hallway, past the small kitchen that smelled of grease and sugar, past the rest rooms and through the rear door.

Ames, tall, wearing a red flannel shirt in spite of the seventy-degree weather, was hoisting a fat green plastic garbage bag into a yawning Dumpster.

"Busy?" I asked.

He wiped his hands on his jeans and turned toward me.

"Last one," he said, nodding at the Dumpster.

That's all we said. Nothing more was needed. Ames was seventy-four, lean, still over six-four, long white hair, a Gary Cooper face of suntanned leather.

DENIAL

Four years ago he had come to Sarasota to find his partner, Jim Holland, who had run away with every nickel he could steal from their company in Arizona, moved to Sarasota, changed his name and became a pillar of society, a hollow pillar made of plaster.

I had helped Ames find Holland. Ames wanted his money and some retribution. Holland wanted to keep everything and get rid of his old partner. I had arranged for them to come unarmed at nine at night to the beach in the park at the south end of Lido Key.

When Ames and I arrived, we crossed the road and walked around the parking lot chain. I didn't know how often the police patrolled the park after closing, but it was hard to keep people out since the beach ran into the park on the Gulf side.

We listened to the surf, the gulls and the crunch of parking lot stones under our feet as I led the way past picnic tables and through a thin line of trees onto the narrow beach. Across the inlet, the lights from the houses looked friendly but far away.

We were early. Holland wasn't there.

I moved to the shore with Ames and looked into the clear moonlit water. A ray about the size of a large kite glided just below the surface of the water no more than a dozen feet out.

"Ames," I said. "It's beautiful here."

"That's a fact."

"Being alive is not bad."

"Depends. You're talking to the wrong man."

At that point, the right man came walking through the trees about thirty yards up the beach. A small white heron skittered away from him. Jim Holland walked erect, sure-footed in our direction, a little man with a mission, hands behind his back. Ames took four or five steps in his direction.

I stepped between them when they were about a dozen paces apart.

"Hold it," I said. "I talk. You listen. You both agreed."

They said nothing.

"Compromise," I said.

"There's no compromise about this," said Ames. "Told you that. He gives me my money back and I let him live."

"Money is mine, my father's," said Holland. "I told you that. He gets out of town and I let him live."

"Cash money," said Ames, standing tall, a rush of warm wind bristling his hair.

The white heron had wandered back and stood a few paces behind Jim Holland in the moonlight.

"That's it," I said. "That's it. We're leaving now. I'm preparing a report and turning it over to the police in the morning. I'm also giving a copy to my lawyer."

That part had been a lie. I had no lawyer.

"Can't work like that," said Holland.

"Can't," agreed Ames.

"I'm not a violent man," said Holland. "I told you, but I see no options here. I've got a business, a wife, children and family honor."

My stomach warned me even before Holland pulled a shotgun from behind his back.

There was nowhere to run and no one to call. I had a vision of a small shark in the water going for my dead eyes.

"This is crazy," I said.

"No argument from me," agreed Holland as he raised the shotgun and moved toward us.

Holland's shotgun was about halfway up when Ames

pulled what looked like a Buntline special from under his shirt behind his back and fired twice at the same time as Holland's shotgun. I was still standing. So was Ames, but Holland went down on his back and flung his shotgun toward the bay. Birds and squirrels went chattering mad in the brush and trees.

Ames returned the long-barreled gun to his belt and turned to me.

"It's done," he said.

"You lied to me," I said. "You said no gun."

"So did Jim. If I didn't lie, we'd be dead men."

He was right and I suddenly needed a toilet. A car, maybe two, raced across the gravel in the parking lot beyond the trees and picnic tables. A pair of headlights cut through, bouncing toward us.

"Gun was my father's. It ends fitting."

Footsteps came crashing through the brush branches and a pair of flashlights found us.

"Put your hands up," came a less-than-steady voice behind the light.

I put my hands up and so did Ames. The two policemen moved toward us past the dead man.

"On your knees," said one of them. "Arms behind your back."

I moved as fast as I could. Ames hadn't budged.

"Can't do that," he said.

"Old-timer," came the voice, drawing nearer, "I'm in no mood."

"Don't go on my knees," said Ames. "For man nor God. I'll take the consequences."

And he did. When they took us in to the station back on Ringing Boulevard, Ames took full responsibility, told the police that I had come to patch up an old quarrel and that

Holland had set us up. He told them I'd tried to stop the killing and that I had no idea that he had a gun or might use it.

It was not with charity and goodwill, but on the advice of a county attorney that they eventually let me go home after starting a file on me.

They kept Ames and I testified at the inquest. Ames was turned over for shooting Jim Holland.

I'd been the only witness. Ames was given a suspended sentence for having an unregistered firearm. He stayed in town, got a job as odd-job man at the Texas and assigned himself the task of being my guardian angel.

"We going somewhere?" he asked.

"Yes."

"Need a weapon?" he asked, following me back into the Texas.

"No," I said.

"We'll be back by one," I said to Ed as we passed him.

"No hurry," Ed said without looking up from his book. "Marie and Charlie'll be here in a little while. I can hold down Fort Apache."

Ames had a motor scooter in his room. He also had various small arms and a Remington M-10 twelve-gauge pump-action shotgun and a yellow slicker that covered it when necessary plus the use of any of the guns of the Old West display on the walls of the Texas. Ames kept them unloaded but all in firing condition.

We got into the Saturn.

"How's Ed's liver?" I asked as I started to drive.

"Swears by acupuncture and Chinese herbs," said Ames. "Seems to work."

"Willpower," I said. "Man owns a bar and can't drink."

"Man does what a man has to do," Ames said.

I would have glanced at him to see if he was joking, but I knew Ames well enough to know that he meant just what he said. I never asked Ames for a joke to tell Ann. I was sure he didn't have any.

He didn't ask where we were going, didn't ask why I pulled off of Beneva and drove down the narrow paved road to the Seaside Assisted Living Facility. The Seaside was a good four miles from the Gulf of Mexico, but it did have a pond with ducks floating on the green water.

I parked in a space between two cars in an area marked RESIDENTS ONLY.

"We're here to see a woman named Dorothy Cgnozic," I said.

The nod from Ames was almost not there, but I knew what to look for. He didn't ask me why we were going to see the woman or why I wanted him with me. If I wanted to tell him, that would be fine. If not, he wouldn't burn with curiosity.

I told him.

"She thinks she saw a woman get murdered here last night," I said.

He looked at me, gray eyes unblinking.

I had asked him to come because he was seventy-four, because people found him easy to talk to, to trust, especially the very young and the very old. He understood.

I took off my Cubs cap. We went inside and found the nursing station down a carpeted corridor. I had been here before to serve papers. It was clean, well lit. There was a slight bustle of chatter behind the counter between a large woman in white with a chart in her hands and a smaller, heavier woman with red hair that looked natural. The red-haired woman was on the phone. The large woman was reading to her from the chart.

Stuart M. Kaminsky

"December eighth," the red-haired woman said. "Chart says that's when the Flomax should stop."

The person on the other end was talking. The redhead looked at the woman with the chart and rolled her eyes upward and then said, "It's your signature. . . . Will do."

She hung up and looked at Ames and me.

An old woman, white-haired, wearing a light blue suit moved next to us at the desk. She leaned on a cane and looked straight ahead at the big nurse.

"We're here to see Dorothy Cgnozic," I said.

"You were here a few months ago," said the large woman with the chart.

"I served some papers," I said.

"And you're going to serve papers on Dorothy?" she asked protectively.

"No. Just want to see her. She called me. My name is Lewis Fonesca. This is Ames McKinney."

"Pleased," said Ames.

If he had a ten-gallon hat, I'm sure he would have taken it off and said, "Ma'am."

Ames is hard to resist. I'm not.

"May I ask what she wants to see you about?" asked the large woman.

I looked at the pin above her left breast. It said she was Gladys Sprague.

"Yes," I said.

"Well, I'm asking."

"My pills," said the woman with the cane.

"Not for an hour, Lois," said the large nurse patiently. "One of us will come to your room."

"It's lunchtime," the woman with the cane said.

"When lunch is over, come back here or someone will come to your room," said the redhead.

"You won't forget?" said the woman with the cane.

"It's all on the charts," said Gladys the nurse with a smile. "We won't forget."

"My tissues," said the woman with the cane.

"We understand," said the large nurse.

The old woman started up the long corridor.

"Mr. . . ." Gladys said.

"Fonesca. And this is Mr. McKinney."

"Right. I'm guessing," said Gladys with a sigh. "Dorothy told you she saw someone murdered here last night."

"Yes," I said.

"No one was murdered here last night," said the redhead. "And no one died. We get about a death a month, sometimes more, but not yesterday and no murder."

"I'd still like to see her," I said.

"Sure," said Gladys. "She almost never gets visitors. She goes to lunch in forty-five minutes. Her room number is one eleven. We like Dorothy. So does everyone else. She helps with the bingo numbers on Tuesday and Thursday, never complains. I don't know what's with this murder business. We have a social worker on call. Dorothy will get a visit from her later this afternoon."

"Our residents sometimes . . ." the redhead started and then went on, "sometimes exercise their imaginations. They want attention, a sense that they are still a part of things."

"It's not necessarily an unhealthy sign," said Gladys.

"Remember Carmine Forest?" asked the redhead.

Gladys shook her head and said to us, "Carmine, what was it, three, four years ago?"

"Three," said the redhead.

"Carmine," Gladys went on, "claimed vampires were

stalking the halls at night, turning the residents into vampires."

"Said he could prove it," Gladys continued. "Said the residents were getting pale, losing blood. Even claimed he had seen fang marks on their necks."

"Which closed almost immediately after they were bitten," said the redhead. "He started painting crosses on the doors with Magic Marker."

"Permanent black marker," said the redhead.

"Got ugly," said Gladys. "Mrs. Schwartz and Mr. Wallstein complained that it was an attack by anti-Semites. They called a rabbi. Carmine called a priest. Rabbi and priest got together and calmed things down."

"Carmine demanded an exorcism," said the redhead. "Priest said the Church didn't recognize the existence of vampires."

"Carmine wrote to the pope," said Gladys. "No answer."

"Then he sent in a letter of resignation from the Catholic Church and said he was going to become a Hindu because they believed in vampires and would send someone to deal with it."

"Did they?" I asked.

"We're still waiting," said Gladys.

"Oh," said the redhead, suddenly remembering. "What about Carla Martin?"

"One one one," I said, starting to move away from the nursing station.

"One eleven, right," said the redhead.

Ames and I went in search of Dorothy Cgnozic's room while Gladys and the redhead recalled whatever Carla Martin's delusion had been. We found the room at the end of a corridor and around a bend. The door was closed. I knocked.

"Come in," came a woman's voice.

I tried the door.

"It's locked," I said.

"Who are you?" came the voice.

"Lewis Fonesca. You called me this morning."

Silence. Then the sound of something padding on the other side. The door opened.

Dorothy Cgnozic was not small. She was tiny, maybe a little over four feet high. She was wearing a bright yellow dress. Her short white hair was brushed back and she had a touch of makeup on her almost unlined face.

She looked at me and then up at Ames.

"Come in," she said, looking past us down the corridor in both directions.

We entered and she closed and locked the door before turning into the room. We moved past a bathroom on our right and around her walker with the yellow tennis balls on the feet. The room was big enough for a bed with a flowered quilt, a small refrigerator, a low chest of drawers with a twenty-four-inch Sony television on top of it and three chairs next to a window that looked out at the tops of trees about forty or fifty feet away.

"Sit," she said.

We did.

"This is my friend Ames McKinney," I said.

"Pleased to meet you, ma'am," Ames said.

"And you, Mr. McKinney," she answered. "You may call me Dorothy."

"Ames," he said.

"If you—" I began.

"Would you like some chocolate-covered cherries?" she asked.

"One," said Ames.

There was a low table piled with books, a Kleenex box

and a pad of paper with a sheet on which I could see neatly handprinted names. She got a small candy box from the one-drawer table at her side, opened it and held it out to Ames, who took one. I declined.

"I don't know which room it was," she said, putting the candy box back and sliding the drawer closed. "I may have gotten it wrong. It was down the corridor in front of the nursing station, toward the end. The door was open. The room was dark but there was light from outside. A person was being strangled, definitely an old person in a robe. She was being strangled by someone big."

"Man or woman?" I asked.

"Don't know. Would either of you like a Diet Sprite?"

"No, thank you," I said.

"Yes, please," said Ames.

Dorothy Cgnozic smiled, rose and moved to the refrigerator. She moved slowly, hands a little out to her sides for balance, and came back with a can of Diet Sprite and a disposable plastic cup. Ames thanked her, opened the can and poured himself a drink.

"The nurses said no one died here last night," I said. "Everyone's accounted for. Maybe—"

"I am eighty-three," she said. "Six operations for bladder, hip and some things I'd rather not mention. My body's going. My brain is fine. My eyesight is nearly perfect with my glasses on and I was wearing my glasses. I saw someone murdered. I told Emmie."

"The night nurse?" I asked.

"Yes."

She reached for the pad with the names and handed it to me.

"List of all the residents as of last Monday," she said. "I'm trying to find out who is missing."

"You think the nurses are lying?"

"Mistaken, confused," she said. "People come and go speaking of Michelangelo."

"Michelangelo?"

"Poetry, metaphor. T. S. Eliot. I'm not displaying signs of Alzheimer's or dementia," she said. "I saw what I saw."

"Maybe the murdered person wasn't a resident," Ames said.

Dorothy and I looked at him.

"Maybe the murdered person was a visitor. Maybe staff."

"In a robe?" asked Dorothy.

Ames took a deep gulp of Diet Sprite and said, "Dark. Light from behind. Maybe it was a coat, not a robe."

"And maybe pigs can fly and geese can give milk," she said. "I saw what I saw."

I think Ames smiled.

"You think whoever did it might want to hurt you?" I asked. "Your door was locked."

"If someone wants to murder an eighty-three-year-old woman in an assisted living facility," she said, "it doesn't take much effort, but . . ."

She reached down for a white cloth bag near the table holding the Kleenex and pulled it over to her. She reached into it, dug deep and came up with a formidable-looking hunting knife in a leather sheaf.

"I will not go gently," she said. "My husband would turn away from me in heaven or hell when we met if I didn't protect myself."

"Cgnozic?" said Ames. "Any relation to Gregory Cgnozic?"

"My husband," she said with obvious pride. "You know his work?"

"A fine poet," Ames said. "Ran with Kerouac, Ginsberg. Heard him once in Butte. Sense of humor. A little like Ferlinghetti."

"People don't remember Gregory," she said.

"More than you think."

"Not many," she said.

She reached back, lifted the box of Kleenex and pulled something from under it. The something was a check for two hundred dollars made out in my name. She had spelled my name correctly.

"You don't have to—" I began.

"It doesn't mean anything if I don't pay you," she said. "I pay you and the service you perform remains mine. You understand?"

"Yes, ma'am," said Ames.

I pocketed the check. I now had one hundred dollars in cash and a check for two hundred dollars in my pocket. They weighed as much as the hopes of two women.

"Anything else?" I asked.

"Prove me right," she said, standing. "Lunchtime. Food's not really bad here. People complain, but it's not really bad. Chicken salad today, but you can always get a toasted cheese if you want and you can get popcorn and coffee whenever you want."

Ames and I both stood. She took the empty can and disposable cup from Ames.

"We'll work on it," I said.

Gladys, the big nurse, wasn't at the nursing station when we went by but the redhead looked up at us from her desk and said, "Well? You don't still believe her?"

"Mind if we go through the motions?" I asked.

"If it will make Dorothy feel better and you don't disturb

any of the residents and you don't run into the boss," she said. "But believe me, everyone is accounted for. Nobody died."

"Could someone have come in to visit a resident during the night?"

"Till eleven," said the redhead patiently. "After that, no visitors. Doors are locked for the night. You have to ring to get in. Emmie Jefferson's note said Dorothy's murder happened at a little after eleven."

"Could she be a few minutes off?" Ames asked.

"Possible," said the redhead. "Does it make a difference?"

We thanked her and went down the corridor and out the door to the parking lot.

"Must be ways to get in here without ringing," Ames said. "I'll scooter back on my own later and check."

"Right," I said. "Gregory Cgnozic was a famous poet?"

I was driving now down the narrow road, past a trio of ducks quacking near the pond.

"No," said Ames. "Just a poet. Happened to catch him that one night in Butte. He was a last-minute fill-in for another Gregory, Corso."

"Was he good?"

"My opinion? Yes. That night in Butte he said John Lennon was the greatest poet of the twentieth century," said Ames. "Audience applauded. Don't think they believed it, though, but he wasn't joking."

"You believe her, about the murder?" I asked.

"Woman saw what she saw," he said.

We went back to the Texas. It was crowded. There was no chicken salad on the menu. Just the items listed on the blackboard above the bar. Burgers of large size with whatever you wanted and chili as hot as you wanted. Ames went to work. I stood at the bar, made a phone call, went for the

Stuart M. Kaminsky

chili and corn bread, worried about Dorothy Cgnozic and drove over to Bank of America two blocks away to cash my check.

Then I drove down Main, parked in the public lot on Main and 301 and headed for the office of Detective Etienne Viviase.

4

THE PLAQUE on his desk read: DETECTIVE ED VIVIASE. His real name was Etienne Viviase, but even his wife called him Ed. He was a little under six feet tall, a little over fifty years old, and a little over two hundred and twenty pounds. Hair short, dark. Face smooth, pink. He was wearing a dark rumpled sports jacket with a tie the color of Moby Dick.

He was seated behind his desk, one of three in the office. The other two were, at the moment, unoccupied, though the closest had a tall pile of reports that was doomed to topple.

"You called?" he said, mug of coffee in one hand, a scone with raisins or chocolate chips in the other.

I looked at the chair across from him and he nodded to let me know it was all right to sit.

"Scone?" he asked. "Coffee?"

"No thanks," I said.

"Am I going to enjoy this conversation?" he asked.

"I don't think so," I said.

He looked at his wristwatch, which resulted in crumbs falling in his lap, which resulted in his brushing away the crumbs, which resulted in him spilling some coffee, which missed his pants leg by inches.

"Five minutes," he said.

"Kyle McClory," I said.

Viviase smiled, but not much, shook his head, but not much, and said, "Not my case."

"Who should I talk to?"

"Me," he said. "I don't think anyone here, especially Mike Ransom, whose case it is, will talk to you."

"His mother asked me to look into it," I said.

"You're not a detective," he said. "You are a process server."

"She asked me. Private citizen."

"Is she paying you, private citizen?"

"Yes," I said.

"Why don't you branch out into skip tracing?" he asked, taking a bite of scone and examining it to see how much he had left.

"I have enough work. Too much."

"Well, I told you. Mike Ransom's working on the Kyle McClory case," he said. "The father's a big-time radiologist. The mother's a local celebrity. She's got a lawyer with a little clout."

"Tycinker," I said.

"We're working on it."

"Can't hurt if I ask some questions," I said.

"It could hurt, but then again it might help," he said. "What do you want from me?"

"What do you know? I mean, what do you know that I can have? I understand there was a witness."

"Hold on," Viviase said, finishing his scone and putting his coffee mug gently on the desk.

He walked over to the file cabinets, opened one in the middle, pulled out a file and came back to his desk. He sat, wiped his fingers and turned on his computer after checking something in the file, which now lay open in front of him.

The computer hummed. He entered something and sat back to wait.

"How's the kid?" he asked.

"Adele?"

"Yeah, and the baby."

"Both fine."

He was about to speak again, but I could see something popping up on the screen. Viviase reached into his pocket, pulled out his glasses, put them on and looked at the words in front of him.

"Looks like . . . ," he said, reading what was in front of him and then checking the open file. "After ten, guy walking past the park saw it."

"Guy?"

"His name is Arnoldo Robles," said Viviase. "He works at a Mexican restaurant, El Tacito."

I said nothing.

"You turn up anything on who killed the boy, you turn it over to me, right?" Viviase asked, leaning back.

"Right," I said.

"Mr. Robles lives on Ninth," Viviase said, scanning the file. "He was on his way home from work, walking up Gillespie past the park. Let's see. Saw the kid running past him, thought maybe he was about to be mugged. Kid turns down Eighth. Robles hears a car behind him. Robles reaches Eighth. Car turns behind the kid, who's in the middle of the street. Kid is running. Car's lights hit him. Kid stops. Holds up his

Stuart M. Kaminsky

hand. Car nails him. Driver gets out to look at the body, then gets back in the car and drives off."

"Why was the boy in the middle of the street?" I asked.

"To get to the other side. I don't know."

"What was he doing in a blue-collar Hispanic neighborhood at that hour?"

"Don't know," said Viviase.

"Anyone ask his friend Andrew . . ."

"Goines," Viviase said, reading it from the file. "Yep. Mike asked him. Goines kid said he had no idea."

"Robles see any other traffic, cars?"

"Doesn't say," said Viviase.

"How fast was the car going?" I asked.

"Doesn't say, but Robles didn't think he was speeding."

Viviase gave me a long look, lips pursed, and removed his glasses.

"He ran the boy down," I said.

"I didn't say that. The report doesn't say that. Right now it's a hit-and-run. Something else turns up, we'll look into it."

He gave me a long quiet look. He wasn't quite encouraging me, but he was a long way from telling me to mind my own business.

"Did Robles describe the car?"

"Let's see . . . Sedan, probably late model, probably four doors."

Viviase closed the file, reached over to put his computer to sleep and said, "Five minutes are up."

"I think I'll talk to Detective Ransom," I said.

"Your funeral," he said. "That's his desk."

Viviase pointed with a pencil at one of the other desks. "He's probably at the hot dog cart outside. Late lunch."

I went in search of Detective Michael Ransom.

The hot dog pushcart was on the sidewalk at the corner of Main and 301. You could see the Hollywood 20 theater across the street.

Two men, both big, both in their thirties, one with short dark hair, the other with even shorter blond hair, were standing by the cart with a hot dog in one hand and a Diet Coke in the other.

"Detective Ransom?" I asked.

The heavier, younger of the two men, the one with dark hair, looked at me, his cheek full of hot dog.

"Yeah," he said.

"My name's Lew Fonesca. I just talked to Detective Viviase."

"So?"

"I'm a friend of Nancy Root's. I used to work for the state attorney's office in Chicago," I said. "I'm sort of her family representative."

Ransom took another bite of hot dog and a drink of Coke.

"I know who you are, Fonesca," he said.

"You mind if I ask you a few questions?"

"Very much," he said.

The other cop turned his back on us and went on eating.

"I'll only take a minute. By the clock."

"First, this is the only meal I've had today," he said, showing me what was left of his hot dog. "Second, I've got a small stack of open felony cases sitting on my desk. The McClory death is in that stack. I'll deal with it."

"I'd just like—"

"Ed told me about you," he said, taking a step toward me. "I am politely asking you to not interfere with my ongoing investigation."

"But—"

"Now I'm firmly asking you," he said, coming even closer.

"If—"

"Now I'm telling you," he said, almost in my face.

I smelled onions and jalapeño.

"Tell Ms. Root I'm working on it. Tell Dr. McClory I'm working on it. And tell yourself not to obstruct justice. Fonesca, I'm a tired man and I think I've got some kind of gastric problem. I've got an appointment with my doctor in the morning. This job can give a person a very bad stomach. Don't make it worse. Now, if you want a kosher dog, I'll pop for it, but you carry it away and don't look back."

I shook my head no, walked down the street, got into my rented Saturn, drove up 301 to Fruitville, turned left and then right at Gillespie Park. The sun was bright. Kids were playing in the park. I turned just past the tennis courts down Eighth. There were cars parked on both sides but enough room for vehicles going in both directions. Kyle could have stayed on the sidewalk but he didn't. Was he just crossing the street? I drove slowly looking for blood, trying to determine exactly where the boy had been hit and killed. There was no blood, none that I could see.

I went to Washington Boulevard, turned right, went to Fruitville and then headed east just past Tuttle.

John Gutcheon sat at the reception desk on the first floor of the three-story Building C in the complex of identical buildings marked A through D.

Building C housed the offices of Children's Services of Sarasota. Buildings A, B and D had a few empty offices but most were filled by dentists, urologists, a cardiology practice, investment advisors, jewelry and estate appraisers, young lawyers and a dealer in antique toys.

DENIAL

John was the receptionist, dispensing advice, directing calls, folding sheets and stuffing them into envelopes and warding off people who had come to the wrong place.

"You want to hear a dentist tale?" he asked when he saw me come through the door.

"Is it funny?"

"No," John said, rolling his eyes. "It's the truth. You want a joke, I'll tell you one when I finish with the dentist business."

John was thin, blond, about thirty and unmistakably and unapologetically gay. His sharp tongue was ever ready to cut off those who questioned his lifestyle by look or word.

"How did your art show go?" I asked.

The last time I had seen him Gutcheon had told me that two of his paintings were going to be shown at the Wardell Studio during the monthly art walk.

"No sale," he said, holding up both hands with a shrug.

"Sorry," I said.

"You didn't see them," he said. "Sally said she'd try to get you to go."

"I'm—"

"Not a people person," he completed. "Yes, that much is obvious. Can I tell you about the dentist thing?"

"Yes."

"Building D," he said. "John Gault, DDS. His real name isn't John Gault but I call him that. You know, Ayn Rand?"

"Not intimately," I said.

"Look who's trying to display a sense of humor," he said. "Anyway, you wouldn't want to be intimate with Ayn Rand. Interesting writer but I hear she was a bitch."

I nodded to show I was listening.

"Well, anyway," he went on. "The dentist. Tooth gets chipped. One back here." He curled up the right side of his mouth and pointed. "Got chipped. Piece came right off in that Chinese restaurant on Clark, the little one. Nice people. Something in the fortune cookie. Cookie says, 'Your plans will soon change.' I went to Dr. Gault the next day and he said I needed two crowns, eleven hundred dollars each. Mr. Lewis Fonesca, I do not have two thousand and two hundred dollars. He says I can pay it out for the next three centuries but I check with other people and my friend Pauly tells me to go to his dentist. You want the result?"

"Yes," I said.

"Well, Pauly's dentist looks at the X-rays, examines my teeth and says, 'You don't need two crowns. There's nothing wrong with that second tooth.' Furthermore, he says the chipped tooth doesn't need a crown, just a filling. He fills it immediately, charges me sixty dollars."

Gutcheon looked at me for a reaction.

"Interesting," I said.

"It is, but I can see you are not one who is interested." He sighed. "The worst part?"

"What?"

"I went to John Gault because he is gay. Betrayed by one of my own. You see the irony?"

"Yes."

"But it's not the irony you want to see," he said. "It's Sally. Go up. Go up. You want a joke? You still collecting them?"

"Yes."

"What do you give a man who has everything?"

"I don't know."

"Antibiotics."

I took out my pad and wrote the joke.

"You didn't even smile," said Gutcheon.

"It's humorous," I said.

"George Carlin once said, 'Don't you find it a little unsettling that dentists call what they do 'a practice'?"

"He said *doctors*," I said, putting my notebook away.

"Well, I amended it to fit . . . never mind."

The phone in front of him rang. He picked it up and I went into the open elevator.

Children's Services took two floors. The second, where I got off, was big, open and filled with partitioned cubicles you could see over. The room was a dirge of voices, every once in a while a word or phrase coming through. Inside each three-sided cubicle was the work space of a caseworker who did his or her best to keep the few square feet from reverting to nature.

Sally's cubicle was to the right. I passed a cubicle in which a short, thin young Hispanic caseworker named Amy Valdez was leaning toward the chair of an even thinner and maybe a lot older and haggard black woman.

Most of the narrow metal desks in the cubicles were covered with files and notes, and on the walls, almost as if it had been an assigned duty, were photographs of each caseworker's family.

It reminded me of the places I used to get my haircuts, the mirrors where young women put photographs of their kids where you could see them. The haircutters wanted to kick the tips up. I never resisted. The last time I had been to one of those places had been more than four years earlier. I cut my own hair, what there was of it to cut.

The caseworkers, like Sally, put their photos up there to remind them that they had a life beyond the cubicles, the weeping mothers, the addicts, the teen prostitutes, abused babies, creatures who attacked and showed their teeth and were classified as human because there was no box to check for "other."

Sally was alone on the phone, her back to me. In a frame on her desk was a photograph of her two children, Michael, fourteen, and Susan, eleven. Sally said they liked me, though they thought I was a little weird. I wasn't sure I liked me but I agreed that I was a little weird.

"This is the third time, Sarah Ann," Sally was saying.

Sally and I had been keeping company, nothing more than that, really, for almost three years. Sally was two years older than I, pretty, plump, dark short hair, perfect skin and a voice like Lauren Bacall.

She worked ten-hour days, half days most weekends, trying to save the threatened children of Sarasota County one by one. There were more losses than saves, but without the people in this office, there would have been no saves but the ones that chance happened to touch.

"I can't keep coming there," Sally said. "It's almost twenty miles each way, but it's not the distance. It's the time. No excuses. Tomorrow. Sometime before noon. Sarah Ann, you be home. You have Jean home. We talk. I take her out and talk to her. You mess up this one and I turn it over."

Sally paused, saw me, nodded, listened to whatever Sarah Ann was saying and then said, "Sarah Ann, tomorrow, before noon. There is nothing more to say. There are no more chances. Good-bye."

Sally hung up.

"She won't be there, will she?" I asked.

"You could tell?"

I shrugged.

"She might," said Sally, swiveling around to face me, "but she won't the next time or the time after that. This one will go to court. And given the judges on the bench, odds are exactly three to one the kid will go back to her mother."

"Drugs?"

DENIAL

"And men. And . . . who knows?"

"I have an idea for an ad," I said. "Television. You find real addicts, young ones, put the camera on them, black and white, and on the screen you put their ages, first names and the drugs they use. Off-camera voice just asks them questions, which they mess up, and the kids who see the ads know that they are watching people whose minds are—"

"You've given this some thought, huh, Lew?"

Then it hit me. I must have shown it.

"What's wrong?"

"It wasn't my idea," I said. "It was . . . my wife's. I'd forgotten until . . ."

"Have a seat," Sally said, pulling the chrome-and-vinyl chair out of the corner.

I sat and took off my cap.

"I'm sorry," I said.

"For what? I'm getting off at seven. Kids want to go to Shaner's for pizza."

"Sure," I said.

"You have a car?"

"Yes," I said.

"Pick us up at the apartment at seven-twenty," she said, smoothing the folds in her green skirt. "Or pick up the pizzas and we'll have them at the apartment. Now, what can I do for you?"

"Kyle McClory," I said. "Name mean anything?"

"You mean, is he in the system?"

"Yes."

She turned, moved the mouse next to her computer, punched in the name, found a file and opened it.

"Not much," she said. "In fact, not anything."

"Try Andrew Goines," I said.

She did.

"Nothing there either," she said. "Anything else?"

"Try Kyle Root. His mother is Nancy Root."

"The actress?"

"Yes."

Sally did some more clacking of the keyboard and turned to me.

"No Kyle Root," she said. "But there is a Yolanda Root. Let's see. She . . . yes, her mother is Nancy Root. Yolanda has a long sheet. Drugs, men and boys, even attempted blackmail on a local businessman when she was thirteen. Went into his office, took off her clothes and demanded money. She picked the wrong guy. Gay. He called the police. Yolanda is, let's see, eighteen now."

"Where is she?"

"Last known address is her grandmother and grandfather, mother's parents, in Bradenton. Grandfather owns a hardware store. You know I'm not supposed to be doing this."

"I know," I said.

"Could lose my job," she said.

"I know."

"You're helping someone, right?"

"Yes."

"What's the worst that could happen? I'd wind up in an office or managing a fast food franchise. Regular hours and no bad dreams about the day."

"And the kids would get all the free leftover junk food they could eat," I added.

"That supposed to be a joke, Fonesca?"

"I don't think so," I said.

"Good. Don't forget about Saturday," she said.

"Saturday?"

"Darrell Caton," she said with a sigh.

Darrell was a fourteen-year-old Sally had conned me into seeing once a week. Big Brother plan. Darrell had no faith in the idea. Neither did I, but we had both agreed to start this week.

"I remembered," I said.

"Sure you did. I'm busy, Lewis," she said wearily. "See you tonight."

She touched my hand, turned her back and picked up her phone.

John Gutcheon was on the phone when I got off the elevator. He waved at me with a stapler and I went into the afternoon.

I parked in the DQ parking lot and went up to my office, where the phone began ringing as soon as I opened the door.

"Lew Fonesca," I said, picking it up.

"No more," came a man's voice, low, a little raspy. "Let it end here," he said.

"What?"

"What happened to the boy, Kyle McClory," he said.

"You know."

"Yes, yes," he said so low that I could barely hear him. "You have to stop looking."

There was no threat in his voice, just exhaustion.

"You did it?" I asked.

"Someone who doesn't need any more pain, doesn't deserve any more pain will suffer if you don't let it just end here," he said.

I took the phone and looked out the window as I said, "I can't."

Whoever it was had either been lucky and called the second I reached my door or he had watched me and called from a cell phone when he saw me get to the office. There were four cars in addition to my rental in the DQ lot. Across

Washington three cars were parked, the sun bright on their windows, so I couldn't see if anyone was inside.

"You don't understand," the man said. "I've got to stop you."

"Why?"

"Seneca said, 'The final hour when we cease to exist does not itself bring death; it merely of itself completes the death process.' We reach death at that moment, but we have been a long time on the way."

My eyes were still on the cars in the lot and on the street.

He hung up. One of the cars, a late-model compact, pulled out of the space on Washington and into traffic.

I went across the street to the Crisp Dollar Bill. The bar was dark and smelled of beer. The bar and the smell reminded me of Mac's Tavern a block from our house in Chicago. My father used to send me there with a glass jar for Mac to fill with draft beer on Saturday nights. There was no music at Mac's, just the silent black-and-white image on the ten-inch screen of the old DuMont television that sat on a shelf and the loud voices of the Irish and Italian neighborhood working men who came to complain, brag and declare the superiority of one nation over another, one baseball team over another. I was informed by my father that no Republicans were allowed in Mac's.

In contrast to those memories, the expensive acoustical system of the Crisp Dollar Bill was playing Bernadette Peters singing "It's Raining in My Heart." Billy the bartender/owner's taste was eclectic. So were his politics.

There were six people I could see in the booths and at the bar. Might have been others in the shadows. There was nothing really shady about the Crisp Dollar Bill. As far as I knew, no one had ever been shot there; though, back when the Chicago White Sox had spring training in the long-gone box behind the Crisp Dollar Bill, there had been lots of after-the-game fights over games in March that really didn't matter when June came.

Billy came over with a Beck's.

"Food?"

"No."

"Two Sousa marches coming up next," he said, moving back toward the bar.

I was in a corner booth in the back on the right facing the door. I nursed my beer knowing that as soon as Bernadette Peters's last plaintive notes ended, the music would blare. It did. "The Stars and Stripes Forever."

"Oh shit," someone at the bar said.

"Departure is always an option," said Billy amiably.

I was halfway through the Beck's, considering what to do next, when the door opened and Ames came in. He knew which booth I was in. He sat across from me.

"I think our Miss Dorothy is onto something," he said.

5

FOUR PEOPLE aren't at Seaside Assisted Living who were there two nights ago," Ames said.

"Someone in the office told you that?" I asked.

"No," he said. "Went to see Dorothy. We took a walk around, talked to people. Came up with a list. Word is no one died the night our Dorothy says she saw the murder."

A new song came on. A tenor was warbling something called "I'm Going Shopping with You." Ames turned his head toward the speaker over the bar.

"That's Dick Powell."

"Right. Give the man a free beer," said Billy from behind the bar.

"What happened to the people who left?" I asked, bringing Ames back to the present.

"Word is one was transferred to a nursing home," he

said. "Another two left on their own. Other went to live with her daughter-in-law."

Billy came over with a beer for Ames and said, "On the house. Got another Powell coming up, 'Speaking of the Weather.' Know it?"

Ames nodded. He knew it.

"You checked with the nurses?" I prompted as Billy walked back to the bar.

"That's your job," he said.

He was right. Ames nursed his beer through Dick Powell before we left.

It took about ten minutes to get to the Seaside and five minutes to be sent into the office of the director, Amos Trent, a serious, heavyset man with a well-trimmed mustache and a suit almost as tan as his face. He said that neither he, nor the nurses, nor any member of the Seaside staff could give information about residents except to relatives. His eyes moved for an instant toward the four-drawer steel filing cabinet in the corner of his office.

"You understand," he said. "Privacy. There are people who prey on older people, offer them everything from jobs stuffing envelopes to life insurance for a dollar a month. We have to be concerned about insurance, liability. One of our heaviest insurance premiums covers privacy of records. I'm sorry."

He got up, put out his hand to Ames and me to let me know the meeting was over. His handshake was firm. So was his decision.

"Okay, then we'd like to see Dorothy Cgnozic," I said.

"You were here earlier, weren't you?"

"We were," I said. "Dorothy's an old friend."

"You mean," said Trent, "Dorothy is old and you are friends, not that you've been friends a long time."

Trent looked at Ames.

"We're friends," he said.

"Well," said Trent. "That's up to Dorothy, but I believe she is sleeping, afternoon nap. We don't like to wake our residents up when they're napping. You understand?"

"Perfectly," I said.

Trent looked at his watch and said, "I've got to get to a meeting. Look, I know about Dorothy's . . . mistake, delusion, dream. She's been telling everyone, the residents, nurses, even the dining room staff about the supposed murder. No one was murdered. Dorothy has, let's see how I can put this, Dorothy has an active imagination. Her husband was a poet."

I didn't see how Dorothy's husband being a poet had anything to do with her having an imagination, but I just nodded.

He was looking at Ames again when he said, "If the time comes when you're inquisitive about assisted living . . ."

I didn't give him any help.

"Father? Uncle?" he tried.

"Mr. McKinney is my friend," I said.

Ames wasn't smiling. Ames smiled almost as little as I did and I never smiled.

"Sorry," said Trent. "I just thought . . ."

"You boning me?" Ames said evenly.

"Boning you?" repeated Trent with a smile.

"Playing with me," he said.

"I wouldn't play with my friend," I said, recognizing the look in Ames's gray eyes.

In a few seconds if Trent didn't leave or we didn't back out, I was reasonably sure Ames would find a way to make the mustached manager of the Seaside suffer.

"Let's go," I said, putting a hand on Ames's sleeve.

DENIAL

"Dorothy doesn't get many visitors," Trent said, folding his hands in front of him. "Please come back to visit."

In the parking lot we got into the car. I backed out of the space and turned down the road past the pond, where two ducks floated.

"He was boning me," Ames said.

"He was," I agreed.

Silence again as we drove south on Beneva and turned at Webber, heading for Tamiami Trail.

"We're goin' back," he said, looking straight ahead.

"Yes."

"When?"

I looked at the clock on the dashboard.

"About two in the morning," I said. "Suit you?"

"Suits me just fine," he said.

I drove Ames to the Texas Bar & Grille, and said I'd pick him up at one-thirty in the morning. That suited him fine too.

Then I headed for El Tacito, the Mexican restaurant where Arnoldo Robles, the man who had witnessed Kyle McClory's death, worked. El Tacito is in a shopping mall at Fruitville and Lime. I found a parking space four doors down from the restaurant in front of a dollar discount store.

I had a friend, James Hahn, back in Chicago. He was an ex-cop who got a PhD in psychic studies at Northeastern Illinois University. He claimed that he could conjure up parking spaces, that by simply concentrating, envisioning and believing, he could make a space available when he arrived where we were going. I tried him on it a couple of times. It seemed to work for him. It never worked for me.

I don't believe in magic. I don't believe in the miracles of the Bible. I'd like to. I'd like to believe that my wife is somewhere, that she is some kind of entity, that she is not simply gone, but I can't. I've tried.

There was an early dinner crowd, about twenty, at El Tac-ito, or maybe it was a late lunch crowd. The air smelled of things fried, sauces hot, and tacos crisp. There were large color photographs on the wall, all of them of hills, mountains, probably in Mexico. Music was playing, guitars and a plaintive tenor almost in tears. I think it was "La Paloma." The people at the red-and-white-tableclothed wooden tables paid no attention to the music. They talked, mostly in Spanish, ate, laughed and raised their voices.

A harried waitress, thin with long dark hair tied back, hurried from table to table taking orders, delivering orders, giving orders when she went back to the kitchen.

"Sit anywhere," she said with a smile.

She had a pile of dirty dishes cradled in her left arm. A wisp of dark hair escaped the band that touched the nape of her neck. She brushed the stray strand away with her hand. She looked tired, satisfied, pretty.

"Looking for Arnoldo Robles," I said.

A trio of men at a back table called to her by name, Corazon. She held up a single finger to let them know she'd be with them in a second or a minute, depending on how much time I took.

"Arnoldo's busy," she said, smile gone, starting to turn away.

"Just take a minute," I said, holding up one finger as she had done.

"You know Arnoldo?" she asked.

I shook my head no. She looked at me from stained loafers to Cubs cap.

"You're not with Immigration?"

I shook my head again.

"Arnoldo has his green card," she said.

"Good."

"Corazon," called one of the trio in the back.

"Then what do you . . . ?"

"The dead boy," I said. "I'm working with the boy's family."

It was her turn to nod.

"He's in the kitchen."

She looked at the back of the restaurant, turned and headed for the three men. I followed and moved past her through a swinging door decorated with bright paintings of flowers, musical instruments and a single word, GUADALAJARA.

To my left was the open doorway to a small kitchen, barely big enough to let the two men in white aprons working in it move. The griddle was sizzling; a red light glowed above the oven in the corner. The air was steamy in spite of an old wall-mounted air conditioner that rattled noisily.

Both men were slightly built, about my height. Both were dark. Both had neatly shaved heads. One man was probably in his sixties, the other in his forties. Both men were moving quickly, hands flying, conducting a kitchen symphony, maybe about to do a juggling act. They were perspiring. The older one quickly reached for a half-full bottle of water and took a few quick gulps. The younger one looked over at me. He had a knife with a broad flat blade in his hand.

"Arnoldo Robles?"

His grip on the knife got tighter.

"Can we talk?"

The older man looked over his shoulder at me.

"What about?"

"What you told the police," I said.

"Who are you?"

"Not the one who was driving the car," I said, looking at

　　　　　　　　　　　　　　Stuart M. Kaminsky

the blade. "I'm working for the boy's mother. I could use your help."

"Busy," he said.

"He's busy," the older man added.

Corazon came through the swinging door, looked at the two cooks and me and then went on through another door where I heard dishes clacking.

"I can wait," I said.

"I don't want any trouble," Arnoldo Robles said.

"I worry about people who want trouble," I said. "I'm not bringing trouble."

The two men's eyes met, and Arnoldo sighed and looked at the ceiling. They said something to each other in Spanish. The older man wasn't pleased or cooperative. He finally shrugged and went back to work.

"Have a seat out there," Robles said to me. "I'll be out in a few minutes."

I went back into the restaurant and found a small table near the window. A few people had left. The waitress named Corazon came up to me, hands on hips, but there was no challenge in the move, just a weary resignation.

"Arnoldo can't sleep," she said. "He says he keeps seeing that boy in the street and the car. . . . He thinks he should have done something."

"You're his . . . ?"

"Wife," she said. "We've got a little boy, eight. My mother watches him when he gets home from school. She thinks some crazy man is out there trying to crash into little boys. She won't let him out to play. Is she right? Is there a crazy man out there?"

"There may be a crazy man out there, but I don't think he's out looking for little boys to run over."

"How do you know this?" she asked.

DENIAL

69

"I think he was just after one fourteen-year-old boy."

"You know this for sure?"

"No, not for sure."

"Then I think maybe we'll keep Carlos inside till he's caught, this driver," she said.

"It can't hurt. How are the tacos?" I asked.

"How are the tacos?" she repeated, shaking her head and smiling. "What do you expect me to say? The tacos are terrible? The tacos are good, the best."

"Two tacos," I said, "and a Diet Coke."

"He's a good man, Arnoldo," she said. "A very good man and a good father."

My turn to nod. She walked away and I waited and looked out the window. The clouds were white cotton. The sun was behind one of them heading for the Gulf of Mexico.

I had finished the first taco when Arnoldo Robles sat down across from me still wearing his apron, a bottle of water in his hand. Corazon Robles was right. The taco was good and big.

"I've got maybe five minutes," he said.

"You look tired."

He shrugged.

"You know this song? The one playing?" he asked.

" 'La Paloma,' " I said.

"Yes, 'The Dove.' People think it is a Mexican song, but it is not," he said, looking at the tablecloth. "It is Spanish and the other famous song in Spanish, 'Granada,' about a city in Spain, is a Mexican song. *Irónico*. You understand?"

"Ironic," I said. "Almost the same word. You look tired."

"Bad dreams," he said. "My wife told you?"

"Yes."

"I dream about that boy, that car," he said.

"I have nightmares too. My nightmares are about my wife. She was killed by a hit-and-run driver."

"I'm sorry," he said. "When?"

"Four years, one month and six days ago."

I took a bite of the second taco.

"Good taco," I said.

"You talked to the police?" asked Robles.

"Yes," I said.

"I don't have anything more to tell you than I told them," he said after a long drink of water. "I was walking home. I see this kid in the street. There's a car behind him. Kid runs down the street, right in the middle, you know? Kid turns, holds up his hand, but the guy in the car just . . ."

"Ran him down," I said.

"Ran him . . . ?"

"Hit him on purpose."

"Looked that way to me," said Arnoldo.

"What was the boy doing in the street?"

"I don't know. I could see him like I see you now. He turns, headlights on his face, and the guy in the car steps on the gas, screeches the tires. I can hear it."

"What did the kid's face look like?"

I kept my eyes on him and worked my taco.

"Look like? I don't know. Afraid and then another look. Don't know what it was and he puts up his hand maybe like he wants the guy to stop, but the guy in the car steps on the gas and I'm just standing there."

"You couldn't see the driver?"

Robles shook his head.

"In my dream, he's a big guy, big shoulders, but I didn't get a good look at him. In his car he was just . . ."

He held out his hands.

". . . like a shape. Like the one in the backseat."

I put down my taco.

"In your dream there's someone in the backseat of the car?"

"In my dream? Yeah, but in the real car too. Someone not so big. Maybe a girl. Maybe a kid."

"You tell this to the police?"

"Yeah, sure, cop named Ralston."

"Ransom," I corrected.

"Ransom, whatever. I told him. He said maybe I was seeing things. I said maybe but I didn't think so. He said maybe the kid who got hit had run onto the street. I said no way. He said maybe the screeching I heard was the driver trying to stop before hitting the kid. I said for sure, no. I could see."

"Anything else you remember?"

"Blood, maybe brains on the street. Boy was dead when I got to him. Car was driving fast down the street. Boy's body all twisted. When I was a kid, I wanted to be a doctor. No more. You really working for the boy's mother?"

I nodded.

"Find the guy," he said. "Find out what it was all about. Let me know. I need to sleep. My wife and I need to know our son is safe on the streets, at least safe from that crazy guy."

He got up. So did I. We shook hands. His was damp with cool moisture from the water bottle. He went back to the kitchen and I dropped six dollars on the table and left.

I started across the parking lot toward my car, reaching into my pocket for the car key. I didn't see it coming. I heard the screech of tires close by and started to look up. I sensed it almost on me. Maybe I held up my hand the way Kyle McClory had done about a week ago. I didn't freeze. I dived over the edge of the fender, my knee hitting something, maybe the headlight, as the car passed by and made a sharp turn at

Stuart M. Kaminsky

the end of the aisle onto Lime. I didn't see it turn. I heard it. I was sprawled on my back, knee throbbing, left shoulder numb, Cubs cap still on my head.

I got up as fast as I could, rubbed my hands against my jeans, picked up the car keys where I had dropped them as I limped toward my parked car.

"Oh my God. Are you all right?" a woman said, rushing across the parking lot. She was small, huge busted with big round glasses, carrying a baby.

"Fine," I said.

"It looked like that maniac was trying to kill you," she said, rubbing the baby's back to comfort him or her, though the baby didn't seem the least bit upset.

"I'm fine," I said.

"Maybe I should call the police," she said. "Driving like that through a parking lot. He could have hit my baby or me. I'm calling the police. You wait here."

"Did you see his license number?"

"No," she said.

"Make and color of the car?"

"I . . . no. But a man was driving it. I think he had a beard or something. I could tell the police that."

The baby decided to cry.

"You could," I said, going to my car.

"You're sure you're all right?" she asked.

"Yes," I said, thinking that I was all right until the next time.

I got in and closed the door.

My hands were shaking. I closed my eyes. I had not been there when my wife had died. The police had pieced together a likely narrative in their report, but it left a universe of imagined scenarios. I had tried to come up with one I could cling to but it kept changing. Sometimes Catherine is struck by a huge Caddy driven by a distracted old man. Catherine doesn't see it coming. She was alive one second, dead the next. Or, sometimes Catherine is frozen in the path of a pickup driven by a drunken, grinning ex-con. Someone she had put in prison.

Now I was juggling three hit-and-run scenarios, Catherine's, Kyle McClory's, mine.

My hands stopped trembling. They hadn't been trembling with fear. They had been trembling because the person who had tried to kill me had opened the curtain, letting in memory.

Since my wife had died, among the things I had lost were fear and a willingness to experience joy.

The woman and the crying baby were back on the sidewalk standing in front of Ace Hardware. I drove slowly. There was a predator on the streets and my knee and shoulder hurt.

I caught what there was of a rush hour as I headed down Fruitville toward Tamiami Trail. The Gulf Coast was in season, which meant lots of tourists, lots of snowbirds. Jaguars, red convertibles with their tops down, a Lexus or two, pickups, SUVs, almost all being driven badly.

Traffic rules in Sarasota: (1) If the light recently turned red, step on the gas and go. (2) If you come to a stop sign, do not stop. Just slow down a little and look both ways. (3) At a four-way stop, it doesn't matter who gets there first. What matters is how big a vehicle you have and how mad at the world you are that day. (4) If there is just enough room for you to fit, you can speed up and cut off another driver. (5) Checking the rearview mirror before changing lanes is optional and checking side mirrors is to be avoided. (6) The law is wrong. It is the pedestrians who should yield to the cars.

Driving badly is an infectious disease on Florida's Sun

Coast. I think it started with native Floridians in pickups and baseball caps who zipped in and out of traffic in a hurry to win the race that had no winner. A variation, in mutated form, had been imported from the North with little old retired men and women who kept their eyes straight ahead, drove a dangerous ten miles under the speed limit, never looked at their side or rearview mirrors even when they changed lanes as they sat with necks craned so they could see over the dashboard. Finally the disease had been passed on to people angry at the pickups, angry with the ancient drivers. This group drove a few miles over the speed limit and had an uncontrollable urge to curse at everyone who hogged or shared the road.

Someone inside one of those cars on the streets of Sarasota with me that day was even more dangerous than all the rest of the drivers on the road. He was the one who had tried to kill me.

6

I PULLED into the driveway of Flo Zink's house on a street off Siesta Drive before you get to the bridge to Siesta Key.

My leg hurt. My shoulder ached. I was thirsty.

The SUV was in the driveway. Before I knocked, I could hear guitars and singing beyond the door. This meant that either Adele was out somewhere with the baby or the baby was not taking a nap. The sound system and the pumping of country-and-western music played several decibels too loud were turned off when Adele's baby was sleeping.

Flo, glass of amber liquid in her right hand, opened the door and smiled at me. Flo is a short, solid woman in her late sixties. She used to wear too much makeup. Now she wears a little. She used to dress in flashy Western shirts, jeans and cowboy boots. She still does.

The music was loud behind her, but nowhere near as loud as when I had first met her. I must have looked at the drink in her hand. She did too.

"Pure, zero-proof Diet Dr Pepper," she said.

I looked at the drink, saw the bubbles and nodded. I had pulled some strings, very thin strings, to get Flo's driver's license back. Adele was a few days away from turning sixteen. She would be able to drive on her own then, but until she could do it legally, she needed a licensed driver in the car. That was Flo.

"Quiz, my sad Italian friend," Flo said, stepping back to let me in. "What Cole Porter song did Roy Rogers make famous?"

" 'Don't Fence Me In,' " I said.

The song was playing throughout the house. I didn't recognize Rogers's voice, but I recognized the song.

"You are a clever son of a bitch," she said. "What are you drinking?"

"Diet Dr Pepper will be fine," I said.

"You know where the kitchen is."

She closed the front door behind me. I limped in and she said, "What's wrong with your leg?"

"Bumped into something."

"Let me take a look. Sit down and drop your pants," she said, motioning toward one of the living room chairs.

"I'm fine," I said.

"And I'm Nicole Kidman. Sit. Drop 'em or roll 'em up."

I sat and rolled up my pants leg. Flo looked down at it. Roy Rogers sang about gazing at the moon.

She looked down at my leg.

"Knee's a little swollen," she said. "Nothing too bad."

She patted me on the shoulder. I winced.

"What's wrong up there?"

"Bumped into something else," I said.

"You are one injury-begging sad sack or a liar," she said.

"Adele home?" I said, rolling down my pants leg, getting up, about to head for the kitchen, just left of the front door off the living room.

"Sit back down. I'll get it," said Flo, holding up her glass and heading toward the kitchen and calling back, "She's home. I'll get her after I bring your drink."

Behind us Roy Rogers sang about starry skies and wanting lots of land.

I didn't want lots of land. I wanted to get back to my small box of a room behind my office. And I could do without starry skies. I liked small enclosed spaces. I hated lying on my back outdoors at night. It made my head swirl. I had felt a little of this before Catherine died. Since she was gone, it had gotten more defined. I welcomed it.

Flo didn't have to get Adele. Adele came down the hallway to the living room, baby in her arms. Adele smiled at me. No, actually, it was a grin. Catherine, five months old, thin blonde hair, was thoughtfully chewing on her mother's hair.

"Mr. F," Adele said. "Want to hold her?"

"No thanks," I said.

Flo came back in the room, handed me a cold glass of Diet Dr Pepper, touched Adele's face, kissed the baby's forehead and scurried off down the hall.

I didn't want a baby's life literally in my hands. I don't trust fate and I know if there is a God or gods, devils or demons, they can play games a certified sociopath might admire.

Flo came back with a colorful Indian blanket and rolled it

out on the living room floor. Adele loosened the baby's grip on her hair and placed Catherine on the blanket on her stomach, facing us. The baby lifted her head unsteadily, hands pushing against the rug, and looked at me. Our eyes met.

"Lew," said Flo. "Lew."

The thought had crept up on me. My wife, Catherine, and I might have had a baby like the one who was looking up at me if a hit-and-run driver on Lake Shore Drive in Chicago hadn't killed her four years ago.

"Yes," I said.

"You all right?" asked Adele, coming to my side.

Roy Rogers had stopped and Johnny Cash was singing about killing a man in Reno as I rejoined the living.

Adele was about my height, blonde, clear-skinned and definitely pretty. She had lost the touch of baby fat shortly after I first met her.

"How's school?" I asked.

Catherine rolled over onto her back.

"Straight *A*'s, arts editor of the paper," Flo said.

Catherine rolled onto her stomach, heading toward the edge of the rug. As she rolled again, Adele stepped over and put her back in the center of the rug. Flo picked up a red plastic baby toy that looked like a ball with handles and placed it in front of the baby.

"How's life treating you, Mr. F.?" Adele said.

I knew how life had treated Adele. Her father had sold her to a local pimp when she was thirteen. Her father had murdered her mother. Adele had gotten into an affair with the married son of a famous man when she was fifteen, who had taken her in. Result: Catherine was named for my wife. Catherine's father was serving a life term for murder. And yet there was Adele smiling, finishing high school, and writing award-winning stories that were sure to get her an invitation to major universities.

"Fine," I said.

"He's been bumping into things," said Flo.

Johnny Cash was finished. The Sons of the Pioneers were now singing "Cool Water."

I drank some Diet Dr Pepper and watched Catherine suck on one of the handles of the circle.

"You know a boy named Kyle McClory?" I asked as Adele sat cross-legged on the rug next to the baby.

"Knew," Adele said. "He got killed about a week ago. Hit-and-run."

"How well did you know him?" I asked.

"Hardly," she said. "He was a freshman. Two years apart in age. Two decades apart in life school. He was a kid. You trying to find the driver, right?"

"Yes. I'm working for his mother."

"Wait, wait," said Flo. "How's knowing about the boy going to help you find some hit-and-run drunk?"

"He thinks maybe Kyle was murdered, right, Mr. F.?" Adele was smiling, her hand gently rubbing the back of the baby, who was totally absorbed with the difficult choice between which handles of the toy she was going to put in her mouth.

"It's possible," I said. "What about Yolanda Root? Kyle's sister."

Adele looked up and said, "Half sister. She wants no part of Doc McClory or his name. He wants no part of her. Probably the only thing they ever agreed on. Her, I can tell you a whole lot about. What are you thinking, Mr. F? Someone ran down her kid brother to get back at Yolanda or something?"

"I don't know."

And I didn't.

Flo had sat on the sofa, diet drink in hand, watching the baby.

"Yolanda's two years older than me," Adele said. "She just graduated. No, I take that back. She wasn't graduated. She was ushered out after an extra year to make up the courses she had flunked. Haven't really been in touch with her much since they handed her the diploma and probably asked her not to come back for reunions."

Bob Nolan and the Sons of the Pioneers sang about someone who was a devil and not a man.

"Yolanda was trouble?" I said.

"Name it," said Adele, gently rubbing her forehead against the top of the baby's head. "Drugs, maybe even a little low-level dealing, men, boys, maybe even girls. She tried to come on to me back when I was with . . . you know. But she wasn't good at it. She was just playing bad girl. You know? Diamond in her tongue, triple rings in one ear and makeup that said put up or shut up. This Goth is watching you. Tolstoy said you play a role long enough, you start becoming the character."

"That's what happened to Yolanda?"

Adele nodded.

"Possibility," I said. "You think maybe someone might try to get back at her by going after her brother? Or maybe she got Kyle into something?"

"No," she said. "She liked the kid, wanted to protect him, be big sister, which didn't play well being who she was. Haven't talked to Yola in, I don't know, maybe a year."

"Andrew Goines?"

"Who?"

"Friend of Kyle," I said.

DENIAL

She shook her head. The name meant nothing to her.

At the door, Flo handed me what looked like a candy bar.

"PowerBar," she said. "Super-high protein."

I put it in my pocket.

"Thanks."

"You don't need an excuse, Lewis," she said.

"Excuse?"

"For dropping in just to see Adele and the baby and, if I can flatter my old ass, to see me. You didn't really need what you got from Adele. Lots of better ways you could have got it."

"Yes," I said. "I do need an excuse."

She put a firm hand on my right arm and said, "Fooling God?" she said. "If he sees you getting too close to someone, he may play another one of his tricks on you?"

That wasn't quite it, but it was close enough.

"Here," she said, handing me something in a small white tube. "Rub it on your knee and shoulder. Hell, rub it on your ass if you've a mind to."

"Thanks," I said, putting the tube in my pocket.

"Happy trails," she said and closed the door after me.

I made some turns, a right onto Webber, a left at Beneva, a U-turn and up to Bee Ridge to be sure no one was following me.

Maybe the guy who had tried to run me down had a life outside the one related to trying to kill me. Maybe he had a job, a family, places he was expected. Maybe he just went after me on his lunch hour. Then again, maybe not.

I drove back down Beneva, stopped at Shaner's and picked up a pair of large pizzas, one with double onions and one with mushrooms and double sausage.

Stuart M. Kaminsky

It was past seven. I drove to Sally's apartment in the Alhambra. I took off my Cubs cap, tucked it into my back pocket and pushed the button. Susan opened the door.

Sally's daughter was eleven, wore glasses, was dark like her mother, and spoke her mind, which at this moment told her to call over her shoulder, "Mr. Smiley Face is here."

Michael appeared, tall, gangly, a head of curly hair and blue eyes, which he definitely got from his father.

"I thought we were going out," Susan said.

"Something came up."

"At least he comes bearing gifts," Michael said.

"Mushroom and double sausage," I said, holding out the pizzas.

Michael took both pizza boxes and with a hand on his sister's shoulder, stepped back to let me in.

Sally came out of the tiny kitchen just off the dining room area. She had changed into a loose-fitting green dress. Michael and Susan had both boxes open on the dining room table and were reaching for pizza slices.

"You're late," Sally said quietly.

"Someone tried to kill me," I said, low enough so the kids couldn't hear me.

"Well," she said. "I just got here a few minutes ago myself and I don't have as good an excuse as you."

"I'm not making a joke," I said.

"I know," said Sally with a sigh. "What's it about?"

"Kyle McClory," I said.

"Tell me about it later," she said, touching my cheek. "I'll get drinks out of the fridge. You grab some plates and napkins."

I had plenty of time. I had almost seven hours before

I had to pick up Ames to break into the Seaside Assisted Living Facility.

There was no point in asking Michael if he knew Kyle McClory. They were the same age, but a culture and school apart. Michael went to Riverview. Kyle had gone to Sarasota High. The schools were ten minutes, endless space and a meaningless rivalry apart.

After the pizza was gone and crumbs cleared away, Susan said she wanted to play a card game called B.S. Sally said she was tired. I said I didn't want to learn anything new. Michael said he would play if Susan did the after-dinner cleaning up by herself. She agreed.

"Please," Susan said, looking first at Sally and then at me. "I'll teach you. It's real easy."

Sally said, "Well . . ."

"I beseech, supplicate, implore and plead," Susan said.

I couldn't resist the display of vocabulary.

We played three games. I won two of them. Susan finally said, "I can't tell when you're lying. You always look the same."

"I'll try to be more obvious when I lie," I said. "Look for twitches, eye movement, finger movements, scratches."

"You have those?" Michael asked.

"No," I said. "Tone of voice helps."

"You always talk the same," Susan said.

She put her cards down and stepped in front of me. There was determination in her eyes.

"Susan," Sally said with what may have been a gentle warning.

"I said I'd do it," Susan said, meeting my eyes.

"Do it," said Michael.

Susan reached over with both hands and began to tickle

me under my arms. I forced a smile; at least I thought it was a smile.

"You're not ticklish," Susan said after about fifteen seconds of trying.

"No," I said.

Susan stepped back.

"You are strange," she said.

I shrugged.

Michael collected the cards and put them away and went to the bedroom to watch the end of an Orlando Magic game. Susan hung around a few minutes longer and then followed her brother.

When they were gone, Sally got up from the table, saying, "Who tried to kill you?"

I told her about the threatening telephone call and the car that almost hit me in the parking lot at the mall.

"I'm not going to say it," she said.

"What?"

"That you have to do a better job of taking care of yourself," she said, moving into the kitchen.

"You just said it."

"Let's call it a night. I've got a report to write," she said. "In addition to which, I'm tired and cranky."

"I've got something to do too," I said, rising.

"Besides going to your room and watching an old movie?"

"Yes. I'm going to a friend's house and we're going to bake a pineapple upside-down cake," I said.

"No."

"I was lying."

"I could tell," she said.

"How?"

"You looked me in the eye and said it without blinking or smiling. Besides, I can't come up with an image of you in a kitchen at night mixing batter."

"I don't think you want to know what I'm going to do," I said.

"Help somebody," she said. "That's what you do."

"It's what you do too," I said.

We were moving toward the front door in the living room.

"We're a match made in heaven," she said and kissed me. "Put your arms around me and mean it," she added, her face inches from mine.

I could feel her breath, smell her hair. Her eyes were large and brown and moist and maybe a little tired. I kissed her back. She opened her mouth, arms around my neck. I felt her breasts warm against me. I told myself not to think of my dead wife. I failed but it didn't stop me from holding Sally and letting the kiss stay warm.

She gently removed her arms, patted my cheek and stepped back, smiling at me.

I opened my mouth to speak but she cut me off with, "Nothing to say, Lewis. Nothing to explain or talk about. It's okay."

She opened the door and I stepped out into the cool darkness. Standing on the landing, I told her more about my day, the person who tried to run me down, about Dorothy Cgnozic. Sally listened, nodded a few times while I talked. I kept it short, very short, and I didn't mention that Ames and I were going to break into the Seaside Assisted Living Facility in a few hours.

"Forty-six eleven Tenth," she said, starting to close the door.

"Forty-six eleven Tenth," I repeated.

"That's where Yolanda Root is staying."

She closed the door.

I watched the parking lot as I moved down the stairs. Nothing moved but the leaves on the bushes from a gentle breeze.

I drove back to the DQ parking lot, checking my rearview mirror for anyone who might be following me.

The DQ was a few minutes from closing. I got to the window in time to order a large black coffee. The thin black girl behind the counter, Teresa, was working two jobs. Teresa was nineteen. She had two children under six years old. During the day she worked in the bakery section of the Publix on Fruitville and in the evening she was behind the counter at the DQ. Her mother watched the kids.

"Want a Blizzard?" she asked, wiping her hands on a white towel. "On me. You're my last customer as a night counter girl. Dave promoted me to day manager."

"Publix?"

"They'll have to get along without me," she said with a smile, showing white, slightly large teeth. "Raise makes up for it and I can see my kids at night, have dinner with them."

"I need the coffee to stay awake," I said.

"Okay, the coffee's on me," she said.

"I accept," I said. "Congratulations."

"Two sugars and cream?" she said. "Right?"

I always took three sugars, but I said, "Right."

She got the coffee and handed it to me. I toasted her with it.

"Did he find you?" she asked.

"Who?"

"Man who was looking for you," she said. "Looked like

he was coming down from a bad high, you know? Shaky, nervous-like."

"What's he look like?"

"Bigger than you, older than you, one of those little beards, real white."

"The man or the beard?" I asked.

"Both," she said.

"When did he come by?"

"Few hours ago, maybe."

"Did you see his car?"

"Didn't notice," she said. "Got to finish cleaning up."

I went to the steps of the two-story office building at the back of the parking lot. I held the coffee cup in my left hand and fished for my keys with my right hand.

I looked back as I went up the concrete steps. There were two cars in the DQ parking lot, Teresa's 1986 Toyota and mine. No cars were parked across Washington. Traffic moved by. It never stopped, but around eleven each night it slowed down to a rumble of trucks and a swish of cars going over the speed limit.

The phone began to ring before I could turn on the lights. I hit the switch, kicked the door closed, pocketed my keys and took my coffee to the desk.

"Yes," I said, picking up the phone.

"I'm sorry," he said.

It was the same man who had threatened to kill me and I was reasonably sure he was the one who had talked to Teresa. He sounded about five levels above nervous.

"For what?"

"Trying to run you down," he said. "I've been telling myself that I just wanted to frighten you, but if you hadn't jumped out of the way, I might have killed you. Are you all right?"

"Nothing broken. Nothing bleeding. Come on up and

we'll talk about it," I said, moving to the window and taking a sip of coffee. He couldn't be far.

"No," he said. "I'm sorry but I really do have to stop you. Please just stop, let me punish myself. Seneca was right when he said, 'Every guilty person is his own hangman.'"

"You going to try again to kill me?"

"You're not going to stop trying to find me, are you?" he asked.

"No," I said.

"Then . . . I'm really sorry. I've got to get home now."

He hung up. I turned off the office light after I hit the switch in the back room where I lived, kicked off my shoes, turned on the television and the VCR and inserted a tape before sitting on the bed, where I hit the button on the remote.

Stagecoach came on. It was dubbed in Spanish. I don't speak Spanish. Julio at the video store down the street had sold it to me for three dollars. I hadn't known it was in Spanish until a few seconds ago. I'm sure Julio hadn't either.

I watched Andy Devine and George Bancroft jabbering at each other in voices that weren't theirs. The guy who dubbed John Wayne tried to mimic the Duke, but didn't come close. I turned off the sound and kept watching. I knew almost every word of the movie.

As I watched, I followed the instructions on the tube I had taken out of my pocket and rubbed the white cream on my knee and shoulder. It went from cold to warm, tingly electric. It seemed to be working.

When the Plummer brothers were dead and John Wayne and Claire Trevor had ridden off in the buckboard, I put in a tape of *The Woman on the Beach*. Joan Bennett spoke English. I finished my now room-temperature coffee.

DENIAL

When the clock said it was time, I turned off the VCR and the lights and dropped the empty coffee cup in the garbage. After a quick stop in the washroom halfway down the walkway outside my office, I went to my car and drove to the Texas Bar & Grille to pick up Ames and commit a felony.

7

AMES WORE his well-worn jeans and a plaid shirt and denim jacket. No slicker. No shotgun. No Stetson on his head. This was a simple break-in.

"Mornin'," he said, getting into the car and handing me a cardboard cup of coffee. He had a cup too.

"Thanks," I said. "Flashlight?"

Ames reached into his pocket and came up with a black penlight not very different from the one I had in my pocket.

Ames didn't put on his seat belt. He never did. It wasn't that he didn't believe they worked. He just didn't like the government, any government, telling him what he had to do to protect himself.

Ames didn't really like anyone telling him what to do for any reason. Even Ed was careful when telling Ames that there was something he wanted done in the Texas Bar & Grille. "Would you do the windows today?" or "Mind getting the garbage out early tomorrow?" were the ways Ed respected Ames's self-respect.

There wasn't much traffic at one-thirty in the morning, but there was some. I sipped coffee, drove and didn't turn on the radio.

"Saw Flo, Adele and the baby," I said. "They're fine."

I glanced at Ames, who nodded to indicate that he had heard, registered and approved of what I had said. That was all we said for the twelve-minute ride. I drove at about ten miles an hour after I turned down the narrow road that led to the Seaside from Beneva.

The front-canopied entrance to the Seaside was dark behind the glass doors. There were cars, seven of them, at the end of the lot. Some of them must have belonged to the night staff. A few of the cars might even belong to residents still able to drive. I didn't park near the other cars. Ames indicated that I should pull into a corner space under a tree where the parking lot lights didn't hit.

"We go in over there."

He pointed to the side of the one-story brick building. We put our coffee cups in the holders by the dashboard, got out and closed the doors quietly. I didn't lock them. We might want to or have to get out of here quickly.

I followed Ames into the darkness at the side of the building. The sky was clear but there wasn't much of a moon, not enough light to keep me from tripping over a bush and pitching forward, losing my hat.

Ames helped me up.

"Lost my cap," I whispered, squinting around my feet.

"Here," whispered Ames, handing it to me.

A light came on in the window three feet from us. We pressed our backs against the wall and inched away. We stopped when we heard the window begin to open.

A tiny woman, white bushy hair, glasses on the end of her nose, leaned out, pulled her robe around her and said, "Jerry Lee?"

She didn't look in our direction, just squinted toward the trees straight ahead of her.

"Is that you, Jerry Lee?"

Something shuffled in the grass by the trees. Whoever or whatever it was came slowly toward the window. When the light from the window hit the gator, which was a good or bad seven feet long, it turned its head up toward the woman, mouth open. Its eyes were a glassy white.

Ames moved slightly at my side. I turned my eyes but not my head and made out a gun in his hand. The gator grunted and turned its head toward us.

"Jerry Lee, be quiet," the old woman whispered.

She threw something out the window into the gator's open mouth. The gator made a gulping sound, took a few steps forward and opened its mouth even wider. The old woman threw something else out the window. Jerry Lee the gator snatched it from the air.

"Jerry Lee," she whispered. "You've got to be quiet. You know I'm not supposed to . . . Someone's in the hall."

She closed the window and a few seconds later the light went out. I could only make out the vague shape of Jerry Lee and hoped his appetite had been satisfied.

There was a click from the gun in Ames's hand as the gator turned its head in our direction and took a short step toward us.

Ames moved past me, took four steps and stood in front of the gator, gun in hand.

"Get out of here," Ames whispered, aiming his gun directly down at Jerry Lee's left eye.

The gator grunted. Ames brought his booted right foot

DENIAL

down on Jerry Lee's snout and took a step back, gun steady in his hand.

"Your move," Ames said calmly to the gator.

The gator shook its head back and forth, trying to decide what to do. Then it turned right and scuttled across the long grass into the darkness between the trees. There was a splash in the darkness.

Ames walked back to me, tucking the gun into his belt under his denim jacket.

"Let's go," he said.

I followed him without tripping to the fourth window, where he stopped and reached up. He pushed the window up and whispered, "It's empty. Least it was this afternoon, when I unlocked the window."

Ames boosted himself up and went through the window headfirst. He made almost no noise. When he was in, he reached back to help me up. I was reasonably quiet.

Ames turned on his flashlight. There was nothing in the room but a bed with a rolled-up mattress, a wooden night table and a wooden chest of drawers with nothing on top of it. There were no pictures on the walls.

Ames motioned to me and turned off his flashlight. We went to the door. He listened, ear to the door, for a few seconds and then turned the knob. He opened the door slowly. The lights in the hall were night dim. He stepped out and motioned for me to follow him.

In the hall, Ames moved to his right with me behind him. There was a turn in front of us with a long hallway. From far down that long hallway came a man's voice. I couldn't make out the words, but could tell that the person was probably talking on the phone because of the silent pauses.

Ames went to the end of the corridor and peeked down the long hallway. Then he turned and motioned for me to

Stuart M. Kaminsky

follow him. He moved quickly across the hallway and into an alcove. I followed, glancing to my left, relieved to see nothing and no one.

I knew where we were now, right in front of Amos Trent's office. Ames tried the door. It was locked. He pulled his jackknife from his pocket, found a thin blade that looked like a toothpick with a tiny forked tip. In no more than four seconds, the door opened. We went in. Ames's flashlight came on as the door closed. I turned mine on too.

We both knew what we were looking for. I went to the desk. Ames went to the file cabinet. We worked fast. I found a few interesting things, including a clearly marked medicine bottle from Eckerd's drugstore containing two Viagra pills, five low-carb chocolate bars, a tube of Thomas Valerian's toupee paste, and a thin catalog of items guaranteed to "embarrass or gross out" your friends and enemies.

Ames was on the second drawer, thumbing through file folders.

"Wrong place," came a voice from the door.

I froze. Ames turned his light toward the voice.

A figure in a blue robe pushed the door closed. I turned my light on him. He was ancient, pudgy, pink-faced, with sparse white hair carefully brushed to the right of his age-spotted scalp. He stood with both hands on a walker.

"Saw you here this afternoon," he said to Ames. "Or maybe it was yesterday. It's easy to lose track of days or time in here."

Neither Ames nor I said anything.

The man flicked on the lights.

"No one'll see the light," he said conversationally. "Even if they look at the door, there's nothing out there but trees, grass, the creek and Rose Teffler's gator. Well?"

"You know what we're looking for?" I asked.

"Dorothy told me," he said. "My name's Ham Gentry, by the way."

"You knew we'd come here?" I asked.

"Hell no," he said. "I'm a night wanderer like Dorothy and a few others, Sid Catorian, Lilly Carnovski. You can hear Sid's wheelchair whining fifty feet away. I just happened to see you when I came out of the toilet at the end of the hall."

"Where is it?" I asked.

He pointed past me to the wall. There was a corkboard a few feet above where I sat. It was covered with neatly posted memos and announcements skewered with colorful tacks. I had looked at the board when I came in. There had been nothing about patient discharges.

"Under the green brochure about Medicare and Medicaid," he said.

I got up, lifted the brochure and saw a report marked, *Discharges, Admissions*. The date at the top was yesterday.

"I saw him put one of those up there a few months ago," said Gentry. There were others beneath it dating back a week.

"Why's he hide it?" Ames asked.

I put the report on the desk and began to copy the information I needed onto the back of an envelope I took out of the trash can under the desk.

"I think he juggles the numbers," said Gentry. "My guess is he uses it to skim moola, *dinero*, a few bucks here and there. Not sure how, but I'm working on it and when I find out, there will be perks aplenty for Hamilton Gentry and his friends."

"Got it," I said, writing down the last of four names and the addresses.

I put the report and the brochure back on the corkboard as close to where they had been as I could remember. Ames and I headed toward the door but Gentry raised his hand to stop us.

Stuart M. Kaminsky

"Just go out the window here," he said. "I'll lock it behind you."

"Thanks," I said.

"Dorothy says someone was murdered here, then someone was murdered here," he said. "Nurses here are damned nice, considering what they have to put up with, but Amos Trent is . . . what the hell, get going."

Ames opened the window, lifted his right leg over the sill, and then his left followed and he dropped into the darkness. I followed him. When my feet touched the ground, the window lock clicked. A few seconds later, the light went out.

I followed Ames along the brick wall and made it past Rose Teffler's window without encountering Jerry Lee.

I dropped Ames at the Texas and headed to my office. There were no cars in the DQ lot. When I opened my office door, I half expected the phone to be ringing, but it wasn't. I didn't look at the information I had copied. I just placed it on my desk in the dark and headed for the back room, where I stripped down to my boxers and lay down on the cot, two pillows under my head. I wasn't sleepy. I watched the lights between the slats of my blinds from occasional cars passing on Washington.

It was, I guessed, a little after three-thirty.

Sleep came, but not quickly.

8

SOMEONE WAS KNOCKING at my door. I opened my eyes. The sun was casting bands of dusty light through the slats of my blinds. More knocking. Not hard. Not insistent, but not giving up either. I reached for my watch, almost got it before it fell off the chair next to my bed. Then I almost fell out of the bed reaching for the watch.

It was a few minutes after eight.

I got up and stood for a few seconds, swaying slightly, blinking, wanting the knocking to stop so I could fold myself back onto my cot.

The knocking didn't stop. In need of a shave, clad in my blue boxer underwear with the little white circles and an extra-large gray Grinnell College T-shirt that I picked up at the Women's Exchange for fifty cents, I was as ready as I wanted to be for visitors.

When I opened the door, the sun greeted me just over the

acupuncture center across Washington Street. A cool breeze and the sight of a man wearing a Tampa Bay Bucs sweatshirt dappled with stains from coffee and liquids unknown also greeted me.

"Digger," I said.

"Little Italian," he said, with a smile showing white, inexpensive but serviceable false teeth.

Digger, until a few months ago, had been homeless. Well, not homeless if you were willing to consider the rest room five doors down a home. Digger, bush of pepper gray hair and nose tilted slightly to the right, was a thinker. Once, when I was shaving in the rest room, he had said, "Why do women complain when men leave the toilet seat up? Why shouldn't men complain when women leave the toilet seat down?"

We stood looking at each other for a few seconds, Digger with his hands behind his back, rocking slightly, me with my hands at my sides, waiting.

"Job's gone," he said, looking over his left shoulder.

I knew what he was looking at, the second-floor dance studio across the street where he had been working as an instructor. Digger had dug deeply into his memory of different times to call up what he called "the Spirit of Terpsichore." The studio had closed a few days ago. No notice. Just gone, cleaned out, empty.

"You want to come in?" I asked.

"I bear no gifts," he said.

"I expect none," I said, stepping back.

He came in and I closed the door.

"Lewis," he said, facing me. "I am optimistic."

"I'm happy to hear that," I said.

"Wrong word," he said. "You are not happy. I have never seen you happy. I have seen you relieved."

"I'm relieved to hear that you are optimistic," I said.

Digger looked at the chair in front of my desk. I motioned for him to sit. He did. I went into the back room, changed into my yellow boxers with the little gray sharks, put on my jeans and a clean short-sleeved white button-down shirt, white socks and white sneakers. Then I went back into the office, Cubs hat in hand, where Digger was examining the sheet of names and addresses from the Seaside I had scribbled.

He looked up as I sat behind the desk and said, "I'm optimistic. My room rent is paid for two weeks. I have prospects, ideas."

"That's good," I said.

"I thought you should be the first one I told because you were the one who lifted me from the chill confines of the WC and the depths of ignominy to the dignity of steady work and eating regular."

Digger was smiling. With people who look like Digger, the conclusion to jump to was that he had spent the night cuddling with a bottle of inexpensive but well-advertised wine or some drug not of choice but of last resort. Neither was true. Digger neither drank nor used drugs. His troubles were deeper than that, rooted, as he put it, in faulty genes, ill-fated life choices, a series of concussions and a god or gods who enjoyed experimenting on him. I knew those gods.

"Ideas," he said, looking down at my list and then back up at me. "I've thought of starting a church, the First Presbyterian Church of the Tupperware. Sell religion and plastic containers that you put things in and pop the tops. On top of each lid will be an inscription: JESUS SAVES; SO SHOULD YOU."

I nodded. Digger leaned forward.

"How about this? A line of candy. Simple chocolates maybe made in the shape of offensive things. I'd call it Good-Tasting Chocolate in Bad Taste. You know. Swastikas.

Stuart M. Kaminsky

Klansmen. That one would be white chocolate, which you know is not really chocolate at all."

"I didn't know," I said.

"What do you think?"

"I think you need a job and a loan," I said.

Digger stopped smiling.

"I paid you back last time," he said.

"That you did."

"Well, I've started finding some dignity. Now I guess I'd better find another job to keep the search going."

I shifted my weight, took out my wallet, removed three twenties and handed them to Digger. I noticed that his hands were clean and his face freshly shaved. He took the money and touched his cheeks.

"Spic and span and speaking Spanish," he said. "Ready to take on the world again."

"Good," I said.

"Any ideas?"

"Can you cook?"

"Continental, Mexican, Italian, Thai, Chinese, French," he said, counting each one off on his fingers.

"Short order," I said. "Griddle cakes, eggs, bacon, sausages."

"With the best of them, whoever they might be," he said.

"Gwen's looking for an early-morning short-order cook," I said.

Gwen's was just down the street, a clean, bright survivor of the 1950s, not a kitsch and cool fifties diner, but the real thing. There was even an autographed poster of Elvis on the wall near the cash register. Elvis had dropped in for breakfast in 1957 when Gwen was a little girl and her parents had owned the place. Now, Gwen and her daughters ran the diner, kept the prices down and the food simple.

"I'm the man for the job," Digger said. "Though I have to confess, I can't really handle all that ethnic cuisine."

"Confession accepted," I said. "You know Gwen?"

"Of course," he said.

"Let me know how it goes," I said, getting up. He did the same.

"Can I buy you breakfast?" he asked.

"Get the job and you can make me breakfast tomorrow."

"How do I look?" he asked.

"Got another shirt?"

He looked down at himself.

"Yes."

"Clean?"

"Spotless," he said.

"Put it on and go see Gwen. Tell her I sent you."

"Here's hoping," he said, moving to the door.

I had long ago given up hoping and I didn't think Digger had much left in him, but he hung on. I hung on. I was never really sure why. That's one of the reasons I saw Ann Horowitz.

I got a clean towel from my closet, took my ziplock bag containing a disposable Bic razor, soap, toothbrush and toothpaste and made my way to the rest room along the railed concrete walkway outside my door.

The rest room was always clean, thanks to Marvin Uliaks, slow of wit, doer of odd jobs on the stretch of Washington Street between Ringling and Bahia Vista. He swept floors, cleaned toilets, washed windows and smiled at whatever cash was handed to him. I regularly gave him a dollar a week. It was worth it.

It was going to be a busy day. I did not want a busy day. I had my list from the Seaside. I had a dead boy whose mother was waiting for something that people called "closure."

Stuart M. Kaminsky

Closure, the end of grief and the answer to why a tragedy burst through their door. I didn't have hope and I suspected that closure, if I ever found it, would close nothing, just open new doors.

When I got back to my office, I sat down and made a list of people to see:

Richard McClory, the dead boy's father
Yolanda Root, the dead boy's half sister
Andrew Goines, the dead boy's best friend
The four people who had been released from the Seaside
    Assisted Living Facility the night Dorothy Cgnozic had seen
    someone murdered

I wanted to go back to bed.

The phone rang.

"Fonesca?"

It was a woman. I recognized her voice. I closed my eyes, knowing what was coming.

"Yes."

"Two today," she said.

"My lucky day."

The woman was Marie Knot. She was a lawyer. She was around fifty, black, no-nonsense face, thin and all business. I wanted to say no, but I couldn't afford to lose her as a client. I was, according to the card with my picture on it in my wallet, a process server.

"I'll pick them up in a little while," I said.

"Need them served before five," she said. "Shouldn't be hard. I have addresses."

She hung up. My going rate was seventy-five dollars for each person served, regardless of how long it took or how much abuse I had to deal with.

I made a few phone calls.

Andrew Goines was in school. When I told his mother that I was working for Nancy Root, she said I could talk to her son when he got home at four.

"I don't really know Kyle's mother," she said. "Talked to her on the phone a few times. His father too. Kyle . . . Andrew could have been with him when it happened."

The familiar sound of a computer printer clacked on her end.

"I work at home," she said. "I'm sorry. I've got to get back online with a client."

"I'll come by at four," I said.

"Mr. . . . ?"

"Fonesca," I said.

"Hope you don't mind, but I am going to call Nancy Root to verify that you're working for her."

"You want her number?"

"No, I've got it," she said. "Got to run."

She hung up.

I found the phone number of Elliott Maxwell Root in Bradenton. Sally had said Yolanda had been living with her grandparents. I called. The voice that answered was young, female.

"Yolanda Root?" I asked.

"Yeah."

Careful, slow, wary.

"My name is Lew Fonesca. Your mother hired me to try to find out who killed your brother."

"What difference does it make?" she said. "He's dead. We're all dead or will be sooner or later."

"Can I talk to you about Kyle?"

"Go ahead," she said. "I'm waiting for a ride. When he comes, I say good-bye, private eye."

"I'm not a private detective," I said. "I just find people."

"Interesting," she said, making it clear that she didn't find it interesting at all.

"Can we talk in person?"

"Sure."

"When?"

"I'm between jobs, sort of," she said. "I clerk a few hours at my grandfather's hardware store on DeSoto near Fifty-seventh. I'll be there between one and three."

"I'll be there," I said.

I started to hang up but she said, "Wait."

"I'm here."

"What the fuck. Yeah, I'd like to know who killed Kyle. They could have stopped, called the police, given him first aid, something, instead of running away."

"Any idea who might want to hurt Kyle?"

"Hurt? It was some drunk or some blind old lady or something," she said. "Hit-and-run. Police said."

"We'll talk at your grandfather's," I said.

"Hey, if you—"

I hung up.

Richard McClory said I could meet him in half an hour at his office on Orange.

I folded my list, tucked it in my back pocket, put on my Cubs cap, locked the door, went through the drive-thru at McDonald's half a block away where 301 joins Tamiami Trail. I ate my Big Mac and drank my Diet Coke while I drove to Marie Knot's office in the complex at the corner of Bee Ridge and Sawyer.

I didn't see Marie, just told the temp at the desk that I was Lew Fonesca. The girl was young, maybe eighteen or nineteen, round face, peach skin, long dark hair. She handed me an eight-by-ten envelope with my name on it and I was out the door checking my watch.

When I pulled into the parking lot of the McClory Oncology Center, I opened the envelope, scanned the two summonses to figure out where they had to be delivered and what they were for. Both were less than fifteen minutes away and neither suggested that the person I'd be delivering it to was particularly dangerous, but one never knows.

I put them back in the envelope, left the envelope on the seat and entered the oncology center in what my watch and the clock on the wall over the television set in the waiting room told me was within a minute of the half hour McClory had given me.

There were four people in the waiting room. Three were men over sixty. One was a woman who couldn't have been more than forty. They all were staring at the television. A woman on CNN was telling them that people were dying in a place thousands of miles away, in a town whose name they couldn't pronounce.

"Sign in," said the woman behind the counter on the right with a smile. She wasn't much younger than the quartet watching CNN.

"I'm not a patient," I said. "I have an appointment with Dr. McClory."

She looked at me, never losing her smile. I didn't look like serious business.

"My name is Fonesca," I said. "Just tell him I'm here."

She picked up the phone and held it to her ear as she pressed a button, paused and said, "A Mr. Fonseca to see Dr. McClory."

"Fonesca," I said.

She nodded at me but she didn't make the correction.

"Yes," she said into the phone.

She hung up, looked at me and said, "Through that door, office all the way straight back."

Stuart M. Kaminsky

I went through the door. A muscular man with a well-trimmed beard wearing green lab pants and shirt came out of a room on my right.

"Changing room is through that door," he said.

"Not a patient," I said. "I have an appointment with Dr. McClory."

He pointed down the corridor and ducked back into the room he had popped out of. The door to Richard McClory's office was open. It was big, with a tan leather sofa against the wall, two tan leather chairs in front of the desk, a swivel chair with matching tan leather behind the large well-polished dark wood desk. The desk was completely clear except for a large black-and-white framed photograph of four men at a small table playing cards. The men, who seemed to be in their sixties or older, sat on folding chairs. One had his hand to his chin as if he were considering his next move. The wall behind McClory's desk was covered in framed degrees, awards and certificates. The one window right across from the door looked out on a parking lot.

"Fonesca?" came the voice behind me.

I turned. He was tall, looked as if he could pass for John Kerry's brother or cousin. He was wearing a white lab coat and a look that suggested it had been a while since he had a full night of sleep.

He held his hand out toward one of the chairs. I sat and he moved behind his desk, leaned forward and folded his hands.

"Nancy hired you," he said.

"Yes."

He looked out the window. An SUV went over a speed bump with a rattle.

"Has anyone close to you died unexpectedly?" he asked.

"Yes," I said.

He looked away from the window at me. It wasn't the answer he expected. There was a flash of something, maybe anger in his eyes. How dare my tragedy be compared with his?

"Kyle was my only son," he said.

I wasn't going to play. I wasn't going to say, "Catherine was my only wife." These were different tragedies, different pains for two different people.

"I know," I said.

"You do this for a living?" he asked. "Exploit people's grief, promise them justice?"

"No," I said.

"No?" he repeated with sarcasm.

"No." I got up and said, "Sorry."

I was on my way out, almost at the door, when he said, "Wait. Close the door. Sit down."

I closed the door and went back to the chair.

"I'm sorry," he said, pushing his hair back with the palm of his large right hand. "I deal with death, the death of near strangers, every day. We save some, save a lot, but some come too late. The families, the wives, parents, children, must feel what I'm feeling."

I didn't say anything.

"Now I'm one of them and I think about the crap I say to them and know that if someone tries to give me that about losing Kyle . . . I'm sorry. I'm tired. I haven't slept in almost three days."

"I know a good therapist," I said.

"Don't believe in it," he said. "You know you're the first person I've discussed Kyle's death with? Everyone just looks at me sympathetically or tells me how sorry they are, but they don't talk to me and I don't want them to. God, I'm rambling."

Stuart M. Kaminsky

"It's all right," I said.

"I suppose. It doesn't matter."

He put his head in his hands for an instant, sighed deeply, looked up and said, "You want to know why I'm a good radiologist?"

I nodded.

"I've been through what about half of my patients have been through. I've had prostate cancer. Radiation. Seed implants. I tell them, I'm living proof that you can survive. It's the survivors of those who don't make it that I can't deal with. You know the side effects of radiation and seed implants?"

"No," I said.

"Well, the one on the table now is the inability to produce sperm," he said. "I can't have any more children, Mr. Fonesca. I'm forty-two years old and Kyle will be the only child I will ever have."

He stared at me, either waiting for a response or seeing through me.

It should have been clear five minutes earlier, but I was sure now. Dr. Richard McClory was self-prescribing to deal with his pain and it looked as if he might be using more than the minimum recommended dose of whatever it was.

"Ask your questions, Mr. Fonesca," he said, leaning back, eyes closed.

"You were supposed to pick up your son after the movie," I said.

"Yes. Kyle and Andrew."

"Both?"

"Yes."

"And when they didn't show up?"

"I called Kyle's cell phone."

"Cell phone?"

"Yes," he said wearily. "There was no answer."

"So you . . . ?"

"Parked in the lot. Looked around. Went inside the lobby. Went back to the car."

"You were worried?"

"I was, God help me, angry. I blamed Andrew Goines. I thought he had convinced Kyle to forget about me and go off and do something stupid. I was going to tell Kyle he couldn't see Andrew again, not when he was staying with me."

"And then?"

"I waited in the car, cell phone on the dashboard. Called Andrew Goines, asked about Kyle. Waited for an hour, gave up and drove home. When the phone rang, I thought it was Kyle with a lame apology asking me to pick him up or telling me he was staying at Andrew's. It was the police."

He opened his mouth and sucked in air. His eyes were red.

"Did Kyle ever run away, stay out all night, do things that—"

"Never, nothing. He wasn't perfect. We weren't buddies. But we weren't enemies either. He was straight. No drugs. No drinking. One of the perks of being a physician is you know such things. It also helps when you go through your kid's drawers and pockets."

We sat silently for a few seconds. He looked at his hands. I looked at him.

"Do what you can," he finally said without looking up. "If you need more money for, I don't know, people who might help . . ."

"Your ex-wife's paying me," I said.

"If you find out anything," he said now, looking up, "you let me know."

"I will."

Stuart M. Kaminsky

"Have you ever felt that you could kill someone?" he asked.

"Yes," I said.

"My job is to save lives," he said. "For the dozens, maybe hundreds I've saved, I think I deserve to take one, the life of the person who murdered my son. Well?"

"I don't think it's in you, Doctor," I said.

"You don't know me," he said with a touch of anger.

"I could be wrong," I said.

There was nothing more to say except to ask for the number of the cell phone Kyle had been carrying. He pulled a flap-top silver cell phone from a pocket, pushed a couple of buttons and gave me the number. I wrote it in my notebook.

A knock at the door.

McClory said, "Come in."

A woman in nurse's whites, probably mid-forties, strong features and eyes that looked at McClory with sympathy.

"Mr. Saxborne is here," she said.

"Thank you," said McClory.

She closed the door slowly, eyes on the doctor.

"Raymond Wallace Saxborne is going to die soon," he said, getting up. "Raymond Wallace Saxborne is almost eighty. Fonesca, between you and me and whatever God is not out there, I am going to have a hard time giving my bedside best to Mr. Saxborne. Kyle was fourteen."

He walked around the desk, past me and out of the office without a word or a glance in my direction.

9

I **SHOULD HAVE BEEN** delivering summonses to two people.
I should have been going to see Yolanda Root, Andrew
Goines and the four people who had been released from
Seaside Assisted Living. I should have gone back to Nancy
Root for more information. I should have done a lot of
things, but I didn't.

Back in my office, I sat behind my desk and looked over at
the painting on my wall, the dark jungle foliage with the
nighttime sky and just the touch of red, and the hint of a
bird.

I picked up the phone and hit the buttons that connected
me to the office of Ann Horowitz. Ann never let a call go by
even if she was in the middle of a confession of matricide
from a raving client. How do I know this? From the calls she
had taken over the past three years when I sat in front of
her, one of which came while I was trying to remember what

might have been a telling dream about . . . I don't know what it was about. When she ended the call, the dream was gone.

"Dr. Horowitz," she answered.

"Are you alone?" I asked.

"Lewis?"

"Yes."

"I'm alone for the next ten minutes," she said.

"I can't do it," I said.

"Do what?"

"Face any more of them."

"Them?"

"The grieving, frightened, angry, depressed," I said. "I've got a list in front of me."

"People you are supposed to help?"

"Why am I supposed to help? I can't help myself."

"You are helping yourself. You're talking to me. Who told you that you had to help those people on your list?"

"I don't know," I said. "It happens. They find me. I'm a magnet for despair."

"What do you think you want to do?" she asked. "Notice I said *think,* because what you want to do may not be what you think you want to do."

I took off my cap and rubbed the top of my head.

"I think I want to buy a cheap car, throw in all my things I want to keep, which probably wouldn't even fill the trunk of a Honda, and drive away."

"Never come back?" she asked.

"Never."

"Where would you go?"

"Away. You're going to say I can't run away from what I am."

"No," she said. I could tell she was eating something.

DENIAL

"You can run. You can hide. Sometimes it works very well. I've even recommended it, but the problem is that wherever you go, you will always be with you. You are your own God, your own judge, your own executioner."

"Freud," I said.

"No, the German actor Klaus Kinski," she said.

"What are you eating?" I asked.

"Ham and cheese on thin white," she said.

"You're Jewish."

"I appreciate your calling this to my attention," she said.

"You don't eat ham."

"I eat ham. I like ham. If God wants to punish me for eating ham, I have little use for her."

"Tradition," I said.

"We were talking about your unwillingness to deal with the problems you've taken on," she said. "I'll deal with my God."

"You pray to your God?" I asked.

"I talk to my God and call it prayer. If my God talks to me, I call it schizophrenia."

"Klaus Kinski?"

"Thomas Szasz. Let's deal with your God."

"I have none," I said.

"Nonsense," she said, chewing. "God is in your head. You created God. Deny other people's God. Deal with your own. You have no intention of running away. If you did, you wouldn't have called me. You would just go. You want me to talk you out of it."

"I don't know," I said.

"You don't have to," she said. "I know. I've been doing this for fifty years. What is on that list of yours? You've got five minutes."

I told her, even mentioned Jerry Lee the gator and ended with my visit to Richard McClory.

"I'm tired," I said.

"Not sleepy?" she asked.

"Tired."

"I'll ask my required question now," she said.

"No, I'm not thinking about suicide. If death wants me, I'm easy to find. I'm not running . . ."

"Got you," she said. "You're not running away from death. You are living a paradox. You want to run from your grief, but you don't want to leave it behind. You want to just let the days go by, but you can't do it."

"You tricked me," I said.

"I'm good at it. I'm not telling you anything I haven't told you before. You listen, but you hear very little. You are a tough case, Lewis, but an interesting one. I've got to go. I hear my next victim coming through the outside door. Go to work, Lewis. Don't go to sleep. Don't go to Key West or Columbia, Missouri. Come see me next week, usual time and day."

She hung up.

I felt better, not good but better. If I hurried, I could get to Yolanda's grandfather's hardware store in Bradenton. On the phone, she hadn't sounded as if she was going to let anyone see her grief, if she had any. That was fine with me.

I drove up 41 past the Asolo, past the Sarasota/Bradenton airport, past malls, one-story chiropractic offices, dentists, Sam Ash's music store, all the fast food franchises known to the world. I listened to Neal Boortz on WLSS. He was talking about airplanes. I'm not sure what he said.

Root's Hardware was in a small strip mall on the north side of DeSoto. It wasn't big. It wasn't small either. Finding

Yolanda was no problem. She stood behind the counter tallying up items for a chunky man with a freshly shaved head and a bushy mustache.

Yolanda wore a yellow tight-fitting tank top, a black skirt, a silver ring in her navel, makeup that would be right at a Halloween party and a sour look that said, *What do you want?*

When the man with the shaved head had gone through the door, little bell tinkling, I moved to the counter and said, "Lew Fonesca."

She looked at me, folded her arms under her breasts and sized me up. I don't think she was impressed. Her mouth was open. She had a silver tongue ring.

"I'm busy," she said.

I saw no customers.

"I'll be quick," I said.

"The Cubs suck," she said, nodding at my cap.

"Things change," I said. "Know anyone who might want to hurt your brother?"

"You could have, like, asked me that on the phone."

"I like to see people I talk to," I said.

"So, you looking?"

She unfolded her arms and smiled. It wasn't a friendly smile. It was a taunt. It was a tease. It was an I-know-what-men-think smile designed to put her in charge.

"You're a pretty girl," I said. "You don't have to hide it."

"Who's hiding anything?" she said.

"Most people," I said. "Kyle. Someone who might want to hurt him?"

"No," she said. "You mean, like, kill? He was, like, fourteen, for God's sake, you know?"

I didn't answer.

"No," she repeated.

"Anyone want to hurt you?" I asked.

Stuart M. Kaminsky

"Me?" she asked, shaking her head and closing her eyes, pointing a crimson fingernail at herself. "You want to get on the list? Take a number. But no way anyone would try to get to me by killing Kyle."

"You got along with him?"

"Sure. He was always trying to show me how he and his friend Andy had done stuff. Kid stuff. He was just, like, trying to impress me."

"Stuff?" I said.

"Water balloons, scratching parked cars with a key or something, you know. Spitting on people from the parking garage by the Hollywood 20, stuff like that, you know. He was a kid."

"So you liked him?" I asked.

She shrugged.

"Sure. That make a difference?"

"Yes."

"Why? He's dead. Like, end of his life, end of story. Go talk to his daddy."

The word *daddy* dripped with venom a coral snake would envy.

"I did," I said.

"All broken up?"

"Yes."

"Fucking hypocrite," she said. "He didn't give a shit about Kyle. Just threw money at him and let him know he didn't want to hear about any problems."

"And your mother?"

Yolanda shrugged again.

"She'll cry you enough tears to fill Robarts Arena. She's an *actress*."

The word *actress* came out with the same venom that had covered the word *daddy*.

DENIAL

"What are your plans?" I asked.

"My . . . what's that got to do with anything? None of your fucking business. I haven't decided yet. You got any ideas?"

The words were clearly provocative, words she had used on men and boys for the past four or more years.

"You'd be a good actress," I said.

She laughed.

"I mean it," I said.

She stopped laughing, looked at me.

"You're not kidding, are you?"

"No."

"I've thought about it," she said. "My mother . . ."

The mask softened a little, but there was no time for it to drop. A man in his sixties, white hair, rugged farm look on his dark face, stepped around an aisle and moved to the counter. He was wearing dark slacks and a white shirt with a blue tie.

"Yolanda?" he asked, looking at her and then at me.

"He's a customer, Grandpa," she said.

"What's he buying?" asked Elliott Maxwell Root.

"A key chain," I said, plucking a chain from a cardboard display on the counter. It had a little laser light on the end that went on when you pressed the blue plastic sides.

"Two dollars and twenty-seven cents," Yolanda said.

I took three dollars from my wallet and handed them to her under Grandpa's watching eyes. She gave me change and a receipt. Grandpa's eyes were watching to see if I was looking at Yolanda in places or ways that might be inappropriate. I considered suggesting that Yolanda might be issued a uniform that covered her, but even in an oversize blue smock, that sexual challenge would burn through.

"Take care," I said to her.

I meant it. She understood.

"I will," she said softly. "Thanks."

Before I headed back to Sarasota, I made two notes in my notebook and checked one I had written earlier. First, where was Kyle's cell phone? Second, according to his sister, Kyle and his friend Andy Goines were into minor vandalism. The note from earlier read: *Robles said there was a passenger in the car that hit Kyle, maybe a kid.*

I stopped at a Walgreens and picked up a disposable cell phone. Then I headed to a camera shop in Northgate Plaza off 301. I had a little trouble finding it. A truck loaded with wooden planks was parked in front. A couple of sweating men wearing work gloves were removing the planks and piling them up. I moved past them into the shop.

It was small; cameras in locked glass cases lined the walls to my right and behind the counter to my left. A young man, maybe twenty-five, grinned at me. He was about six feet tall and couldn't have weighed more than 120 pounds. His grin was cadaverous.

"Wayne Bennett?" I asked.

"Yes," he said.

I took out the summons and handed it to him. He looked at the envelope and then at me.

"This what I think it is?" he asked.

"I don't know," I said. "What do you think it is?"

He placed the envelope on the counter and wiped his palms on his shirt.

"They want me to tell what I saw Jesse doing," he said.

"I don't know," I said. "I don't know who Jesse is."

"Jesse will kill me," he said. "No, I mean he might really kill me. You try to help a friend . . ."

"Your friend Jesse might want to kill you?"

"He hates prison," said Bennett.

"Most people do," I said.

"Not more than Jesse," he said.

I had nothing to say.

"What am I going to do?" he asked.

"Be where it tells you to be when they tell you to be there," I said.

I left without looking back. If I paused, he would tell me his story. I couldn't handle any more stories. They filled the air wherever I went, invisible, ghostly. Ann was right. There was no hiding from ghosts, mine or other people's.

My next stop was on Longboat Key, one of the high-rise, high-priced condos on the bay. I pulled up to the guard gate and an old man in a khaki uniform and a matching cap came out of the small shack with a clipboard.

"You're here to see . . . ?"

"You Benjamin Strayley?"

"Yes," he said, puzzled.

I handed him the envelope.

"She did it," he said with a sigh. "She really did it, didn't she?"

"I don't know," I said.

"The bitch," he said, shaking his head. "Sorry, I don't usually use language like that but . . . the bitch did it. You know how long we've been married?"

He looked as if he really expected an answer or a guess.

"Forty-one years," he said.

Catherine and I had been married nine years when she died. There was no point in telling this to Benjamin Strayley, who slid the envelope under the clip on his board.

"Forty-one years," he repeated. "I didn't even want to move down here. Her idea. All my friends, family are in Danville."

"I'm sorry," I said.

There was a car behind me.

"I'll open the gate," Strayley said. "Turn around and you can go right out."

"Thanks," I said.

He went back in the shack.

I bypassed my office, parked in front of Gwen's diner, ordered two grilled cheese sandwiches and a chocolate shake and found out that Gwen had taken Digger on as a fill-in short-order chef.

A few people knew that Gwen's real name was Sheila. Her mother had been Gwen. When her mother died, people saw the sign on the roof of the one-story building and assumed the woman who owned it and bustled behind the counter and in the kitchen and from table to table was Gwen. She accepted without correcting.

Tim from Steubenville was sitting at the counter. I joined him. Tim was a regular, close to ninety. He lived in an assisted living home a short walk away at the end of Brother Geenen Way. He spent as much time as he could at Gwen's reading the newspaper, shaking his head and trying to get people into conversations about eliminating the income tax, abolishing drug laws, ending almost everything the "damn government" was involved in besides having an army, paving the highways and providing a police force.

There was very little left of Tim from Steubenville beyond his convictions. Blue veins undulated over the thin bones in his hands as he drank his coffee from a white mug.

"I tried Digger out," Gwen said. "He can cook the easy stuff, good enough for breakfasts. He'll make enough to live on if he's careful, and the food's free if he doesn't overdo it."

I thanked her.

"No favor," she said. "I can use the extra help in the morning now that my firstborn is out producing grandbabies."

Gwen was buxom and full of energy with curly brown hair that she was constantly brushing back with her arm. She poured me a cup of coffee. I put in two Equals and a lot of milk from the small metal pitcher.

"Banana cream?" she asked.

"Sure," I said.

She winked and went off to get me a slice of pie.

"She shouldn't pay him more than the free market will bear," said Tim. "Minimum wages are an infringement of free enterprise. If the market says she has to pay him twenty dollars an hour, so be it. If the market says she only has to pay him four dollars an hour, so be it. Free market."

He held up his mug as if he were toasting what he had just said. I held my mug up too.

When I finished the pie, I felt better, but *better* is a comparative term; better than what? Better than when? Gwen was talking to two men at a booth who looked like truckers. Something she said made them laugh. I put four dollars on the counter and got up.

"I say," said Tim, looking at his almost empty coffee mug, "almost every damn government agency should be shut down. Now, tomorrow. That's what I say."

I knew. He had said it before. The next thing he would do if I didn't escape would be to go through the list of government departments that should be dismantled. He usually started with OSHA, but sometimes the FDA came first.

"You know it's damn unconstitutional to deprive Americans of their right to get their damn prescription drugs wherever they want," he said.

　　　　　　　　　　　　　　　　Stuart M. Kaminsky

"You were a constitutional lawyer?" I asked, immediately regretting it.

He turned his head to me and said, "I worked the line in an automobile assembly factory for almost fifty years. I don't need a damn law degree. Just read the Constitution."

"I will," I said. "Gotta go."

It was almost three. I hurried to the Gillespie Park neighborhood, got out of the car and walked the same route Kyle McClory had walked before he died. I turned on the cell phone I had bought and punched in the number Richard McClory had given me. There was no answer. I didn't expect one. I was listening for the ringing on Kyle's phone, looking in the bushes and grass. Nothing.

I tried for the fifth time. I was about where Kyle had been standing when he was hit. This time someone answered. Or, to be more accurate, someone was breathing hard on the other end.

"Hello," I said.

More breathing.

"Hello," I repeated.

"Fonesca," he said with a sigh. It was the voice of the man who had told me to stop looking for who killed Kyle.

"Can we talk?" I asked.

"No," he said. "I should have thrown this thing away as soon as I picked it up. I'm going to do that now."

"What happened? The night you killed Kyle?"

"No," he said. "Just listen to me. Listen. You've got to stop. Please. I don't want to kill you. I've . . . I . . . just stop. No one will be helped by you finding me."

"I'll find you," I said.

"You're going to make me kill you, aren't you?"

"You sound like you'd rather not," I said.

"I can't think of another choice," he said.

"Well, since it's my life we're talking about, maybe I could come up with some alternatives."

"I don't think there are any," he said.

"How about—" I began, but he turned off the phone.

10

HEADED for the Goines's home off Gulf Gate. It was easy to find. A quiet street. Modest one-story two-bedrooms. I parked in the driveway next to a Kia mini-SUV and went to the door.

The woman who answered about fifteen seconds after I rang wore jeans and a yellow man's shirt with the sleeves rolled up. She looked at me over the top of her round glasses.

"Mrs. Goines?" I asked.

She looked too young to be Andrew Goines's mother, at least at first glance. Her skin was clear, her eyes blue, her hair short, straight, blonde.

When she spoke, I added a decade to my first impression.

"Yes," she said.

"Lew Fonesca," I said. "I talked to you earlier about your son and Kyle McClory."

"Oh yes, sorry," she said. "I thought you were someone

here to try to sell me something or donate to saving the world or supporting a political hack. I'm working on a grant for the Sarasota County Film Commission. Almost finished. Come in."

I followed her in. The entryway was small. The living room to my right was small. The dog that came bounding out of nowhere was big, big and hairy and brown. He tried to stop his rush at me but slid on his nails on the tile floor and bumped into me. I didn't fall but it was close.

"Clutch," she said. "Get out of here."

Clutch was panting, tongue out, looking from me to her.

"Out," she repeated.

The dog took a few steps into the tiled living room and then looked back at me.

"Out," she repeated.

The dog slowly, almost mournfully disappeared through an open sliding door.

"I did call Nancy Root," she said. "She told me you were working for her. Mr. Fonesca, Andy got a little, well, nervous when I told him you were coming by. He was better, but not much, when I told him I'd talked to Kyle's mother about you."

"How has he reacted to Kyle's death?" I asked.

She shook her head and said, "Odd; he seems—maybe I'm just imagining it—frightened. He puts on a front, but the more he says everything is fine, the more I'm convinced everything isn't fine. He won't talk to me about it."

"Andy's father?"

"Dead," she said. "He was a helicopter pilot in Afghanistan. It went down. Everyone on board died. The captain who came by said it wasn't downed by enemy fire. As if that makes a difference."

"Andy?"

Stuart M. Kaminsky

"Andy's in his room," she said. "I told him you were coming. Don't expect a lot of cooperation."

"You said you didn't know Kyle McClory well."

"Not well," she said. "Tell the truth, the few times he came over he worked a little too hard to be likeable. Tried to say what he thought I wanted him to say. Couldn't get past that. Can't say I really tried too hard to break through. Poor kid."

"Andy?"

"Oh, sure," she said. "Come on. Call him Andrew, at least to start out. My guess is if you call him Andy, he'll tell you to call him Andrew. If you call him Andrew, he'll tell you to call him Andy."

I followed her through the living room into an alcove with three doors. The door in the middle was the bathroom. That door was open. The door to the right was obviously Mrs. Goines's bedroom. The door to the left was closed and a yellow plastic streamer said, VERBOTEN.

She knocked.

"Yeah," came the boy's voice.

"The man I told you about is here," she said.

"Changed my mind," he said.

"Andy, he's working for Kyle's mom," she said. "Give him five minutes."

"I haven't got anything to say that'll help him."

"You never know," I said. "Five minutes is all I need."

Long pause, the door opened. Andy Goines, barefoot, cut-off jeans and a Def Jam T-shirt, stood in front of me. He was short, stocky, round pink face, dark hair brushed straight back. He looked at me and clearly wasn't impressed.

"Okay," he said. "Come on in. Five minutes. I'm watching the clock."

Andy's mother excused herself, saying she had to get

back to her grant proposal. Andy kicked the door closed behind me.

The room was clean, the bed made with a plain green blanket and four green pillows. A black director's chair sat next to the bed. Nothing on the wood floor. CDs and DVDs neatly stacked on shelves next to a low dresser on top of which sat a television set and a CD deck on top of a DVD deck. There was a speaker on each side of the dresser. Next to the dresser was a small desk with a computer and chair. The desk wasn't cluttered. A blue backpack sat on the chair.

On one wall were two posters, both framed, lined up next to each other. One poster was for one of the *Lord of the Rings* movies. On it, Sean Astin was leaning over Elijah Wood, his hand resting on Wood's shoulder. In Wood's open palm was the bright gold ring. The other poster was Eminem. I knew who it was because his name was printed in bold blood red across the top of the poster. Eminem was holding a microphone in one hand and pointing at me. Eminem looked angry.

On the other wall were three posters, all brightly colored sports cars. One car, a convertible, was red. The second car was a squat, dark Humvee with what looked like teeth, and the third car, a yellow Mini Cooper.

"Okay if I sit?" I asked.

"Suit yourself," he said, his hands plunged into the pockets of his jeans.

I sat in the director's chair. Andy Goines stood across the room in front of the television set.

"I've got nothing new to say about what happened to Kyle," he said.

"Tell me again, please."

"You a Cub fan?" he asked, looking at my cap.

"Yes," I said.

Stuart M. Kaminsky

He shook his head. I thought he was going to say something like "loser" or maybe he was thinking it.

"We went to the movie, got out," he said flatly. "We were supposed to be picked up by Kyle's dad. Kyle called him. We had time. We walked around the block. Kyle told me he'd meet me in front in a few minutes. Had something he had to do. He ran through the parking lot. I thought he had to find a toilet or something. I went out in front. Kyle didn't show. I called my mom and asked her to pick me up. That's it."

"You didn't see Kyle's dad?"

"Nope, but I wasn't looking for him."

"You didn't think something happened to Kyle?"

"Nope. He did stuff like that. Went off. Called me the next day to tell me something cool he'd done. It happened."

I nodded and said, "What phone did you use to call your mother?"

"Kyle's," he said.

"But Kyle wasn't with you. Did he give you his phone?"

Andrew Goines looked at his watch. He was definitely uneasy.

"Wait, now I remember. I called from the pay phone in the Main Street Book Store."

"Main Street Book Store doesn't have a public phone," I said, not knowing if they did or didn't.

"I don't know. Maybe I called from the Hollywood 20," he said. "What's the difference?"

"What time did you call your mother?"

"What time? How the hell would I know? Maybe ten, fifteen minutes after we got out of the movie."

Since one lie had worked and the kid looked beyond nervous, I went for two more.

"I checked the movie times," I said. "You got out at

nine-thirty. You mother says you called her at about ten-thirty. That's an hour."

"We were talking, following some girls we knew," he said.

"Who were the girls?" I asked.

"You mean their names?"

"Yes," I said, taking out my notebook.

"What's this? *Law & Order?* They were just girls we see at school in the halls and stuff. They didn't even look at us."

"Kyle was your best friend, right?"

"Yeah, so?"

His hands were out of his pockets and his palms were beating gently against his thighs. I looked at the poster.

"Frodo and Sam," I said. "Kyle was Frodo. You were Sam."

"You saw the movies?"

"Read the books," I said. "Long time ago. Sam saved his friend."

"You've got a point? You saying I could have saved Kyle or something?"

He took a small step forward. The crack in his voice was small, but it was there.

"I don't know. What happened to Kyle?"

"I told you. I told the police."

I was shaking my head no.

"You don't believe me? You calling me a liar?"

"You put it that way, I guess I am, but I think you've got a reason to lie," I said. "I think you're scared."

"Of what?" he said, aiming for defiance but hitting fear.

"Of who," I said. "He called me."

Andy Goines tilted his head to one side.

"What? Who called you?"

"The man who killed Kyle," I said.

"You are shitting me, man," he said, his voice rising,

pointing a finger at me the way Eminem was across the room on the wall. Only Andy's look was definitely not anger but fear.

"No."

"You're lying. Why would he call you?"

"To tell me to stop looking for him," I said. "I think he tried to run me down the way he did Kyle."

Andy Goines was shaking now. He pulled the backpack from the chair by the desk, dropped it on the floor and sat down, hands rubbing his legs.

"Did he say anything about me?"

"No," I said.

"I think he's going to try to kill me. Oh shit. Shit. Shit."

He was pounding his fists on his legs now. He bit his lower lip and looked at Eminem for help, didn't get any and turned back to me.

"Help me find him," I said.

"Shit," he said once more. "He went crazy, man."

"Kyle?"

"No, that guy."

"Kyle's sister said you and her brother were into doing things?"

"She's a lying whore. What kind of things?"

"Scratching cars, dropping water balloons."

He looked at me and began blinking fast.

"You know, don't you?"

I shrugged.

"I mean, we shouldn't have done it, but we were just shitting around. It wasn't the first time. Other guys up there did it."

"Did it?"

Andy got up and sat down again.

"Okay, after the movie we went to the top of the parking

garage. You know, the one behind the 20. We leaned over and waited for people to go by and we spat down on them, tried to hit them. Then we'd duck back before they could look up and we listened to hear if they said something that'd show we had a hit."

"You spit on people's heads?"

"Four levels up," he said. "It's not easy."

"I'm sure it takes a lot of skill."

There was a lot more I could say, but I stopped. I didn't want him to stop now that he was going.

"We hit a guy with a girl," he said. "Then a while later we looked down and saw this older guy with white hair. He was with a girl. They were walking real slow, right on the walk under us. We dropped big ones on them."

He stopped. Andy was breathing hard now.

"You've gotta understand," he said. "It didn't mean anything. Just messing around. You messed around when you were a kid, right?"

"No, not like that," I said.

He ignored my answer and started to rock in the chair.

"Anyway, we heard a scream," he said. "Like someone got hit by a rock or something. It was just spit. Kyle and I looked over the roof and the guy with white hair was looking up at us and the girl was holding the top of her head and screaming real weird-like."

Andy went silent, remembering, and then went on. "Well, anyway, we moved back from the edge of the roof and started to go back to the ramp. I was the one who heard it first."

"It?"

"Footsteps, someone running, like an echo," he said. "That crazy son of a bitch was coming up after us."

"You're sure?"

"Sure? We were at the ramp when we looked back and there he was screaming at us like a nut. For spitting. We ran. He didn't catch us. We hid out in the main-street bookstore on the second floor for about ten minutes and then came out to wait for Kyle's dad. And there he was."

"Kyle's dad?"

"No, the crazy guy. In a car coming right up in front of the movies. There was someone in the back, but I couldn't see. He saw us. We ran like hell back down the sidewalk toward the parking lot. When we hit the lot, we heard a car screeching into the parking lot. It was him, same car."

"What kind of car?"

"Taurus. Blue. Late model. No more than a year old. He saw us, came flying over the speed bumps. We ran through the lot and went over the fence on Fruitville. Ran across the street, almost got hit by a pickup. Then we went down the first street. I don't know what it was."

"He was still following you?"

"He must have seen us go down the street. We were half a block down, running, when we heard the car turning behind us. We didn't know where we were. I followed Kyle between two houses. A couple of guys, Mexicans, yelled at us, asking us where the hell we thought we were going."

"The guy in the car?"

"Didn't look back," he said. "Went through a yard full of old tires and stuff and ran around down 301 and into the Walgreens on the corner. We went to the toilet in the back and locked ourselves in. I'm telling you, that guy was nuts."

"You decided to separate," I said.

"Yeah, but not until we got out of the toilet and saw the guy running out of the store. The girl at the checkout counter said she thought a guy who just left was looking for us. She said we could catch him if we hurried."

DENIAL

"That's when you decided to separate?"

He nodded.

"We looked through the window and saw him pulling out of the lot," Andy said. "He wasn't going to give up. So we split up. I went back toward the 20. Kyle went back around the drugstore. That's it. Who'd ever think someone would kill a kid because he spit on his wife or daughter? Have to be nuts."

"You'd recognize him again if you saw him?"

"I'm pretty sure, yeah. White hair, little beard. Pretty big guy."

"Old?"

"Yeah, like your age, maybe."

"Anything else?"

"He had a bumper sticker," Andy said, looking at *The Lord of the Rings* poster. "Saw it when he pulled out of the drugstore lot. Manatee Community College parking sticker."

"How do you know that?"

"My mom has one, blue and white. She teaches a course there Thursday nights."

I got up. So did Andrew Goines.

"You're going to tell the police, aren't you?"

"Soon," I said.

"You have to tell my mom?"

He had quickly gone from being a cocky fifteen-year-old to a frightened ten-year-old.

"She wouldn't understand," he said. "That's why I didn't say anything to the police. Kyle was dead and I wasn't sure it wasn't just an accident. But now . . ."

"Now?"

"He called you. You said he called you, right?"

"He did," I said.

"My mom thinks I'm some kind of perfect kid," he said.

"She's all the time telling people how much I'm like my dad. I'm not like my dad. She's going to find out, isn't she?"

"About the spitting?"

"Yeah."

"I don't know. Maybe not for a while. Maybe not any time."

Andy Goines looked at his watch.

"Almost fifteen minutes," he said. "I told you I'd give you five. You done?"

"I'm done."

"You're going to find him, right?"

"Yes," I said.

"Thanks."

He awkwardly held out his hand. I shook it. His palm was wet. He walked with me to the front door. His mother was in another room talking on the phone and tapping something out on the computer at the same time. I didn't wait to say good-bye.

"I should have stayed with Kyle," the boy said. "I should have been there to help him. My dad would have."

"He might have run you down too," I said. "Then your mother would have to go on without your dad and you. It's hard to go on alone."

I was going to add, "Trust me," but I didn't trust people who said that. It almost always meant that I had just heard something I definitely should not trust.

He closed the door behind me.

I stopped to report to Marie Knot that I had handed out the two summonses and to pick up a check for my work. Then I drove to the DQ lot and parked. It was a little before six. I got a double burger and a large chocolate cherry Blizzard, went up to my office and turned on the light.

The phone was ringing.

"Fonesca," I said.

"I was watching you. I could have killed you," he said. "You didn't see me."

"Thanks for not killing me," I said, sitting behind my desk, Blizzard and burger in front of me.

I took off my cap and waited. He was sitting out there no more than a few hundred feet away. He had seen me go through the door.

"Can't you understand?" he pleaded.

"Explain it to me," I said. "Come on up to my office. I'll split a burger and a Blizzard with you."

"It's useless, isn't it?" he asked.

"You mean trying to get me to stop looking for you? Yes, but it doesn't hurt for us to talk. Call whenever you like."

He started the car he was in. I heard it over the phone and out the window.

"How's your knee?"

"Never hurt much," I said, moving to the window to see if I could spot the car. I didn't. "Well, maybe for a minute or two."

"Your shoulder?"

"Seems all right. Don't you have a philosopher to quote?"

"You're joking," he said. "You're mocking me."

"No," I said. "I'm interested."

"Do you believe in God?" he asked.

"I don't know. Depends on when you ask me."

"God," he said, "is a concept by which we measure our pain."

"Which philosopher said that?"

"John Lennon."

He hung up before I could ask him if he had ever heard of a poet named Gregory Cgnozik who was another admirer of

Stuart M. Kaminsky

the dead Beatle. I walked out the door. At the railing, which rattled when I leaned on it, I looked up at the clouds, fluffy billows, reddish in the reflection of the sun. I watched them drift south. I don't know what I wanted from the clouds, from the moment. Peace? A minute, five minutes of peace?

I could have started visiting the people who had been released from the Seaside the night Dorothy Cgnozic had supposedly witnessed a murder, but it wasn't in me.

I went back inside and made two calls while I finished eating.

Call one was to Nancy Root. She wasn't there. I told her machine I was making progress and would report to her soon. Call two was to the Texas Bar & Grille. Ed Fairing answered after three rings and said, "Texas," over the rumble of voices. I could almost smell the beer. I asked for Ames, who came on a few seconds later.

"What have you got planned for the next two or so days?" I asked.

"Working on my models, reading, breathing easy," he answered.

"Think you can make a trip in the morning and maybe one in the afternoon to Manatee Community College?"

"I can," he said.

"Paying job," I said. "Go through the parking lot looking for a late-model Ford Taurus, blue with an MCC parking sticker. Check the front of the car for dents, blood or some repair or paint touch-up in the last few days. If there's more than one Taurus that matches, write down the license tag number. Tell Ed it's important."

"Ed's no problem," Ames said. "I'll start in the morning."

That was it. Enough for one day. Too much for one day. I wanted to lie down and watch a VHS of Joan Crawford in *Possessed*, followed by *Seven Keys to Baldpate*, the version with Richard Dix. I wanted to sleep for about eight or nine days.

But it wasn't to be. The knock at my door came at the point in *Possessed* where Joan Crawford was about to shoot Van Heflin.

I went to the door half expecting that the guy who killed Kyle McClory would be there ready either to talk or shoot me or both.

I didn't recognize him for a second or two, but he was familiar.

I didn't recognize Detective Etienne Viviase because he was wearing sneakers, brown slacks with a big buckle shaped like an Indian-head nickel and a University of Florida baseball cap and sweatshirt. The gator on the shirt grinned at me. The detective did not.

"Detective," I said.

"Process server," he said. "I'll make this quick. My wife and kids are parked out there and my Peanut Buster bar is probably melting."

"Want to come in?"

He looked over my shoulder at my office and said, "No thanks. Know a man named Maxwell Root?"

"Hardware store in Bradenton," I said. "Father of Nancy Root. Grandfather of Kyle McClory."

"And," said Viviase, "grandfather of Yolanda Root. He says you harassed his granddaughter."

"Just asked her some questions," I said.

"How about Dr. Richard McClory and Andrew Goines? You ask them questions too?"

"Yes, but—"

"Anonymous caller," he said. "Call transferred to me because Mike Ransom has the day off and Lichtner on the desk knew I'd dealt with you a few times in the past. The caller, a very nervous man, said you were harassing the friends and family of Kyle McClory."

"You check with McClory and Goines's mother?"

"They have no complaints."

"Yolanda Root?"

"She says you were, quote, an asshole, but that you weren't harassing her. Don't feel too upset about the 'asshole' comment. She had equally unoriginal insults for McClory."

"So what brings you to my door with a Buster bar melting below? Just Nancy Root's father's harassment claim?"

"Who made that call with all that bullshit about your harassing people?"

"The guy who ran down Kyle McClory," I said. "He tried to run me down too."

"Really? When was this?"

"Yesterday. Mall on Fruitville and Lime. Good Mexican restaurant there."

"The one where Robles works. Have any plans for telling Ransom?"

"Not until I know the name of the caller," I said.

"And you know this guy who called killed the McClory boy?"

Someone called, "Dad," from the parking lot beyond the railing. Viviase looked over his shoulder and shouted, "Be right there."

"He told me," I said. "He practically told me."

"When?"

"He calls me a couple of times a day," I said. "Wants me to stop looking for him. Said he'll have to kill me too if I don't stop."

"You're a suitable case for treatment," Viviase said.

"I'm in treatment," I said.

"You getting close to finding the guy?"

"Yes."

He thought for a few seconds.

"When you do, if you do, let me know," he said. "Remember the case is Mike Ransom's and he'd get more than a little pissed off if a process server came up with his hit-and-run killer."

"It was murder," I said.

"Great," said Viviase with a sigh. "Better and better."

"Ed," came the voice of a woman from the DQ lot. "Your ice cream is now cold chocolate peanut soup."

"Dump it and I'll come down and get another one," he called.

I was half afraid he was going to ask me to meet his family. He didn't. He just turned and walked toward the steps. I closed the door and went back to my bed. The pause button froze Joan Crawford, gun in hand, wild look on her face. I pressed her into action. She fired six bullets and the scene faded to black.

11

DAWN CAME DULL GRAY. Fog. I could have and would have stayed in bed another hour or two or three if the phone hadn't been ringing.

I considered permanently disconnecting it but then there would be even more people coming to my door.

I looked at my watch. Eight-thirty. The phone kept ringing. It could be him, Taurus the Philosopher with more threats, pleas and warnings. I slowly took out my soap and shaving gear and put them in my gym bag. The phone kept ringing.

I pulled a clean gray pullover polo shirt over my head and went into the office.

"Fonesca," I said, picking up the phone.

"Nancy Root," she said. "When you called last night, I was in a show. Then, this morning I found out that my father called the police and said you were harassing Yola. I just got off the phone with him. I was furious. Please don't let him stop you from finding whoever . . . I find it so damn hard to say it."

"I won't let it stop me," I said. "You didn't tell me you had a daughter."

"I'm sorry. I didn't think it was important."

I didn't say it, but I thought it. Not important that she had a daughter? Not important that I talk to her? Both?

When I didn't say anything, she asked, "Was it?"

Yolanda Root had told me about her brother's and Andy Goines's vandalism. I had used what she told me to get Andy Goines to open up. In the scheme of things, yes, it was important.

"I may have something for you in the next few days," I said. "No promises."

"You know who did it?"

"Give me a few more days."

"But . . . yes, all right. Richard called me. He said you'd seen him."

"Yes."

"I'm sorry."

I wondered what she was sorry for. For going to see her ex-husband? For how he might have behaved?

"It's okay. I'll call you when I have something."

"Can you meet us later?" she said. "Richard and me."

"I've got—"

Someone took the phone from her and said, "Fonesca, how soon can you get to my office?"

It was Richard Tycinker.

"One-thirty," I said.

"Good." He hung up.

I took my list of names and forwarding addresses of those four escapees from Seaside, went down the stairs with

Stuart M. Kaminsky

my gym bag, picked up a coffee to go and an Egg McMuffin from McDonald's and drove down Bahia Vista to the YMCA, where I did four miles on the treadmill, did the round of machines, nodded to a few of the regulars, who nodded back at me. We didn't know one another's names. I didn't want to know their names.

When I finished, I showered, shaved, used the roll-on deodorant, got dressed and went back out into the fog. I had coaxed and sweated myself back into a state resembling life.

I drove up Lockwood Ridge to University Parkway, turned right and found University Gardens, beflowered, gated and nowhere near a university.

The sheet on the seat next to me said Ellen Gallagher now lived here with her grandson and his wife, Ralph and Julie Church.

I told the guard at the gate, a woman of more than average weight and less than average height, that I was there to see the Churches.

"Sorry, no churches in University Gardens," she said. "You must be looking for St. Thomas's a few miles east."

"No," I said, "I mean Julie and Ralph Church."

"Ah," she said with a smile.

Her brown eyes met mine.

"I knew that," she said. "Couldn't resist. You can go nuts here alone and I've been on since five this morning."

"It was a good joke," I said.

"You're not smiling."

"I don't smile."

"Your name?"

I told her and she checked the list on her clipboard.

"Don't see your name here. They expecting you, the Churches?"

"Tell them I'm from Seaside."

"Check," she said, moving back into the shack and picking up the phone. I couldn't hear what she was saying but she was back out again in a few seconds.

"You know how to get there?" she asked.

I said I didn't so she gave me directions to 4851 Tangerine Drive Circle. The gate went up and I passed Tangerine Drive, Tangerine Parkway, Tangerine Drive Street, Tangerine Drive Avenue and made a right turn onto Tangerine Drive Circle.

The house was small with a finely manicured lawn of something that resembled but wasn't grass. There were no cars in the driveway so I pulled in and walked up the narrow brick path to the front door, which opened before I could push the button.

An old woman in a flowery dress and a necklace of colorful beads stood before me. Her hair was white, neatly frizzled, her skin unblemished but slightly wrinkled.

"Ellen Gallagher?" I asked.

"Yes," she said.

"You were at Seaside Assisted Living?"

"Yes."

"May I ask why you left?"

"Who are you?"

"Miles Archer," I said. "Assisted Living Quality of Care Office."

She pursed her lips, thought for a moment and said, "Let's see. The food is mediocre. The conversation inane. The staff patronizing. The lure of twice-a-week bingo resistible. The complaints of my fellow inmates repetitious. I doubt if I was much better but I didn't have to listen to me. Reasons enough?"

"Why now? I mean, why did you pick that day to leave?"

"Because my grandson and his wife invited me, as my own children had not," she said. "They just moved here from

Buffalo. Want a sandwich? Some coffee? My grandson and his wife are at work."

"No, thank you," I said.

"Foggy," she said.

"Yes."

"I was a high school English teacher for more years than you've been on earth," she said. "Now I have the run of the house, my own television with cable."

"That's great."

"I told you that because I thought I was beginning to see the I-feel-sorry-for-the-old-lady look on your face."

"No," I said. "I always look like this."

"Any more questions?"

"No," I said.

"Then have a foggy day. I've got an Ann Rule book I want to get back to."

She closed the door. I turned and took a few steps. The door opened behind me.

"Here," she said. "Take this."

She handed me a very large chocolate chip cookie and went back into the house, closing the door.

I ate the cookie as I drove east on University to I-75 and then went south, getting off about ten minutes later at the first exit to Venice. The new address of Mark Anthony Katz, the second name on my list, was a low-rise apartment complex in Osprey, which was still under construction; piles of dirt dotted the landscape. There was no gate. There were no guards. There were plenty of trucks rumbling in and out.

Mark Anthony Katz's name was on Apartment 4, Building 2, first floor. I knocked. The building smelled like fresh wood and concrete. I knocked again and was about to give up when the door opened.

A lean old man with a wisp of hair on his speckled head

DENIAL

stood in front of me. He wore a long-sleeved orange cardigan buttoned to the neck and held on to a walker. Across the walker was a bumper sticker that read: I CAN'T REMEMBER SHIT!

"Mr. Katz?"

"No soliciting," he said. "You see the signs?"

"I'm not selling anything," I said.

"Not insurance?"

"No," I said.

"Cemetery plots, subscriptions to *Things to Do When You're Nearing Death* magazine?"

"No."

"You don't want me to sign some petition to save the manatees, whales, seals or sea grass?"

"No," I said.

"I miss anything?" he asked.

"I don't think so."

"So what the hell do you want? And who the hell are you?"

"Archie Goodwin, Consumer Advocates for the Retired," I said.

"Bullshit," he said. "I watch Nero Wolfe on television. I can't remember shit, but I do remember names."

"My mother was a Wolfe fan," I said. "Father's name was George Goodwin."

He regarded me with prune-faced distrust.

"I want to know why you left Seaside."

"Why? You want to talk me into going to the Assisted Living Home for Retired Housepainters or to join Geriatrics Anonymous?"

"Can I come in?"

"No," he said. "No offense. I just don't want you knocking me down, stealing whatever I've got and leaving me to crawl to the phone."

"Fine. Why did you leave Seaside?"

"Don't need it. Drove me nuts. I don't like people much. Winn-Dixie's right over there." He pointed. "I can take a taxi anywhere I want to go, including the movies at . . ."

"Sarasota Square," I supplied.

"Right. I can't remember shit."

"I know."

"How do you know?"

"It's written on your walker."

"It's been a nice visit, Goodwin," he said and closed the door.

I checked him off my list, got in the Saturn and headed toward escapee number three. Her address was on Orchid, the east side of 41 where the houses were smaller, the costs were lower and the lawns not all kept neat and trim.

Finding the house was easy. It was a one-story white frame that needed a coat of paint. I parked on the street. Next to the house was a weed-filled lot with a sign on a stick saying the lot was for sale.

The woman who opened the door was big, probably about fifty. She was built like an SUV and wearing a business suit. She looked like she was on the way out or had just come in.

"Yes?" she said.

"I'm looking for Vivian Pastor," I said.

"Why?"

"Just have a few questions."

"About?"

"Why she left Seaside," I said. "I'm with the Florida Assisted Living and Nursing Home Board of Review. It's routine. Is she here?"

"Yes."

The woman blocked the door.

"Can I talk to her?"

"You can, but I don't think you'll get your answer from her," she said. "I'll tell you what you need to know, but it will have to be reasonably fast. I've got to get to work."

"I'd like to talk to Ms. Pastor," I said. "Actually, I have to. Board rules."

She looked at her watch, sighed and said, "Come in. Vivian is my mother-in-law. I didn't think they were taking proper care of her. I'm Alberta Pastor."

She held out her hand. I took it. She had a grip that could crack walnuts.

"My name is Lew Fonesca."

I followed her into the small dark living room filled with a 1950s padded couch and two matching chairs with indentations where people had plopped for decades. There wasn't much light coming through the windows, whose curtains were closed, and the single standing lamp in the corner was vainly trying to hold back the darkness with a sixty-watt bulb.

"I promised my husband, David, God rest his soul, that I'd take care of his mother."

She opened a door and we stepped into a small dining room with a round wooden table for four. At the table sat a very small old woman with bent shoulders and large glasses that made her eyes look enormous. She was wearing flannel pajamas with red and blue stripes against a white background. In her hand she held an advertising insert.

"Mother," Alberta Pastor said. "This man wants to ask you a few questions about Seaside."

"See what?" the old woman said, bewildered.

"The place I got you out of," the younger woman said patiently. "Where you were living. Remember?"

"Haven't I always lived here?" the old woman asked.

"No, Mother," Alberta said.

"Ma'am," I said. "Why did you leave Seaside?"

The old woman looked at the younger woman in confusion.

"The place you were staying," I tried.

"I don't understand," the old woman said with a smile.

"Dementia," Alberta Pastor said to me. "It's been getting worse. They said they could take care of her, but she belongs in a nursing home or here with me. I don't break my promises. For David's sake, I'll keep her with me as long as I can. I've got a woman who comes in to look after her while I work. She should be here any minute. She's late. Vivian used to watch game shows, read, but now . . ."

"I had breakfast," the old woman said. "Didn't I?"

"Yes, Mother," Alberta said patiently.

"Am I hungry?"

"I don't know. Are you?" Alberta asked.

"I don't know," answered the old woman. "See, what did I tell you?"

"About what?" I asked.

"I don't know," the old woman said with a laugh.

"Enough?" Alberta asked me.

"Yes," I said.

The old woman went back to looking at the ads for toothpaste, Diet 7-Up and cans of Planters cashew halves.

Alberta Pastor led me back to the front door.

"Anything else I can tell you?" she asked.

"Nothing I can think of," I said. "Thanks."

I was back in my car. Three checked off. All among the living. Only Gertrude Everhart remained. Her new address was the Pine-Norton Nursing Home on Tallavast just north of the Sarasota/Bradenton airport.

The Pine-Norton was sprawling, pink stucco, new and no

trouble finding. I went through the automatic doors at the entrance and stepped out of the way for a young black nurse's aide in a blue uniform pushing a shriveled old woman in a wheelchair. The woman's head was leaning to the left as if her neck was no longer strong enough to support it. The door just to my right had the word OFFICE in black letters on a white plaque next to it. The door was open.

A woman, probably in her thirties, but she could have been younger, was staring at the computer screen in front of her, her nose a few inches from it. She was frowning.

I knocked and she looked up with a harried smile.

"Can I help you?" she asked.

She was pretty, nervous, with ash blonde hair that wouldn't stay in place.

"Gertrude Everhart," I said. "I'd like to see her."

"You are . . . ?"

"A concerned friend of the family," I said.

The woman puckered her lips as if she had bitten into a lemon.

"Mrs. Everhart was admitted yesterday," she said.

"Her choice?" I asked.

"Her . . . yes, she came voluntarily."

She turned her chair around, faced a file cabinet, opened the third drawer from the bottom and pulled out a file. Then she turned back to me.

"Friend of the family?"

"Guardian angel," I said.

"You know her son then."

"Yes," I said. "How is Gertrude?"

She tapped the file on her desk, made a decision, opened the file and scanned it quickly.

"Mrs. Everhart is suffering . . . no, I'm not supposed to use that word. I've only been here two weeks and, well, anyway,

Stuart M. Kaminsky

Mrs. Everhart, Gertrude, has a degenerative condition in her lower limbs. She is, as you probably know, confined to a wheelchair."

I nodded.

"She is also, let me see . . . early stages of glaucoma, high blood pressure, recurrent bladder infections, emphysema . . . You want the whole list?"

She looked up.

"No," I said. "Can I see her?"

"She just went out with Viola," the young woman said, looking back at the computer screen.

"Old lady in the wheelchair?"

"Uh-huh. You know anything about computers?"

"They exist," I said.

"About how they work?"

"In mysterious ways," I said.

She looked up and said, "Thanks a lot."

I left. Down the paved driveway lined with parked cars, Viola the nurse's aide was slowly pushing Gertrude Everhart, which meant I had started with four and then there was none. Everyone in the Seaside on the night Dorothy Cgnozic said she saw a murder was accounted for.

No, I thought as I got back in the car, there was still the staff, but Dorothy had said she saw the nurse on overnight duty. I drove past Viola and Gertrude, turned on Tallavast and headed for 301 past the airport.

The problem was, I believed Dorothy Cgnozic. I just didn't have a corpse.

The red-haired woman behind the desk at Seaside Assisted Living was filling in a report, pausing every few seconds to scratch her head with the back of the pen she was using.

I hadn't seen her before. She kept working without looking up and said, "Yes."

"I'd like to see Dorothy Cgnozic," I said.

"Relative?"

"Friend."

"The residents are having lunch."

"When will they be done?"

She looked at her watch.

"Ten minutes. You know her room?"

"Yes," I said.

She looked at me.

"Maybe you should just wait here till she's finished."

"Sure."

There were some wicker chairs in a little alcove next to the nursing station. A television set on a metal platform about six feet high was tuned to the game channel. I watched the young Alex Trebek get people to answer questions backward for a few minutes and listened to the redheaded woman mutter to herself.

I got up and moved back to the counter.

"Any of the staff quit or out sick?" I asked.

She scratched a nail just over her left eyebrow and said, "You looking for a job?"

"Definitely."

"You want to fill out a form?"

"Yes."

"Don't bother," she said. "There are no vacancies, no openings, nothing new coming up, nobody out sick. People like working here. The hours are terrible. You're surrounded by the befuddled and dying. The central office in Orlando is always changing the rules. But the pay is good, very good. Anything else?"

"No."

"They may be hiring at Beneva Park Club," she said. "What can you do?"

"Try to learn from my mistakes," I said.

She leaned back, stretched high, yawned and said, "A little levity is always welcome. Now if you'll just . . ."

A trio of elderly women were coming toward me down the corridor to my left. One of them was talking nonstop, loud. The other two were listening, or not. One of the nontalking women was Dorothy Cgnozic, pushing her walker.

"The war, the war, the war," the talking woman said, waving her arms. "The man talked about nothing but the war till the day he died. Same stories. Jeep driver for General George S. Patton. Chased through some forest by seven or eight Nazis with those funny helmets. What his buddy John Something said when mortar shells were falling on them. What Eli the Jew did with his bayonet knife to a German he jumped on in a fox pit."

"Foxhole," Dorothy corrected.

The talking woman didn't care or didn't hear.

"Drove me crazy, those stories. Told them to the kid who delivered the groceries, the mailman, the insurance man, the guy at the Texaco station who couldn't even understand English."

"Dorothy," I said as they moved behind me.

She looked over and stopped.

"Mr. Fonesca."

The red-haired woman behind the desk with the pen tapping on the form in front of her nodded to show that I was vindicated and not a mad intruder.

"He got his wars confused at the end," the talking woman said as she and the other woman left Dorothy behind to talk to me. "Korea, Vietnam. Came up with the notion that he had been part of the invasion of Japan."

I walked with Dorothy down the corridor behind the talking woman. When we were out of earshot of the redhead, Dorothy said, "Did you find out who I saw get murdered?"

"No," I said. "The staff is all accounted for. The residents are all accounted for. The four people who left are all accounted for. No deaths."

"It's no go," she said. "My husband used to say that. It's no go the picture show. It's no go the Roxy. You can watch with wonder when Merman sings, but don't go getting too foxy."

I didn't get it.

"Variations on Louis McNiece," she said.

"Ah."

"He was a poet, like my husband. I saw what I saw. Someone was murdered. Find out who and prove I'm not halfway to dementia. Find out who and tell the police. Find out who and what and why and I'll tell every nurse, social worker, physical therapist, visiting children pretending they're doctors, administrators. You're sure none of the people who were released is dead?"

I pulled the list out of my pocket as we walked and read, "Ellen Gallagher, living with her grandchildren."

"Not a socializer."

"Mark Anthony Katz. Lives on his own."

"Proud, crotchety."

"Vivian Pastor. With her daughter-in-law."

"Big. Lives for bingo. Checks off the days. Good for four cards a night."

"Gertrude Everhart is in a nursing home," I concluded.

"Now there's a poor woman whose mind is definitely going," Dorothy said. "Sometimes I think that's a blessing."

She stopped walking and put her thin hand on my arm.

Stuart M. Kaminsky

"Do not give up," she said. "You need more money?"

"No," I said. "I need more ideas."

"Yes, you do," came a voice behind us.

I turned to look at Ham Gentry, the pudgy pink man with the walker who had caught me and Ames in Amos Trent's office. He shuffled his walker next to Dorothy's. I had the sudden fantasy that they were about to race down the hallway.

"You have any?" I asked.

"Ideas? One. Ask more questions," he said.

"I'll do that."

"I will too," he said. He looked at Dorothy. "We both will. I believe in this woman."

He was breathing heavily, definitely not ready for a walker race. He patted his chest and said, "Fish cakes. Taste all right, but don't sit well. The sands of time are falling. Get moving. A man who believes in the Chicago Cubs," he said, pointing to my cap, "cannot give up this easily."

I nodded, said I'd be back in touch with Dorothy and watched the two of them move slowly down the carpeted corridor.

It took me less than ten minutes to get to Richard Tycinker's office. The woman at the reception desk looked up at me, checked her watch and said, "They're waiting for you in his office."

I moved past her down the gray-carpeted corridor and knocked at Tycinker's door. He told me to come in. I did and closed the door behind me. He was sitting behind his desk. Nancy Root, Richard McClory and Yolanda Root were there too, as far apart as they could be. McClory sat in one of the chairs across from Tycinker. Nancy Root sat on the black leather sofa. Yolanda Root sat in a matching black leather armchair against the wall.

"Nancy says you're close to finding the man," said Tycinker.

"I think so," I said.

"Nancy, Dr. McClory and Yolanda would like to talk to you. I suggest you go into the conference room."

I nodded. Tycinker got up from behind his desk, moved to the door I had just come through, opened it and waited for us to follow. We did. Nancy was first, then Yolanda, then McClory. I was next, with Tycinker last.

He motioned to his right. I knew where the conference room was.

"You'll have complete privacy," he said. "Take as long as you need. There's coffee brewing and soft drinks and bottled water in the refrigerator."

He opened the conference room door, waited till we were inside and then left, closing the door behind him.

I wasn't sure who was in charge or what this was about. The table was freshly polished. The large windows looked out at a line of five evenly spaced palm trees. Yolanda went to the refrigerator, got a Pepsi and sat at the far end of the table popping the can. Nancy Root, looking strained, sat on one side of the table facing the window. McClory, needing a shave and looking as if he was hungover, sat across from his ex-wife with his back to the window. I sat at the end of the table across from Yolanda.

I took off my cap and placed it on the table, waiting for someone to tell me what we were doing here.

"Go ahead," Nancy said, looking at her ex-husband.

"Look," he said, not to me but to her.

"We agreed," Nancy said.

Yolanda took a gulp of Pepsi and gave her former stepfather a look of open contempt and muttered, "Wimp." McClory pretended not to hear.

"Kyle was my only child," he said.

"He knows that," said Yolanda. "And he was my only brother and Nancy's only son. Jeez."

Nancy suddenly stood up.

"You're not going to do it, are you?" she asked, glaring at McClory.

"I'll do it," he said without enthusiasm.

Yolanda shook her head and pursed her lips.

"Richard," Nancy said firmly. "You and Yola wait outside."

"Great," said Yolanda sarcastically. "We've got so much to catch up on."

"Look, Nancy . . ." McClory said.

She looked but said nothing.

McClory got up slowly, resigned, looked at me, brushed his hair back with his hand and came around the table. Yolanda across from me rocked and bit her lower lip, said, "Shit," and got up. McClory and Yolanda left the room, closing the door behind them.

Nancy Root sat again and faced me. She was wearing a little too much makeup and a determined look that seemed more than a bit strained.

"Kyle is dead," she said. "The man who did it is alive. I understand that if you find him and turn him over to the police, a number of things could happen."

I wasn't sure where this was going, but I nodded.

"He'll get a lawyer," she said. "Maybe plead innocent."

"Maybe."

"Will there be enough evidence to convict him?" she said.

"I think so," I said.

"You think so, but you're not sure."

"He'll be convicted," I said.

"Of what?"

"The charge? That's up to the prosecutor," I said.

"I've been in enough courtroom dramas to know that murder in the first degree is unlikely," she said, eyes holding mine.

"I—"

"He can say it was an accident, that he didn't mean to run him down," she said. "He can . . ."

She closed her eyes.

"He might plead guilty," I said. "I think he's feeling guilty."

"But he'll live," she said. "He'll be alive and Kyle is dead. He won't get the death penalty."

She was right. There was nothing for me to say and I knew now what was coming next and why she had told McClory and Yolanda to leave the room.

"I think we should stop here, Mrs. Root."

"No," she said, shaking her head. "I want him dead. We want him dead. It's not enough, but the thought of him being alive when Kyle is dead is too much to live with. You understand? Every day I'll know Kyle is buried in that coffin and the man who ran him down is alive, waking up every morning, eating, showering, reading, working at something, watching television. That is unacceptable. Do you have any idea of how we feel?"

"Yes," I said. I knew exactly how she felt.

"The horrible irony is that Kyle's death and that man have brought the three of us together," she said with a laugh that wasn't a laugh. "If you call what you just witnessed being together."

I said nothing.

"Well?" she said. "Do I have to be more specific?"

"No," I said.

Stuart M. Kaminsky

She wanted me to find the man who ran Kyle down and kill him.

"Good. You know what I want and I don't have to say it. Richard will pay fifty thousand dollars, cash, nothing signed, no income to report."

"I'm sorry," I said.

"What about that old man, your friend?"

"Ames?"

"Mr. Tycinker tells me he killed a man a few years ago."

"Ames isn't a hit man," I said. "And he can't be bought."

"Then," she said with a sigh, "when you find him, let me know before you go to the police. One of us will . . . do it."

"Makes me an accessory," I said.

"I know about your wife. What would you do if you found him, the person who killed her?"

"I don't know," I said.

"Do you believe in God, Mr. Fonesca?" she asked.

"He asked me the same thing," I said.

"He?"

"The man who killed Kyle."

"You talked to him?"

"He calls me," I said. "He's falling apart. I don't know."

"Know what?"

"If I believe in God."

"Do you believe in an afterlife? Any kind of an afterlife? Nirvana? Anything?"

"I don't think about it," I said. "I work hard at not thinking about it."

"It takes a great deal out of you, doesn't it, not to think?"

"Yes," I said. "When I find him, I plan to turn him over to the police. You want to end my services?"

"If I said yes, you'd just stop looking?"

"No," I said. "I'll keep looking. I'll find him."

She slumped back.

"Am I fired?" I asked.

She waved a hand and looked out the window at the trees.

"No," she said.

I wanted to give her some comfort, tell her that she would find some peace in simply knowing her son's killer was found, was punished, was exposed. But I knew it wouldn't work and if I tried it, it would be a lie.

"Do what you have to do," she said.

I got up, took my cap and went to the door. In the corridor Yolanda was leaning against a wall, arms folded, looking at the floor. McClory was pacing. They both looked at me and knew that I had turned down Nancy Root's offer.

McClory walked past me without meeting my eyes and headed down the hallway. Yolanda started to ease by me and into the conference room. She stopped, turned toward me, her face inches from mine.

"He's a wimp. You're a wimp. If I get the chance, I'm going to stab the guy who killed Kyle. I'm gonna stab him and keep stabbing him and hope that he begs for his life and cries while he dies."

"It's not so easy to murder someone," I said.

"He did it," she said.

"I don't think it was easy for him," I said.

"You don't . . . you feel sorry for him?"

She seemed to be waiting for me to respond. I had no response.

"I'll find him," I said.

About ten minutes later, I parked back at the DQ and walked south on Washington to Gwen's. There were no fish cakes on the menu but the chalk list on the blackboard on the wall a few feet from the Elvis poster said meat loaf was. One space was left at the counter. I sat next to a thin, young guy with a beard, long hair in a braid and a faraway look in his glazed eyes as he ate a burger. On the other side of me was a regular at Gwen's, a guy with muscles in a white T-shirt with a stitched blue outline of a stationary bike over the pocket, the emblem of the gym down the street. He was drinking soup. No Tim from Steubenville.

"Digger show up this morning?" I asked Gwen when she came back with my meat loaf.

"Showed up, did just fine for the first day," she said. "You just missed him. He made the meat loaf."

"Looks good," I said.

"Enjoy," she said, grabbing the almost full coffeepot from the burner behind her and heading around the counter to make the round of the tables.

Something, I thought, pouring ketchup on the plate in an open space between the meat loaf and french fries.

"Huh?" asked muscles.

I didn't know I had said it out loud.

"Just something I'm trying to remember," I said.

"You're the guy who lives in the office behind the DQ."

"Yeah."

"You work out?"

"At the Y," I said.

"I can get you a good price at Milt's Gym," he said. "Just a few feet from your place."

"I'll think about it," I said.

"Good price," he repeated. "Remember what you were trying to remember?"

"Not yet. Something someone said to me today."

"Right training, right food, right herbs can get your memory kicking ass," he said.

I could not come up with a concrete image of my memory, let alone an image of it or me kicking ass.

"It'll come," I said.

"Don't bet your left arm on it," said the blond guy with the beard through a mouth full of burger.

"I won't," I said.

"Not that I know what anyone would want a fucking left arm for," he said. "I mean one that wasn't his."

"Maybe the same reason someone would want a pound of flesh."

"Pound of flesh?"

That pretty much ended the luncheon repartee. We finished in silence. Muscles left first after going into the pocket of his T-shirt and coming out with a business card he handed to me. I put it in my pocket.

I finished next, looked at the check, nodded at the blond guy, who was staring at his plate, left a dollar tip and paid Gwen at the cash register.

"Pretty nice day," she said, glancing out the window.

I nodded.

There was no one on the sidewalk. People didn't stroll in Sarasota, but cars did flash by. I was about twenty feet from the DQ lot and almost next to Milt's Gym when I heard it. It sounded like a car behind me coming up the sidewalk. I started to turn. It was a car coming toward me on the sidewalk.

Tinted windows. Small car, tires on the right side in the street, on the left almost scraping the wall. There was a break in oncoming traffic. I jumped to my right into the street in front of a blue pickup truck. The pickup driver swerved to his

Stuart M. Kaminsky

left, missing me by a few feet and almost colliding with an oncoming squat convertible. The car on my tail turned with me. Whoever it was did not seem concerned about who or what was coming or going. This was a person with a clear mission, to run me down.

12

A CAR SCREECHED out of the DQ lot in front of me and headed right at me. One car behind. One car in front. Me in the middle trying to find space to cross the street to the other side. I was trapped ten feet off the curb. The car with the tinted windows swerved back toward the sidewalk. I stood on the white line. The right fender of the car coming toward me grazed the right fender of the car behind me, which was back on the sidewalk. I heard a headlight pop.

I made it across the street and looked back over my shoulder. The car with the tinted windows that had tried to run me down was skidding across the street and into the northbound lane. It roared on, glass from the broken headlight tinkling behind. The other car that had come out of the DQ lot was turning down the narrow street just past Gwen's.

People were streaming out of Gwen's, including Gwen, who shouted across the street, "Lew, you all right?"

I nodded.

"Damnedest thing I ever saw," said a black guy with a sandwich in his hand. "Looked like they were trying to squash you right between them."

"Melanie's calling the cops," Gwen said. "You better come back in and wait."

I shook my head no, crossed the street and moved toward the DQ. I couldn't talk. Not fear. Memories.

When I got inside my office, I went to the desk, sat with a reminder of the taste of recent meat loaf. My knee was throbbing slightly. My shoulder ached. My hands were trembling.

My phone started to ring. I stared at it for five rings and picked it up, expecting Taurus the Philosopher.

"Yes," I said.

"Not here," said Ames.

"What's not where?"

"Parking lot at the college," he said. "Seven Tauruses. None with fender damage."

"I know," I said.

"You know?"

"He just tried to kill me," I said.

"You'd best call the police," said Ames. "I'll be right there."

"I don't think I have to call them. They'll be here in a few minutes."

And they were, less than twenty minutes after Ames hung up.

When the knock came at the door, I was staring at the painting on my wall of the dark jungle. I was having trouble seeing the spot of color. I counted on that one small spot. I hoped it hadn't vanished.

"Come in," I called.

Etienne Viviase entered, back in detective garb, sport jacket, loose tie. He didn't say anything, just sat in the chair on the other side of the desk and shook his head. I watched him fold his arms and turn his eyes toward me.

Finally, with a sigh and a blowing out of air, he said, "Well?"

"Not very," I answered.

"Well, what happened?"

"Someone tried to kill me," I said. "Maybe it was an accident. A drunken driver."

"Came right up on the sidewalk and didn't stop?" he said. "Witnesses say whoever it was would have rolled right over you if another car hadn't sideswiped him."

"If they say so," I said. "I was busy."

"Didn't catch a license number? Part of one?"

I shook my head no.

"I don't want to be here," he said.

I knew how that felt.

"For some reason, the department has decided that you and I have a relationship. Your name comes up, it lands on my desk."

In a way, we did have a relationship.

"My day is not brightened and my burden not lightened by my encounters with you," he said.

"I'm sorry."

"Your apology will be taken into consideration. About a week ago a kid gets run down and killed. You start looking for the driver. About half an hour ago someone tries to run you down. It does not strike me as a coincidence. Enlighten me, Fonesca."

"I'll have some information for you soon," I said.

"If you're alive to give it to me."

"Did you ever have one of those feelings that you knew

166   **Stuart M. Kaminsky**

something, heard something, saw something that would clear up a crime, but you can't quite remember what it is?"

"I've been a cop for a quarter of a century," he said. "I have the feeling at least twice a week."

"I need a little more time," I said. "If—"

The phone was ringing.

"Why don't you get an answering machine?" Viviase asked.

"Had one for a while," I said. "Didn't like it."

The truth was that I dreaded seeing that light blinking, knowing there were one, two, three, five messages waiting for me, telling me something I didn't want to hear, asking me to do something I didn't want to do, like calling back. It was easier to just pick up the ringing phone, not have time to think about who or what it might be.

I picked up the ringing phone.

"Will you stop now?" the man on the other end said, his voice quivering.

"No," I said. "But we can talk."

Viviase looked at me.

"You owe me," the man said.

"You tried to kill me," I said.

"You don't understand. I saved your life."

"Who is that?" Viviase said, standing.

I put the phone against my chest and said, "The man who killed Kyle McClory."

Viviase started to reach out for the phone, changed his mind and nodded for me to go on. I put the phone to my ear and said, "You saved my life?"

"I was in the parking lot outside your office waiting for you," the man said. "I think I was going to talk to you. I saw you coming, saw the car behind you bump up on the sidewalk. I cut him off."

DENIAL

"Why?"

"I can't explain," he said. "I mean, I can explain but if I do . . . I saved your life. Doesn't that mean anything?"

"I didn't ask you to save my life," I said.

"It doesn't mean anything that I saved you?"

"It means something," I said. "I just don't know what it means."

I looked at Viviase, who wanted to know what was going on.

"Santayana was wrong," the man on the phone said softly.

"At the Alamo?"

Viviase was more than puzzled now.

"George Santayana," the man said. "To knock a thing down, especially if it is cocked at an arrogant angle, is a deep delight to the blood."

"He was wrong?"

"The blood forgets but the soul remembers."

He hung up.

"What the hell was that?"

"He's sorry he killed Kyle McClory," I said.

"I'm glad to hear that," Viviase said. "Who is he?"

"Not sure," I said, "but he wants to be found. He didn't try to kill me a little while ago. He saved my life."

"He wants to kill you, but he saved your life?"

"He doesn't want to kill me. He thinks he might have to."

"Why?"

"He's afraid."

"Damn right," said Viviase.

"Not for himself," I said.

"He told you that?"

"No," I said. "I heard it in his voice."

Stuart M. Kaminsky

Viviase put his hand to his forehead and said, "You know you're a little nuts, don't you?"

"Yes," I said. "It's what keeps me sane. Can I buy you a Dilly Bar?"

"You can," he said, "but you may not. I can have your process server's license revoked. You know that?"

"Will you?"

"No," he said. "I've got to go. There are people out there who want to be helped."

He got up, went to the door, turned back as if he was going to say something, changed his mind and left.

When Ames knocked at the door about twenty minutes later, I told him to come in. He did and moved to the window air conditioner and turned it on.

"You're sweating," he said.

I touched my forehead. He was right. Ames stood in front of the desk, his hands folded.

"Want me to go back to the college tomorrow?" he asked.

"We'll find him tomorrow."

"Sure about that?"

"You know who George Santayana was?"

"Philosopher."

"Our man is probably a philosophy professor or maybe classics or English. His Taurus definitely has a dented fender now, right side. He has white hair, a white beard, tall."

Ames nodded. We would go to the departmental offices at the college, ask the right questions, find the man who both wanted to be found and didn't want to be found, who was willing to kill me but didn't want to, who was in anguish I fully understood.

"Why don't we go now?" he asked. "Just stop by the Texas and I'll get a dogleg."

I wanted to tell him that I didn't plan on moving for hours, maybe not till the next morning, and only then because I had been seduced by responsibility.

Someone had tried to run me down. No doubt about it. But if it wasn't the philosopher on the phone, who was it?

The phone rang again. I stared at it and for a few seconds wondered if it was really ringing or I was just imagining it. It rang five times. Ames looked at me and then at the phone.

"Gonna answer it?" he asked.

I picked it up and said, "Yes."

I really meant no, no to almost anything.

"Mr. Fonesca, I've been trying to call you for hours."

"I've been busy," I told Nancy Root.

"What have you found?"

Her voice was steady, strong, clear, but with an underlying effort.

What had I found? That the world is without form and void, that nothing is predictable, that the just and the unjust, good and bad, suffer or survive at about the same rate. That my mother's God, if he was out there, had played a major game with us. He had built in an impulse, no, a drive, to survive, even when common sense told us that survival was, ultimately, impossible and painful. From her voice, from what had happened to her, I had the feeling that Nancy Root would understand, but I didn't say any of this.

"It's only been a few hours. I told you I should have some answers for you soon," I said.

"The man who killed my son is insane," she said.

"It might be a woman," I said.

"No, he called me."

Ames leaned against the wall near the door, watching me. "What did he say?"

"That he was sorry," she said. "He was crying. I couldn't

Stuart M. Kaminsky

understand all of it. He told me to make you stop looking. He . . . pleaded with me. He was so pathetic."

"You've changed your mind about wanting him dead?"

She ignored my question and went on. "He said he had to see me. That I'd understand if he could just talk to me. Then he hung up in the middle of a sentence. I had the feeling that he wasn't just feeling frightened, sorry for himself, that there was something else at stake."

"My question," I reminded her.

"Yes," she said. "I still want him dead. Nothing he can say would bring Kyle back and you did tell me that he had intentionally run down my son."

"That's what the witness says."

"Then—"

I heard a voice behind her. She said something I couldn't make out and then came back on the phone.

"There's someone at the security desk who says he has to see me," she said. "Corrine says he's a big man with a white beard. It might be . . . ?"

"It might be," I said. "How good is the person on security right now?"

"Ron? He's a retired policeman. He's at least seventy and—"

"Tell him to have the man wait. Tell him you'll see him in a little while. Tell him you're in the middle of a show."

"I am," she said. "It's Friday. Matinee. Intermission. I have to go back on in a few minutes."

"I'll be there in fifteen minutes," I said. "Do you have a gun?"

"No," she said.

"Don't do anything," I said.

"Are you worrying about his hurting me or my hurting him?"

"Both," I said.

She hung up.

"We rolling?" asked Ames.

"We're rolling," I said.

13

I **EXPLAINED** to Ames as we drove up 301 to DeSoto and then went west past the greyhound track on our left and then the airport on our right. There was a long wait at the light at Tamiami Trail. The Ringling Museum of Art sat about three hundred yards in front of us behind the iron fence. The light changed. I went across the Trail and made a right turn into the Florida State University Asolo Center.

The parking lot was almost full, with visitors to the museum and to the matinee performance. I drove past the large box, which housed the theater, the Sarasota Ballet and the Florida State University graduate program for acting students.

I found a parking spot near the backstage entrance, pulled in and got out with Ames coming around and joining me as I moved up the concrete steps toward the door. It had taken less than fifteen minutes.

I had tried to think about what I would do when I stood in front of the man who had wept on the phone, but nothing would come. Whatever happened would happen. I had no plan. I glanced at Ames and saw that he had a plan; it consisted of showing me a very small pistol in the palm of his right hand.

"Double derringer," he said. "A forty-one-caliber rimfire."

"I don't think we'll need that," I said.

"Can't hurt," he said.

"Yes, it can."

He shrugged. We had no time to discuss it. We went through the door, Ames hiding the weapon in the palm of his large hand.

The security counter was on our left. A man in a blue uniform, lean and spectacled, stood behind the counter. There was no one else in view. The double doors leading backstage were closed.

"A man," I said. "Big, white beard, wanted to see Nancy Root."

The man behind the desk looked at us.

"Who're you?" the guard said.

"Friends of Miss Root," I said. "Where's the man?"

"Left," he said. "Nervous. Asked how much longer the show was. Not much room to pace in here. He went outside, walked around a little and then went off to the right, walking fast. You want to see Miss Root, you'll have to wait too."

"Is there any other way in?" I asked.

"Couple," he said. "Can't open them from outside and if they open from inside, it lights up on the board back here."

"Except for the entrance to the theater?" I said.

"That's right."

"If he comes back, don't let him in to see Miss Root," I said.

"Not up to me," he said. "Up to her." He looked us over. A short dark man wearing a baseball cap. A tall old man in flannel shirt and an old cracking leather jacket. "You're not cops."

I didn't confirm his keen observation. I went back outside with Ames next to me. We hurried around the building and up the steps to the theater. The doors were open. The play had to be nearly over.

An old woman in a white blouse and blue skirt stood talking to a young man behind the refreshment counter in front of us. They looked us over as we moved quickly toward them. The woman held a finger to her lips to let us know that we should be quiet. She whispered, "Show's almost over. Can I help you?"

"Big man, white hair, white beard," I said. "Did he come in a little while ago?"

"Yes," she said. "Very odd. He said he had to get in. I told him he had missed more than half the show, but he went to the box office and bought a ticket."

"He's in the theater?" I asked.

"Oh yes."

"Where?"

"Balcony," she said. "Plenty of seats on the main floor, but I didn't want him to disrupt the actors, so I thought—"

"We really have to find him," I said.

"Performance will be over in about fifteen minutes or so," she said.

"We really have to find him now," I said.

"Why?" the young man behind the counter said.

I tried to think of a good lie that would get us in. I failed, so I said, "You know what happened to Nancy Root's son?"

"Yes," said the woman.

The young man nodded.

"I think the man with the beard was driving the car," I said. "I'm working for Miss Root."

"I'm calling security," said the young man.

The woman looked confused.

"Good idea," I said, starting toward the stairs on my left, half expecting the old woman to try to stop us. She didn't.

We came to the mezzanine landing and went up another flight of carpeted steps and moved through a closed door into near darkness. We could hear voices, the projected sound of actors' voices that said, *We're actors. We're not talking normally. We're projecting. We expect you to pretend that you don't notice.*

I groped my way through a hanging velvety drape with Ames at my side. A voice from the stage below us, Nancy Root's voice, said, "And you think that would stop me? Fifteen years together and you think a few words can stop me now?"

The light from the stage was bright enough to make out the seats in the balcony, though the people in them were shadowy.

"Not here," Ames whispered before I could see faces.

Most of the seats weren't filled. People were scattered.

From the stage, a man's voice said, "Stop you? With words? You're right. I know you too well to think that common sense would make any difference. No, Maddy, I'm going to kill you."

I motioned Ames down narrow steps and looked over the balcony into the orchestra seats. Ames did the same. The man wasn't there. On the stage, Nancy Root, in a blonde wig, stood in a living room, arms folded, facing a tall, burly-looking man with wavy brown hair and a knowing smile. She

Stuart M. Kaminsky

was wearing a blue dress showing cleavage. He was wearing a tuxedo. He was holding a gun.

I was trying to think of where we could stand to see the seats in the mezzanine and the rear of the ground floor when Ames nudged me and pointed across the theater at a box seat at the mezzanine level.

A single figure sat in it, a burly man with a white beard. His hands gripped the bronze rail in front of him as he looked down at Nancy Root.

I was moving back up the steps to return to the steps to the mezzanine level when the man looked over at us. Our movement had caught his eye.

Our eyes met. He recognized me. I didn't recognize him but I knew who he was. He got up and stepped back quickly into the shadows of the box. Ames and I hurried up the last few steps, went through the drapes and headed for the door and the steps beyond, which would take us to the mezzanine level.

The box where the man had been was empty, the door open.

On stage, Nancy Root was saying, "I have a cliché for you, Norman. You won't get away with it."

"Why not?" the man asked with a touch of amusement.

"Because," she said, "I'm recording everything we say. Don't bother to look around. It's voice activated and the microphone is extremely well hidden."

"You're lying," he said.

"Am I? Well, there is one way to find out," Nancy Root said. "I don't recommend it for either of our sakes."

Ames and I were back in a dark corridor just beyond the box seat. The man hadn't passed us. There was an emergency exit to the left. This time Ames led the way. We were on a bare concrete landing. Bare concrete steps with a metal railing led down. Footsteps clanged below us.

"Wait," I called.

The footsteps stopped.

"Let's talk," I said.

Ames, derringer in hand, started slowly, quietly down the stairs back against the wall. I leaned over the railing. There was no one in sight.

Somewhere below us the man, his voice echoing, said, "Not here. Not now. I have to take care of things. Take care of her before—"

"Nancy Root?"

"No," he said. "Oh God, I should have let her kill you."

"Her?" I called.

"The woman who tried to run you down," he said.

I could hear him move, heard the echo of running feet below. First the man. Then Ames hurrying down. I started after him, my sore knee slowing me down, and reached the ground level in time to see Ames go through a door and turn to the right. The door started to close. I pushed the door back open and followed him.

The security guard came through a door in front of me and said, "What's going on?"

I didn't answer. I followed Ames.

"I said, What's going on?" the guard repeated.

A turn in the corridor. Dressing rooms. Something that looked like a small lounge. An almost empty room with a polished wooden floor and floor-to-ceiling mirrors on one wall.

I was closing in on Ames, who pushed through a door into a small, empty theater with seats graded upward about fifteen rows. There was a dim light coming from the small stage to our right and exit lights behind us and across from us.

We headed for the exit and pushed through a door and found ourselves back in the lobby with the old woman and the young man behind the refreshment counter.

"That way," shouted the man, pointing to the entrance to the theater.

We ran through the doors into the late afternoon.

Fear, anger, desperation, adrenaline had kicked up the speed of the big man in front of us. He had a lead of about thirty yards.

Ames slowed down a little and said, "Damn arthritis."

I moved past him, losing my Cubs cap. I was in good shape, at least for running, but my knee did more than just slow me down. I didn't know what I'd do even if I had been able to catch up with the man, who was a good four or five inches taller than I was and at least fifty pounds heavier.

The man got to his car, opened the door, sat heavily and slammed the door. I was in the middle of the aisle. He was parked between two cars facing into the space. He backed out, swinging the rear of his car in my direction with a wailing squeal.

I moved between two parked cars. I could see the dented fender, the broken light. He was almost even with me. He looked over the passenger seat and met my eyes. I'm not sure what he saw. I'm not sure what I was feeling. I definitely wasn't thinking.

He shifted into drive and started forward.

A shot, the sound of a firecracker, came from the small gun in Ames McKinney's hand. Ames was standing in the driveway now. The bullet hit the rear window of the car as it started forward. It made a hole but didn't shatter. Ames fired again. The bullet pinged off the trunk as the driver made a sharp left turn.

"Two pellets," Ames said. "That's it."

He held up the empty little gun.

"Let's go," he said.

"No," I said, imagining a wild car chase, imagined the clearly desperate man losing control, a crash. "We'll find him. Now we know where to look."

We went back through the stage door, where the fuming security guard stood with his hands on his hips and greeted us with, "What the hell is going on here?"

"Miss Root will explain," I said.

"She'd better," he said. "I've got to write this up, you know."

"I understand."

"I don't need this kind of crap, you know."

"I know," I said.

"I get crap about this, I'm quitting. I can always bag groceries at Publix or Albertsons."

He went back behind the counter, pulled out a pad and began to fill out the form, shaking his head the whole time while we waited for Nancy Root.

She came out about five minutes later, still in costume and makeup.

"Where is he?" she said, looking at Ames and me.

"Got away," I answered.

"I saw him in the box stage right, didn't I?"

"Yes," I said.

"He's insane, isn't he?" she asked.

"Something like that," I agreed.

I wondered if the person who had run down my wife had felt anything like the kind of guilt as the bearded man. I hoped he did.

Nancy Root and I looked at each other. Her mask of makeup didn't cover the pain in her eyes. I knew that pain.

Stuart M. Kaminsky

I saw it in mirrors when I had to look or mistakenly looked. She was an actress. She would have to look in mirrors as long as she worked at her profession. She was young. She had a lot of years to look at those mourning eyes.

14

WE SHOULD GO."

Ames spoke softly, seated next to me, looking straight ahead as I drove down Tamiami Trail.

"In the morning," I said.

"Suit yourself."

Ames wanted to go to Manatee Community College and track down the bearded philosopher. I wanted to eat something very bad for me, full of carbohydrates, maybe a couple of Big Macs or a chocolate cherry Blizzard. Maybe both. Or maybe I'd try something different. Then I wanted to put on a clean pair of underwear and go to sleep. It was just before five at night.

We said nothing as we made the turn at Fruitville just past the quay. I turned on the radio. Someone on WLSS was interviewing a woman named Sunny who ran a shelter for stray cats. She had several hundred of them, knew all their names, played them symphonies to keep them calm, assured all listeners that she wasn't a crazy cat lady.

"Roland and I keep the yard clean," the woman named Sunny said, as if she were the happiest person in Sarasota, possibly the world. "And there are temperature-controlled little nooks for all of them."

Sunny didn't want money. She had plenty. Her husband, Roland, was a retired CEO of a corporation called InterTelex.

I imagined a hundred cats grinning, pawing, leaping, fighting, cuddling, rolling and jumping. Orange, black, white, striped, furry, hairless.

For a minute or two I managed to push reality from my mind, put it in a green fragile bubble and let it quiver away to wait. Catherine had wanted a cat, but neither of us was home during the day and she didn't think it would be fair to a cat to leave it alone.

A week or so before she had died, I made up my mind to surprise her on her birthday with two cats. I'd get them from the humane society on Halstead, or maybe it was Broadway. I wouldn't name the cats and I wouldn't use whatever name the humane society had tagged them with. I would let Catherine name them.

I lost Sunny's bouncing voice and the cats faded away. The bubble came floating back and for an instant I imagined a baby.

"Easy up," said Ames, reaching out and turning the steering wheel as I drifted into the left lane just before we came to 301.

I stopped imagining and straightened out as Ames changed the station. The golden oldies station came on. Cyndi Lauper was belting out "Girls Just Want to Have Fun." She sounded too much like Sunny the Cat Lady. I turned off the radio and turned right.

DENIAL

We made it to the DQ parking lot, where Ames's motor scooter was chained against a metal post.

"I could go it on my own," he said.

"No, I'll go with you in the morning."

"Lock your door tonight," he said as he got out and then leaned back through the door, his hand open, the derringer lying in it. "Two shots. Pellets are already loaded."

"I don't need it," I said, looking at the tiny weapon.

"Someone trying to kill you?"

"Looks that way," I said.

"Want me camping out in front of your door all night?"

"No."

He reached farther into the car, the gun inches from my hand. I took it and nodded.

Ames closed the door and headed for his scooter while I parked in an open space closer to my office home.

Dave was at the DQ window. Dark tan, wrinkled skin, bleached-out hair from hours on his boat in the Gulf, he said, "Lewis, you look like a bulimic manatee."

Even at my best I doubted if I could come up with the image of a bulimic manatee.

Dave owned the DQ franchise and four others on the Gulf coast. He filled in from time to time to remind himself of what it meant to work the counter and to prove to himself that he was still working at making a living.

"Chili and a Blizzard," I said.

"Chocolate cherry?"

"Surprise me," I said. "No, don't surprise me. Chocolate cherry. Large."

"I'm thinking of calling the sizes tall, grande and venti," he said. "Like Starbucks. Think they'll sue?"

"I don't know," I said.

"Hope so," he said. "Great publicity. They ask me to stop.

I tell the newspapers, argue that they don't have trademarks on words like *tall, grande* and *venti*. Then I get the publicity free, business picks up. I reluctantly give into the pressure and come up with different names, maybe have a contest to name the sizes. What do you think?"

"Donald Trump and Warren Buffett will both come to you with big offers."

I paid him.

"Dreams don't cost anything, Lew," he said, turning to prepare my chili and Blizzard.

Oh yes, they do, I thought. Dreams could be very expensive.

A pair of teen girls were behind me. I moved out of the way and stood in front of the pickup window. The girls were talking about someone named Shelly. Like Yolanda Root, the two girls used the word *like* at least once every other fragment of a sentence. They were wearing almost identical jeans and T-shirts with words on them that I didn't recognize.

It took me about fifteen seconds to figure out that the "Shelly" they were talking about was the dead poet.

"Like, he's got these great metaphors," said one girl.

"He is so cool," said the other.

" 'The moonbeams kiss the sea,' " said the first girl. " 'What are all these kissings worth, if thou kiss not me?' "

"Can you imagine, like, Bill Sherman saying something like that?" said the second girl.

"As if," said the first girl. "Bill Sherman is a carved-out empty hunk."

"Bingo," said the first girl.

They both laughed. I shuddered once. The second girl glanced in my direction. They were both looking at me now, aware that I had been listening to them. I turned to the window as Dave came up with my order. He looked up at the sky and said, "Tomorrow should be clear. Want to go out with me on the boat for a few hours?"

"Busy," I said. "Rain check."

The last time I had gotten on a boat in the bay, the owner, complete with white captain's hat, had tried to kill me.

I moved past the girls with my bag and didn't look at them.

Were they fourteen like Kyle McClory? Did they know him? Were they closer to sixteen, like Adele? Did they know her? Did they think about vulnerability or mortality? I was afraid the answer was yes.

In my office, the phone was not ringing.

Maybe I should get that answering machine.

I sat at the desk, ate and drank, and tasted nothing. "Bingo," I said out loud.

The word meant something. It was the key to the question that had been coming back to me, the question whose answer I needed if I were to . . . what? Prove Dorothy right? Find the truth about the bearded philosopher?

Nothing more came. Then I noticed both the chili and the Blizzard were gone. I didn't remember enjoying or finishing them. Comfort food had failed to comfort.

It was almost six. I was in my white boxer shorts with the little red valentines. I wore my extra-large University of Chicago T-shirt. The phone had not rung. I was too tired to turn on the television and the VHS player and push in a tape. Covers over my head, I closed my eyes.

A knock.

Not here, I thought.

Another knock.

I've not returned.

Two short hard knocks.

I pushed back the covers, pulled on my pants and went to the door. It was Arnoldo Robles.

"I tried to call," he said.

I stepped back so he could enter and closed the door.

"I remembered something," he said.

"Have a seat," I said.

"No time. Got to get back to El Tacito. I could be making it up or imagining it or maybe even dreaming it," he said. "But that other person in the car, the one that killed that boy, I think she was smiling at me through the back window just when the car hit the boy, big kind of goofy smile like she was happy to see me."

"You just remembered this?"

He sighed and shook his head.

"No, everything happened just like that and I thought maybe I was seeing things," he said. "Maybe I thought the police would think I was making it up."

"You could recognize her again if you saw her?"

"It's crazy," he said, running the fingers of his right hand through his thick hair. "I had this feeling that I'd seen her before, or her twin brother or sister or something."

"Where did you see this twin?"

"Don't know," he said. "But I'll think about it. You find the driver yet?"

I considered saying that the driver had found me, but if I told him the story of the bearded philosopher, Arnoldo Robles might begin to wonder if the man might have the key witness against him on his hit list. It was, in fact, a possibility.

"No," I said. "But I think I'm close. I'll let you know."

"Could have been my kid on that street," he said. "I keep thinking about that, you know?"

"Yes," I said.

We stood for a few seconds. There wasn't anything else to say.

"Well," he said. "I better go."

I opened the door and as he walked through the door said, "Thanks for coming."

"Sure," he said and turned left toward the stairs.

I dreamt of cars. Cars and cats. The cars were in a demolition derby on Main Street. Cats dashed and leaped out of their way. Clowns, little people, Charlton Heston, Sammy Sosa. Women, children and someone who might have been me dashed from door to door trying to get away from the metal on metal, metal on flesh. The doors were all locked. I didn't see them but I knew they were there, Adele with the baby in her arms, Flo in her Western boots, Ames on his scooter.

There was a parting of cars for an instant and two cars were coming at each other, the same two cars that had collided down the street with me in the middle. In the middle of reality. In the middle in my dream.

I stood frozen. It wasn't fear. It was more like resignation. The cars missed me by inches, plowed into each other, spraying my back with tiny shards of glass from a broken window.

On the sidewalk were the two girls at the Dairy Queen and Dorothy Cgnozic with her arms around them. Together they yelled, "Bingo," and I woke up.

I dressed in my clean second pair of jeans and a short-sleeved denim shirt and picked up a clean towel, soap and razor and headed barefoot for the door. When I opened it, Darrell Caton was standing there, or rather he was leaning against the metal railing five feet from my door. I didn't trust the railing. I didn't trust Darrell either. His arms were folded. The last time I had seen him, his mother, whom he resembled, was standing in the same pose in Sally's cubicle.

Darrell was thirteen, thin, black and angry. He had been given a choice. Shape up or go into the system, juvenile detention, maybe a series of foster homes. His mother was twenty-eight years old and reluctantly ready to give up on him.

He was wearing an unwrinkled pair of dark pants and a clean, dark blue T-shirt.

Darrell, who for all I knew was still a lookout for a crack dealer in Newtown, said nothing.

Sally had conned me into being Darrell's Big Brother. It was difficult to tell if the idea appealed less to Darrell or to me. Our lack of enthusiasm for the experiment was the one bond we had.

"Darrell," I said.

"Well, you got that right," he said.

"What . . . ?"

"Saturday," Darrell said. "It's Saturday. Nine in the morning."

"Saturday," I repeated, shaking my head knowingly.

"You forgot," said Darrell flatly.

"That it was Saturday or that you were supposed to be here?" I asked.

Darrell said nothing, just waited.

"I forgot both," I said, realizing that there was no point in going out to Manatee Community College. There probably wouldn't be anyone there on the weekend.

"Want me to go back home?" he asked.

"How did you get here?"

"Walked," he said.

He lived just off Martin Luther King Drive in Newtown, about two miles away.

"No, give me a minute. I've got to clean up."

He looked puzzled.

"Bathroom, down there," I said.

"You sleep in your office last night?"

"I live in my office," I said. "Just go in and wait. I'll be right back."

He unfolded his arms, pushed away from the railing and stepped past me without a hint of energy or enthusiasm. I closed the door behind him and moved down to the bathroom shared by the tenants of the building and, until recently, by Digger, who had frequently spent nights there stretched out, head on a folded jacket or sweater.

The building had no name, just an address. I had nodded or avoided nodding at a few of the other tenants over the past four years as we passed each other. This was not upscale Sarasota property, but it wasn't ready just yet to be knocked down and trucked away to make room for a bank. Not yet.

There was a level above mine with offices probably just like mine. I'd never been up there, though I had seen a few people go up the stairs and come down them, leading me to believe there was something resembling life up there.

The office next to mine, toward the stairs, was almost always dark. A white plastic sign on the door with black chipped letters claimed the office was that of Walters Estate Planning & Investments. If the Walters people couldn't do better than this location, I wondered how anyone would have any faith in their financial advice.

On the first of each month, I dropped a rent check in an envelope through the mail slot of Walters Estate Planning & Investments. The check was made out to Marciniak Properties, Inc. for $320. When I rented the office, I had called the number on the FOR RENT sign.

The person, a man with an accent I couldn't place, told me the office door was open; the key was on the windowsill inside. All I had to do was drop a check for the first month's

Stuart M. Kaminsky

rent made out to Marciniak Properties through the Walters slot and the place was mine. No lease. No conditions.

"You pay on the first of each month," the man on the phone had said. "You don't pay, the lock is changed and you are out. You understand?"

"Yes," I had said.

"You've got any problems, make a note, stick it through the mail slot. Don't call me. You understand?"

"Yes."

He hung up. I never saw him, never saw anyone going in or out of Walters Estate Planning.

I washed and shaved. I was hurrying, nicked my chin with the twice-used disposable Bic and spent a couple of minutes stopping the dot of blood. While I administered to my wound, I tried to think of what I would do with Darrell Caton.

I had the bearded philosopher to find and the person who had murdered the still-unidentified and unlocated Seaside Assisted Living victim and whoever had tried to run me down a few hundred feet from where I was now standing. More important, who might take another shot at me. If Darrell was with me when I got killed, the mourning period for both of us would probably be very brief.

When I got back to the room behind my office, Darrell was looking through my videos.

"Never heard of any of this shit," he said.

"A gap in your education," I said.

"This stuff all black-and-white?" he asked, holding up the box for *Beat the Devil*.

"Most of it," I said as I put towel, soap and shaving things on a shelf.

Darrell was shaking his head.

"And you live here?" he said, looking around.

"Yes," I said, sitting on the cot and putting on my socks and shoes.

"My mom and I are shit poor and we got more room than you. We got our own bathroom too."

"Sounds nice," I said.

"It's shit nothing," said Darrell emotionlessly. "Man."

"What?"

"How you supposed to help me? White guy who lives like this?"

"You want me to help you?"

I was dressed now. I picked up my Cubs hat and fitted it on my head.

"You gonna wear that?"

"I'm already wearing it," I said.

"Anybody I know see me with you and they gonna laugh at me right out on the street or kick my ass when they get me alone," he said.

"You want me to help you?" I repeated.

"No," he said. "I want you to keep my ass out of the system is what I want. You want to help me?"

"I like your mother," I said.

Darrell pointed a finger at me.

"Man, you don't know my mother."

"Saw her at Sally's office," I said. "All I needed to see. She endures."

"What?"

"Nothing. Anything you want to do today?"

"You got money?"

"Some."

"Eat something, go see a movie," he said. "That's what Sally said we might be doing."

"Fine. You like DQ?"

"It's okay."

"What kind of movie you like?"

He shrugged and said, "Ones where people get shot and stuff."

"A concise and well-defined aesthetic," I said.

"What?"

"Nothing," I said. "I was being a smart-ass."

"Whatever. You're bleeding."

I had folded DQ napkins in my pocket. I took one out and dabbed it on my shaving wound. There wasn't much blood.

I sat on the cot. Darrell put the tape down and turned to me. There was a knock at the door. It was probably the first time since I had moved into these two small rooms that I welcomed a knock at the door.

I got up and let Ames in. He was wearing his yellow slicker, no hat. The slicker suggested that he was hiding a weapon with considerably more kick than the derringer he had given me.

"Ready?" he asked.

"I've got—"

The slicker parted; a shotgun I recognized appeared suddenly in Ames's hands. It was leveled just past me. I turned. Darrell stood there with the derringer in his right hand.

"No," I said, pushing the shotgun barrel away. "That's Darrell."

"Darrell?" asked Ames.

"I'm his . . . I'm spending some time with him today," I said. "Sally's idea."

Ames understood.

"I'm going home," Darrell said, handing me the derringer. "Crazy old man comes in with a shotgun. You got a candy-ass little gun. Crack houses in town that don't carry this much heat."

Ames returned his shotgun to the sling under his yellow slicker.

"Ames thought you were the person who's trying to kill me," I explained.

"Say what? Someone's trying to kill you?"

"Yes."

"Who?" he asked, definitely interested.

"I don't know," I said.

"You don't know who's trying to kill you," said Darrell. "At least where I live you know who's trying to kill you. And all you got to protect you is that crazy old fool and this cap gun?"

Ames took three steps toward the boy, who took three steps back.

"Apologize," said Ames.

"I apologize, man," Darrell said, looking at me for support.

"What are you apologizing for?" Ames asked.

"I dunno," said Darrell. "Whatever."

"You called me a crazy old fool," Ames said evenly. "I don't take that from men or boys."

"I'm sorry, hey."

Ames shook his head and looked at me.

"Saturday," I said. "The college is closed."

"I know," said Ames.

"Then why did you come armed for elephants?"

Ames dug into the pocket of his slicker and came out with a folded sheet of newspaper. He handed it to me and I unfolded it.

"Turn it over, bottom of the page on the right," Ames said.

I found it.

Stuart M. Kaminsky

"It's him," I said.

"It's him," Ames agreed. "Face seemed familiar. When I was stacking the newspapers in the recycle bin back of the Texas I found this. In last week's Friday section."

"Hey," said Darrell, moving toward the door. "It's been real great, but I'm goin' home now."

"Wait," I said.

Darrell didn't look at me. He looked at Ames, whose eyes met his. Darrell stopped.

The man in the small picture was the bearded philosopher. His hair wasn't as white and he was smiling. The small article next to his picture said he was John Wellington Welles, PhD, professor of modern philosophy at Manatee Community College. He had written a book, *The Destruction of Moral Definition*. He was giving a talk in the Opera House on Main Street at 3 P.M. Admission was free. There would be copies of the book available for sale, which Professor Welles would be happy to sign.

"You guys dealers?" Darrell asked. "Guns?"

"No," I said. "Sometimes we find people."

"Like private detectives on those old television shows?" he asked.

"Something like that," I said.

"You don't look like it."

"We fool a lot of bad guys that way," I said.

I looked at my watch. Plenty of time to do something with Darrell and get him home before three. Maybe there was an early movie.

"Ever been to Selby Gardens?" I asked.

"No, what's that?" Darrell asked.

"Place where you look at flowers and trees," I said.

"Forget that," said Darrell. "You been there?"

"No. But Ames has."

The boy looked at Ames.

"I been there," he said.

"Don't sound like nothing to me," Darrell said.

"Jungle Gardens," I tried. "Animals, birds, gators, snakes."

"You been there?"

"No," I said.

"You been anywhere?" Darrell asked.

I felt like saying, *To hell and back,* but said, "A few places."

"You said DQ and a movie," Darrell said. "You backing out?"

"No, but Ames and I have to catch a killer."

"Today?"

"This afternoon."

"You shittin' me again, right?"

"No."

"Kin I go with you?"

"You wouldn't have fun."

"More fun than looking at flowers and snakes," he said.

"We've got stops to make. Then you'll have to hear a white guy with a beard talk about things you won't understand," I said.

"Like?"

"The destruction of moral definition," I said.

"What's that mean?"

"Things are getting worse," I said.

"What things?" Darrell asked.

"People don't care as much as they used to about what's good and what's bad," I said.

"Everybody knows that. Old Wyatt Earp here, he gonna blow the mother away?"

"If I have to," said Ames.

Darrell smiled and said, "Way cool."

Stuart M. Kaminsky

I made a couple of calls. Before I got back that night, there would be a surprise storm and a golfer at Bobby Jones golf course would be struck by lightning and killed. Before I got back that night, someone would come very close to killing me.

15

DIXIE CRUISE lived in a two-room apartment in a slightly run-down twelve-flat apartment building on Ringling Boulevard a block from the main post office.

I had called the office of Tycinker, Oliver and Schwartz, but not about their client Nancy Root, not exactly. I wanted to reach Harvey, who had a windowless office in the rear of the law firm next to the washroom. Harvey was the firm's open secret, a computer hacker who, except for a slight problem, could easily be making as much money as Donald Trump was paying whoever was still standing at the end of a season of *The Apprentice*.

Harvey was an alcoholic. He would stop for weeks, months, and then disappear. The firm tolerated his crashes from the wagon, encouraged him to seek help through AA or a therapist, but Harvey resisted.

I knew someone would be at the law office even though it

was Saturday morning. In fact, Saturday mornings were busy with clients who had full-time jobs during the week.

Oliver's administrative assistant—who back in the days long past would have been called a secretary—said Harvey was not in, was not expected, could not be reached at home, might never come back or might show up Monday morning.

I went to my second choice, Dixie Cruise. She was home.

Dixie worked at a coffee bar on Main Street. She was slim, trim, with very black hair in a short style. She was no more than twenty-five, pretty face and wore big round glasses.

Dixie had the down-home Florida accent of any Bobby Joe or Billy Bob. Dixie was also a computer whiz second only to Harvey. She had the added advantage of always being sober.

Harvey's services were free, part of my retainer agreement with the law firm. I had to pay Dixie but her rates were low, very low, fifty dollars an hour, minimum of one hour.

When I knocked at her door, Dixie opened it, a grilled cheese sandwich in one hand. She looked at me, Ames and Darrell. I introduced them.

"I'm finishing my brunch," she said. "Come in."

We went into her tiny, neat living room/dining room/ bedroom then into a slightly smaller room devoted to two computers with supporting gray metal boxes, stacks and speakers.

"Got to pick up my mom and dad at the Tampa airport at noon," she said, sitting in front of a computer and pushing a button. The computer hummed.

"This shouldn't take long," I said.

She adjusted her glasses, took a bite of her grilled cheese sandwich, placed the sandwich on a paper plate next to the computer and began letting her fingers dance above the keyboard without touching the keys.

"Name?" she asked.

Darrell and Ames stood watching.

"John Wellington Welles," I said.

"You're kidding me, right?" she said, turning to look at me.

"No."

"John Wellington Welles is a character in a Gilbert and Sullivan show, *The Sorcerer*. My mom was in it when I was a kid. She took me to every darn rehearsal for a month."

"It's his name," I said.

"I'm gonna get me a lot of Gilbert and Sullivan hits. Can you narrow it down some?"

"He's a philosophy professor at MCC," I said.

"Got it," Dixie said and started her journey on the Internet highway after inserting a CD in a slit in the computer.

The CD began to play. A woman began belting out a song.

"The Pointers," said Darrell.

Dixie paused to look at the boy with a smile.

"My mom plays this stuff all the time," said Darrell.

"Your mom has good taste," Dixie said, turning back to the screen.

Dixie's fingers moved in time to "Fire." The images on the screen kept flashing by as she clicked, pointed, clicked, scrolled. One screen showed a man who might be a much younger version of Welles. I didn't have time to read any of the words near it or on the other pages.

"Bank, bank, bank," Dixie sang in place of the words on the CD. "Can't hide from the Heart of Dixie."

We watched. Dixie took snatches of the grilled cheese sandwich. Three, four, seven, ten minutes. "Fire" became "Automatic."

Finally, she pushed a button, sat back with her hands

behind her head and waited while one of three printers on the table to the right of the computer began to make noises.

"Laser life," she said.

"Most cool," said Darrell.

"You know the Net?" she asked.

"Know what it is," said Darrell.

"Want to come over sometime, I'll teach you stuff," she said.

The printer hummed.

Darrell looked at me.

"Ask your mother," I said.

Dixie reached over and handed me three sheets that had spewed out of the printer.

"Want bank records, debt report, medical history?"

"Maybe," I said, reading the sheets she had handed me.

As I finished each one, I handed it to Ames to read.

I learned that John Wellington Welles was fifty-two years old, born in Canton, Ohio, to Clark Welles and Joyce Welles, both deceased, both high school teachers, he of math, she of English. John Wellington Welles, who had no siblings, had a BS degree in sociology from Syracuse, an MA in linguistics from Cornell and a PhD in philosophy from Columbia. He had taught at Northeastern University in Boston for fourteen years, left a tenured full professorship to move to Sarasota to work at MCC, lower pay, lower prestige and no tenure.

He had a long list of publications, including a book called *Introduction to Ethics*, articles in journals, though the latest one had been published six years earlier. Six years earlier, Welles's wife had died, cancer. They had one daughter who was now nineteen.

I had his current address, in Bradenton, the make of his car, a Taurus, and even how many payments he had left on it, six. He was paying $234 a month. His house was fully paid for and evaluated at $149,000, which did not put him in the high range of homeowners. Two arrests, both within the last six years, both for assault, neither of which had led to a conviction.

"Assault," Ames said.

"Can you find out about these assault arrests?" I asked Dixie.

She nodded, took her hands from behind her head and began the search. Darrell moved close, looking over her shoulder, mouth slightly open. The rapidly changing light and colors did a light show across his face.

It took about five minutes.

"Both arrests in Boston," she said. "I'm not printing this stuff out and I'm getting it off my hard drive as soon as I'm done."

"Why?" asked Darrell.

"Because," Dixie whispered, "it is not legal."

Darrell grinned at both Ames and me. I leaned over to read about Welles's arrests. No alcohol involved. No weapons involved. One incident happened in a department store a day before Christmas. Welles attacked a man named Walter Syckle, broke his nose. Syckle dropped charges. No reason given for the assault. The second arrest was similar. Welles punched a twenty-year-old man in line at a supermarket. Released. Charges dropped. No reason given for the assault.

"Has a temper," said Ames.

"Looks that way," I said.

That was all I could get from Dixie. I gave her six twenty-dollar bills. I'd charge it to Nancy Root. Dixie folded the bills, slipped them into her shirt pocket and said, "Thanks," and then, to Darrell, "I meant it about coming back here. Bring your mother."

"She won't be trusting you. She'll say you must want something and she got nothing to give."

"Bring her," said Dixie. "I'll grill cheese sandwiches and we'll surf for all kinds of good stuff."

Ames, Darrell and I left and went to the car.

"You wondering what I'm wondering?" I asked Ames.

"Yes."

"Why did he leave a tenured job at a university for an untenured one at a community college?"

"Maybe pushed out," he said.

"Or maybe he was running away," I said.

"People do it," he said. "Something happens. They run."

He meant me.

"Want to go to Welles's house?" Ames said.

"What'd he do?" asked Darrell from the backseat.

"Something he seems to feel very sorry about," I said. "We'll get him away from the house, at the talk."

Ames nodded.

I drove back to the DQ, five minutes away, and got Darrell and myself medium chocolate cherry Blizzards and a Dilly Bar for Ames. We sat at one of the metal tables in front of the DQ, the sky rumbling and dark but the rain not yet falling.

"Never had one of these," Darrell said, working on his Blizzard. "It's good."

I'm not sure what I was going to say. My eyes were following the cars flowing by; my thoughts were following not much of anything.

A big truck with RED RIVER CITRUS written on its side over the picture of an orange rumbled by and jerked over a bump.

A blob of my Blizzard fell in my lap. The truck was gone. Another blob fell but I moved my legs in time. I looked at the cup in my hand. It had a small round hole on one side and another one on the other side.

"I think someone just shot at me," I said.

"Shit," said Darrell. "You're dripping."

"Yes," I said.

Ames was up, right hand under his slicker as he looked up and down the street. There were three people in the DQ line. No one was walking down the street.

"You all right?" he asked, not looking at me.

"Yes," I said.

"Someone really shot at you?" asked Darrell.

I put the Blizzard down. The dripping had slowed. The holes were now above the drink line.

"Welles," Ames said.

"I don't think so," I answered.

I tried to stand but my legs wouldn't move.

"Sure you're all right?" Ames repeated.

I wasn't all right. I was numb. It didn't seem real. Reality is noise, a car skidding toward me, a punch or a doctor telling someone he has a year to live. This had been noiseless.

"You callin' the cops?" Darrell asked.

"No. Let's go," I said.

"Where?" asked Darrell, excited.

"To see some very old people," I said.

"Shit, that's no fun."

"One of them has a pet alligator."

"One of those baby things?" asked Darrell.

"A big one," said Ames.

"Name's Jerry Lee," I said.

"Could have hit the boy," Ames said in a husky whisper, following me to the car.

"Yes."

Ames went silent as we got in and closed the doors. I looked at him. His face was rigid, the muscles of his jaw twitching slightly.

"Yes," I said.

"I get my barrels on him, I'm pulling," he said.

"Maybe we can come up with an alternative," I said.

Ames just shook his head once. It was a definite no. Ames rode at my side with the shotgun in his lap and his eyes scanning the faces of the people in every car that passed us.

At the stoplight at Hillview we pulled up next to a big, yellow Lincoln with a tiny bespectacled woman driver with curly white hair. She turned her head toward us and found herself looking into the eyes of Ames McKinney. She turned her eyes forward again, watching the traffic light.

When we got to the Seaside, Ames motioned for us to stay in the car. He got out, shotgun under his slicker, and looked around before motioning us to get out.

"Where's the gator?" asked Darrell, looking around.

"Behind the building," I said.

"We gonna look at it?"

"Maybe," I said, leading the way through the glass doors of the Seaside, which slid open automatically.

The office doors to our right were closed for the weekend. We made our way to the nursing station, where a tiny black woman in a blue nursing smock was dispensing medicine to an ancient old man with a large freckled bald head. The man took some pills on his tongue, accepted a small plastic cup of water from the nurse and washed down the medicine with a quick gulp.

The man looked at the three of us, blinked and said, "Is there a carnival in town?"

"John," the little nurse admonished, taking back the plastic cup.

"Well, I mean it," John said. "Look at them. I worked a carnival summers when I was a kid. We had a couple of Negro midgets."

DENIAL

"I ain't no midget," said Darrell.

"You ain't?" John said, looking astonished. "You fooled me. This other fella, though," he went on, pointing a bony arthritic finger at Ames, "definitely runs a shooting gallery."

"John," the nurse warned wearily.

"He's carrying a gun right under that yellow raincoat," John said.

"John likes his little jokes," said the nurse, who looked beyond tired.

"I like a good bowel movement too from time to time," he said. "I don't ask much."

With that John turned his back and shuffled down the hall.

"Can I help you?" the nurse said, turning to us. She was black, thin, in her mid-forties and obviously tired.

I read the name tag on her uniform. It said EMMIE.

"You're the night nurse," I said.

"Most nights," she said.

"You were here the night Dorothy Cgnozic reported that someone had been murdered."

"I was," she said. "My first night on the job, people checking out, woman tells me she saw a murder. Crazy night. Who are you?"

"Friends of Dorothy's," I said.

"Sometime I'd like to hear the story of how that friendship began, but not today. I'm on my second straight shift. Can you believe two nurses came down with some kind of flu? I've been on almost fourteen hours."

"Sorry," I said.

She shrugged and said, "Time and a half. I'm not complaining, not with two-year-old twins to raise, just tired."

"Dorothy told you she just saw someone murdered?" I asked.

Stuart M. Kaminsky

"Yes, she thought it was a woman. I looked in the room. No body, nobody missing. Checked the log, day-shift releases, and night maintenance man. I think maybe Dorothy had a bad dream."

"The room where Dorothy said she saw the murder," I said. "Where does the window open to?"

"Back of the building," said Emmie. "Nothing but dark, woods, snakes and a crazy half-blind gator with a bad temper."

Darrell looked at me. He was smiling. The existence of the promised gator had been validated.

"We've got a patient who keeps feeding the damned thing. One day that Stevie Wonder gator is going to take her arm off."

"Jerry Lee," Ames corrected.

"Who?" she asked.

"Gator's name," Ames said.

"Whatever," she said with a sigh. "You want to see Dorothy?"

"Yes," I said.

"Know where her room is?"

I told her we did and she moved behind the desk to sit heavily in the wooden chair and close her eyes.

Dorothy was fully dressed and sitting in the small uphol-stered and faded salmon-colored chair next to her bed. She was watching something on television but turned it off with her remote when she saw us.

"Mr. Fonesca and Mr. McKinney," she said with a smile. "And the young man?"

"Darrell Caton," he said, not sure whether he should of-fer his hand, starting to hold it out, then changing his mind and pulling it back to his side.

"You found the murderer?" she asked.

"No, not yet."

"You find out who got killed?"

"No, but I think I'm getting close. Has anyone tried to get you to stop me from talking about the murder?"

"No one's asked me to stop, nobody but the nurses and some of them just look at me like I'm a dotty old coot keeping herself busy with a harmless delusion."

"Want to take us to Rose Teffler's room?" I asked.

"That's not where the murder happened," Dorothy said.

"But on the same side of the building a few doors down from her room?"

"Suppose so," said Dorothy. "Waste of time. I already asked her if she heard or saw anything."

"Still—" I started and she interrupted with, "Okay. Let's go."

We walked down the hall, a bizarre quartet, probably looking like a spoof of the walk down the corridor at the beginning of *Law & Order*. We went to the right, though the most direct way would have been back past the nursing station.

It took us about five minutes to get to Rose Teffler's door. Dorothy moved slowly with her walker. A sprig of some dried flowers hung on the door. Their color was almost gone.

I knocked. No answer from inside, though Ames did cock his head as if he had heard something move behind the door. Then the door opened.

Rose Teffler was tiny, no more than four foot six. She squinted at us with suspicion and Dorothy said that we had some questions.

"What about?" the old woman said.

"The night Mrs. Cgnozic saw someone a few doors down being attacked," I said. "If someone committed murder and took the body out during the night, they would have to go past your window."

"What time?"

"After eleven at night," I said.

"I'm not up at that time," she said. "Always get nine hours of sleep."

"You get up to feed Jerry Lee," said Ames.

Rose Teffler looked at Ames with fear.

"They don't care about the gator, Rose," Dorothy said. "Everybody knows you feed the gator."

"They do?"

"They do," Dorothy repeated. "These people don't care about your feeding Jerry Lee."

"I do," said Darrell.

"The night—" I started, but Rose Teffler was already saying, "Yes. I thought Jerry Lee had gotten whoever it was. Lots of noise. Heard Jerry Lee out there thrashing around. I was about to feed him. Someone screamed or something. By the time I got to the window and opened it, all I could see was someone or something slouching away next to the building. Looked like the Hunchback of Notre Dame."

"Charles Laughton," I said.

"Lon Chaney," Rose corrected.

"Right," I said. "Sorry."

"Maybe it was Charles Laughton," said Rose. "You won't tell about Jerry Lee."

"No one left to tell except Trent. No one tells him anything," said Dorothy, but Rose wasn't listening.

We left and walked Dorothy back to her room, promising her that we'd get back to her soon.

"I know what I saw," she said, sitting in the chair next to her bed. "Wait."

She reached back to the bedside table to her right. She opened the drawer and came out with a box of Girl Scout Thin Mints. She handed the box to Darrell.

"Thanks," he said.

Darrell, Ames and I moved out of the room. Behind us Dorothy clicked on the television remote and the long-dead people on a laugh track I'd grown up with found something very funny.

We passed the nursing station. Emmie was now drinking a cup of coffee. She nodded at us.

"Get anywhere with Dorothy?" she asked.

I told her we had and we went down the corridor and through the sliding glass doors. At the end of the building we turned left where Ames and I had been two nights ago.

The grass, shrubs and trees were thick, and through them you could see patches of the small marsh beyond.

"We gonna find the gator?" asked Darrell.

"Not if we're lucky," I said.

Ames had his shotgun out. The windows of the rooms of the residents in this wing of the Seaside were to our left. The ground was soggy.

I kept my eyes on the ground.

"What're you looking for?" asked Darrell.

"Something that doesn't belong here," I said.

We were under Rose Teffler's window now.

"Like this?" asked Darrell, reaching down to pick up something.

He turned to show us a slipper, dark blue. He handed it to me. I handed it to Ames.

"Hasn't been here more than a week, maybe," Ames said.

Ames and I were thinking of the same possibility. Someone could have taken the dead body out through the window

Stuart M. Kaminsky

and carried it past here. The slipper could have fallen off the body.

"Gator could have come thinking he was going to be fed," I said.

"Maybe he was," said Ames.

"You mean that old gator ate someone?" said Darrell gleefully.

"Let's keep looking," I said.

We did. No blood. No body parts. No second slipper. No evidence. We did manage to draw the attention of an old, nearly blind gator named Jerry Lee, who came slithering out, head raised through the thick reedy grass.

"There he is," shouted Darrell.

Ames had his shotgun out. He was aiming it toward the slow-moving animal. Ames's hands were steady.

"You gonna shoot him?" asked Darrell.

"If I have to," said Ames, gun cradled firmly against his shoulder.

I pushed Darrell behind me. Ames was between us and Jerry Lee, who looked as if he might be smelling us out instead of looking at us. He slithered forward a few feet.

Something flew from behind me. A box of Girl Scout Thin Mints hit the alligator in the snout.

"Got him," said Darrell.

"You got him mad is all," said Ames.

Jerry Lee was coming faster now. The window behind us opened. Jerry Lee was a dozen yards away now and coming toward us.

Something else flew from behind me, but this time it wasn't a box of cookies. It looked like a chicken leg and thigh. Jerry Lee opened his mouth and took it in.

"He shouldn't eat during the day," said Rose Teffler.

"I saved that from lunch. Was going to give it to him tonight, but now . . ."

Jerry Lee chomped. We hurried back around the building to the parking lot. I was carrying the soggy slipper.

Darrell was beaming with delight as we got in the car.

"Where we goin' now, hold up a bank or something?"

"We're going to a lecture," I said.

16

I **FOUND A SPACE** in the library parking lot. The library is less than ten years old. It is big, white and has pillars that look like they came out of a soft-serve ice cream machine. I've never been inside the building but Ames tells me it's bright, has a nice pair of staircases, is easy to use, contains computer stations and has far fewer books on its shelves than he would like.

Ames was a reader. He always had a stack of four or five library books on the single table in his small room at the Texas, less than three blocks away. He also had a five-level bookcase filled with paperbacks and hardcovers he had picked up at garage sales. Most of the books were biographies of historical figures, but there were even a few poetry books and a novel or two.

Ames, Darrell and I crossed the street and went into the lobby of the Opera House. The Opera House was and is really an opera house. This was the first time I had entered it but I knew that much and more from Flo, who, when her husband, Gus, was alive, had been a donor, not out of a love of opera but as a tribute to a social system she and Gus had been part of.

I'd grown up with opera, Saturday's Texaco broadcasts from the Met. My grandmother listened to the opera on Saturday more often than she went to church on Sunday. She heard them all, but her heart was only really into the Italian operas, particularly ones she had gone to when she was a girl in Italy.

For a long time the Opera House had been a movie theater. Flo told me that DeMille's *The Greatest Show on Earth*, which was shot in Sarasota, premiered at the Opera House with Charlton Heston onstage after a circus parade including some of the actors in the movie. But now it was an opera house again, about one thousand seats, boxes at the rear of the main floor, carpets, paintings of donors on the walls, nice brass fittings in the toilets.

We were purposely late. It was just after three. I was hoping Welles wouldn't spot me in the audience. I was hoping the lights would be turned down. I was hoping there would be a big crowd to hide in. I was wrong on all counts, though it took him a while to find me.

The lights were up though not bright. Fewer than two hundred people were scattered on the main floor. The balcony was closed.

There was a podium on the broad stage in front of a blue curtain that looked like velvet. A woman stood at the podium. Behind her sat John Wellington Welles. Ames, Darrell and I sat behind four women about twenty rows from the stage. In front of the stage was a table with two stacks of books.

The woman, lean, green suit with a glittering red jeweled

Stuart M. Kaminsky

pin on one lapel, was at the podium reciting Welles's writing and teaching credentials. Welles sat to her right on a folding chair trying to pay attention or at least pretending to pay attention. He was doing a bad job either way.

His eyes wandered but not toward the audience, not yet. Then his head bowed as if he were listening to a eulogy. He sat with his legs apart, hands folded almost in prayer. His hair needed brushing. His eyes needed Visine. His tie needed adjusting and his jacket needed to be donated to Goodwill.

"They gonna show a movie?" Darrell whispered.

"I don't think so," I said.

"They got popcorn, candy? Some shit like that?" he asked.

"No," I said.

One of the women in the row in front of us turned. I was sure she was going to tell us to be quiet. That was her plan but when she saw us she changed her mind. When she looked at me, I took off my Cubs cap. When she looked at Ames, he ignored her and adjusted his yellow slicker. When she looked at Darrell, he glared back at her.

The woman turned forward again.

The audience, what there was of it, was divided into three groups—college students, older women, and me, Darrell and Ames.

"And following his lecture, Dr. Welles will answer questions and sign any copies of his book you wish to buy. And now it is my great pleasure to introduce you to Dr. John Welles."

The applause was dusty polite. This was no rock music sensation, no rising star in the Democratic or Republican party, no best-selling author of an apocalyptic novel.

Welles slouched to the podium, adjusted the microphone, leaned toward it and said, "The destruction of moral definition."

It was the same voice I had heard over the phone, the same person who had threatened, pleaded with me to stop my search for him.

There was a glass of water in front of him. He picked it up and drank and then looked out at the audience, his hands clutching the sides of the podium. The pause was long. There was shuffling in the seats. The woman who had introduced him and who now sat where Welles had sat in the folding chair held a benevolent hopeful smile.

"What is moral?" he asked. "The question is more than rhetorical. It is the essence of what I have to say. Before we can address its destruction or decline, we must first know what we mean. To even hope for success, all conversation must contain a common agreement of the meaning of the words we are using."

He paused again and shook his head as if someone invisible had just whispered a truth in his ear.

"Morality," he went on, "in its most simple and most illusory sense means a code of conduct. There are those who assume a universal morality, a universal code of conduct based on humanistic principles, often elusive humanistic principles. Where would such principles come from? Are we born with them? Are they simply common sense? If we follow this path, we are caught in a never-ending maze in search of definitions. For what is common sense?"

He looked to the audience as if he expected a challenge or question. There was none. He drank more water.

"And then there are specific moralities," he went on. "Christian morality and Nazi morality differ at their very core conceptions.

"Nazi morality was based on simple principles, monstrous principles. Aryans were superior beings. Because they were superior, they deserved to rule. All others are inferior.

Stuart M. Kaminsky

Because they are inferior, they do not deserve to exist. This was a given, a supposedly undisputable truth. What is Christian morality based on? Doing good, following the golden rule because it is just and moral and obvious? No, the basis of Christian morality is not that people will behave with a benevolent God-given moral sense, but that they will display a moral sense because there is a reward for doing so."

A hand shot up in the audience. Welles ignored or didn't see it. He went on.

"The reward: eternal life, heaven. Christianity is not built on the principle that moral behavior is to be engaged in simply because it is right, but because God wills it and will reward those who practice it. And when one fails to do what the community and they agree is right, they can still gain entry to heaven by a quick repentance and a belief in salvation through Jesus."

The hand shot up in the audience again. This time Welles saw it and wearily paused, nodding at the young woman, who stood and said, "In your book you say—"

"Forget the book," Welles said, waving away the young woman, his stack of books on the table below him, the past. "A. A. Milne, in addition to creating Winnie the Pooh, once said that if Jack the Ripper was ever caught, his defense would be that he was only behaving according to the human nature dealt to him."

"I don't see—" the young woman said loudly.

"No," Welles said. "You do not see. Morality is based on the assumption that he who commits an immoral act will be aware of and troubled or plagued by his own guilt. But what if he doesn't recognize his act, the rape, slaughter or torture, as immoral? Is there such a thing as a moral monster?"

He paused for the young woman to answer, but she was clearly confused and sat down.

DENIAL

"What's he talkin' about?" Darrell asked me.

"His conscience," said Ames.

"All of our consciences," said one of the women in front of us, turning to face Ames.

"No, ma'am," said Ames. "Just his own."

"*Exemplo quodcumque malo committitur, ipsi Disclicet auctori. Prima est haec ultio, quod se Judice nemo nocens absolvitur,*" said Welles. "Juvenal in the Satires. Whatever guilt is perpetrated by some evil prompting is grievous to the author of the crime. This is the first punishment of guilt, that no one who is guilty is acquitted at the judgment seat of his own conscience."

"But," came the shout of a young man in the audience, "what if the guilty person is a sociopath or a psychopath and doesn't believe he is guilty of anything?"

"Then he is fortunate," said Welles. "He is protected by his own madness. Punishment will never come, only retribution."

"Do you believe in the death penalty?" someone shouted.

"I'm living it," Welles said.

"What does that mean?" asked the man who had shouted.

"What does that mean?" Welles repeated, as if asking himself the question for the first time. "It means that the consequence to a person with Judeo-Christian moral principles who violates those principles knowingly is accepting his inevitable punishment."

"And," called another voice from the audience, "are there times when a person should knowingly violate those principles, break the law?"

"Yes, if he is willing to accept the consequences," said Welles.

There was murmuring in the audience. Welles drank some more water and looked around the audience for the first

Stuart M. Kaminsky

time. His eyes met mine as he scanned. His eyes held mine as he said, "The guilty, those with a conscience, very often seek their own punishment. But sometimes, not often, but sometimes, something transcends simple morality, simple guilt."

"What?" asked a young woman.

Welles was still looking at me.

"Responsibility for others," he said.

He forced his eyes from my face, sighed deeply, closed his eyes and said, "Ladies, gentlemen, I've been speaking nonsense from the same kind of heat-oppressed brain as that of the Bard's Macbeth. I'll stop here and had you paid to enter this theater, I would gladly refund your money. As it is, I suggest that those of you who were considering the purchase of my book, keep your checks and cash in your pockets and handbags and go out and buy yourself a trinket or a good dinner."

Welles turned to his right and headed offstage. The audience was murmuring in confusion. The woman who had introduced Welles stood up, bewildered.

"He's drunk," said one of the women in front of us.

"Let's go," said Ames.

The three of us rose and sidled down across the seats to the aisle. We moved to an exit door near the stage and pushed through in time to see Welles go through a courtyard next to the Opera House and turn right.

"I'll get him," said Darrell.

Ames grabbed Darrell's shirt and pulled him back.

"Man's got a gun," Ames said.

"You sure about that?" asked Darrell.

"Sure enough," said Ames.

"How we gonna stop him then?" asked Darrell.

Ames pulled back his slicker, showed his sawed-off shotgun and said, "I've got a bigger one."

"You gonna shoot it out with him?"

"If I have to."

It was a strange chase. We ran across the street, got into my rental car and I pulled out of the space with a screech of tires, almost colliding with a very large white Cadillac.

I tore out of the entrance, made a right and ran a light going in the direction Welles had run. I made another right but didn't see him or his damaged Taurus.

"Lost him," said Darrell. "I knew I should have chased him. I would've tackled him like Warren Sapp."

I slowed down.

"What're you slowing down for?" asked Darrell. "Let's find him."

"I know where to find him," I said. Dixie had given me Welles's address. "I'm taking you home."

"No way," said Darrell from the backseat. "I'm goin' with you."

"Not this time," I said.

"This is shit, man," Darrell said, leaning back in the seat, arms folded, scowl on his face. "This is shit."

Darrell and his mother didn't live far away, and it was on our way to Bradenton. The building was a low-rent public housing building that had once been middle-class apartments and was now a step up from the streets.

Darrell got out of the car at the door. A quartet of old black men sat in front of the building in folding chairs, talking. They watched as Darrell said, "You gonna shoot the sucker?"

"Not if we can help it," I said.

"He's some kind of crazy. You know that?"

I wasn't sure if he was talking about Ames or Welles.

"Yes," I said.

"Hell," said Darrell, who turned and started to walk toward the old men.

"Next Saturday?" I called through the open window.

"Yeah," said Darrell, his back turned. "Whatever."

We drove away.

"What do you think of Darrell?" I asked.

"Like the boy," said Ames.

After that speech, we drove in silence up Tamiami Trail toward Bradenton.

17

THE HOUSE was about two blocks south of the Manatee River, old, small, wood frame, painted white. The paint was old, streaked with dark stains. The roof was covered with decaying brown leaves from the tall oak whose branches hung over it. The lawn was dappled with clumps of moist leaves, which matched the ones on the roof.

The house had a tiny porch with a wooden railing and just enough room for a pair of lawn chairs. The surrounding houses were similar but there was no consistent design on the block and there were no people in sight.

We heard a machine, maybe a lawn mower or chain saw, echo in the distance when we stepped out of the car. The neighborhood smelled moist and musty. I was parked directly behind the car that must have been John Wellington Welles's, the Taurus that had killed Kyle McClory. No, the car hadn't killed him. The driver had.

Ames and I walked up the narrow, cracked concrete walk. The street looked weekend peaceful until the door opened and Welles stepped out. He was no longer wearing his jacket and tie. His shoulders sagged and the gun in his hand pointed in our direction.

We stopped. No one spoke.

"There are so goddamn many things I could have done," Welles finally said, looking at the gun in his hand. "I could have planned it all better. I could have planned it. No, I couldn't. I didn't. In the poker game of life, emotion will almost always push common sense out of the way and take over."

The gun in his hand lowered slightly.

"Who said that?" I asked, inching forward.

"I did," he said. "My insurance . . . now that's another tale. If I shoot myself, there's no money to take care of Jane."

"Jane?" I asked.

I knew Ames was reaching slowly, very slowly for the shotgun under his slicker.

"I should have simply stepped on the gas on the way back here and slammed into a wall," Welles said, shaking his head. "But what if I lived? It's a dilemma. I'm not sure what happens with the insurance if you shoot me."

"I don't understand," I said.

"You don't? No, of course you don't."

The door was open behind him, but not the screen door. Welles turned and called, "Janie."

Someone stirred in the darkness beyond the screen and then appeared slowly, warily. Welles pocketed the gun as a woman who seemed familiar stepped out and looked at us. She wore a blue dress with a bright yellow-and-red flower print. She smiled.

"My daughter, Janie," Welles said, putting his arm around the girl. She smiled more broadly.

Her face was familiar because it was the same open, round face of all people with Down's syndrome. She had seemed familiar to Arnoldo Robles because he had seen others with that face on television.

"Hello," she said to Ames and me, still smiling.

"Hello," I said. So did Ames.

"Can I go watch the rest of the movie?" she asked.

"Yes," said Welles, kissing her on top of her head.

She gave him a big hug and went back inside, disappearing in the darkness.

"Janie's nineteen," Wells said. "Already old for someone with Down's. Her mother died of cancer. There's been no one to take care of her but me since. You understand why I didn't want you to find me? Why I was willing to kill you?"

"Yes," I said.

"But I couldn't do it."

"You shoot at me at the Dairy Queen?" I asked.

"Shoot at you? No. When?"

"Why'd you kill the boy?" Ames asked.

Welles rubbed his eyes with a thumb and a finger and then blinked.

"We were coming out of a movie at the Hollywood 20. Janie likes movies, movies that don't show people getting hurt. We were walking to the car, talking. I told her we would stop for ice cream. She was happy. Then it happened."

He went silent again and sighed.

"You know the parking garage behind the 20?"

"Yes," I said.

"They were on the roof," he said. "They spit, both of them, spit on Janie's head. At first I thought it was from a bird. Then I heard them laughing. Janie was bewildered, trying to clean her head and face with the back of her hand. Then she started to cry. You can't imagine what it's like to hear that confused crying. I looked up, saw their faces. People flowed past us trying to ignore my crying baby, my violated baby. I took her quickly to the car, sat her in the backseat, handed her some napkins, told her to sit and relax, that I would be right back."

Welles's shoulders sagged and he sat heavily in one of the lawn chairs on the small porch. The chair creaked. Ames took a step forward. Welles managed to get the gun from his pocket and aim it in our direction.

"No, not yet," he said. "You've got to hear it all. I ran up the steps of the garage. I heard one of them above me on the fourth level shout, 'The crazy bastard is coming up here.' I wanted to get my hands on them, strangle them, make them weep like Janie, throw them off the roof, spit in their faces. When I got to the roof, they were about fifty feet away near the down ramp. One of them, the one I . . . he laughed at me. I ran. They were much faster than me. They ran down the ramp shouting taunts."

Welles was tapping the barrel of the gun against the aluminum arm of the chair. He was remembering, shaking his head.

"I kept running, almost lost them in the crowd of people waiting in line at the 20 for the next shows. I shoved through people. People cursed me. I didn't hear the words. Then I saw them and they saw me, and they began to run again, run down Main toward downtown. Do you have any idea of how I was feeling?"

"Yes," I said.

The thought of this happening to my Catherine, my dead Catherine.

"Yes," I repeated. "I do."

"I went back to the car," Welles went on, speaking faster now. "Janie wasn't crying now. She was just huddled against the door, her head against one open palm. I sped out of the parking lot and started looking for them. They saw me and I saw fear and it drove me. I wanted to frighten them. I wanted them to wet their pants, to fall on their knees and beg for forgiveness. I wanted them to apologize and weep at Janie's feet and tell her she was beautiful and should never cry. But that didn't happen."

He stopped again. Now he was tapping the barrel of the gun gently against the right side of his head.

"I found the one boy on Fruitville," he went on. "He saw me and crossed. I moved into the far lane, cutting off a car that must have barely missed me. The boy ran down the street. I was right behind him now. I could see he was growing tired of running. Oh God, I wanted to frighten him, grab him by the hair. I had a cold, half-full cup of Dunkin' Donuts coffee in one of the holders on the dash. I wanted to get in front of him, throw coffee in his face. I wanted him to wet his pants. I wanted to see fear, terror, but that didn't happen."

He looked at us, trembling.

"He stepped in front of the car," I said.

Welles nodded yes and said, "He walked right down the middle of the street. I was moving slowly, only a car length away when he turned and held up his middle finger. He gave me the finger. He gave Janie the finger and made a face, a bug-eyed blank face, ridiculing my daughter. I stepped on the gas, hard. I think there was a screech. It might have been the tires or me or Janie or the boy. I hit him. He went down. I went right over him and stopped. I wanted to stand over him, tell him I hoped he suffered. He was dead. The cell phone was right next to his hand. I picked it up. I don't know why. I got back in the car and kept going."

Stuart M. Kaminsky

There was more, but he had said almost all that he had to say.

"I told Janie that the boy was fine and that he was sorry and that he had said he thought she was beautiful. I took her to Friendly's for a chocolate ice cream sundae. You understand?" he asked, looking first at me and then at Ames. "I'm not asking you to forgive me. It's not your right."

He let out a laugh, a single self-pitying laugh and added, "Can you believe that when I was a boy I wanted to be a priest? Exposure to logic disabused me of the calling. Sometimes I think God had a black suit and collar waiting for me and when I didn't claim it, he let me think I was safe for a while, then gave me my wife and my poor baby, took my wife and moved those boys on the roof to—"

A car came roaring around the corner behind us.

"I made a call when I got home," Welles said, calmly looking at the approaching car. "Maybe my saving your life counts for something. I've lost all sense of what I've studied most of my life, moral definition. Watch out for the woman who tried to run you down. I could see it in her eyes, in the few seconds before she scraped past me. She doesn't have my curse of hesitation and guilt. If anyone shot at you, it was that woman. It wasn't me."

The car, which had come around the corner behind us, stopped. Ames kept his eyes on Welles, who looked beyond us at the person getting out of the car. I turned and saw Richard McClory, jaw tight, hurrying toward the path where Ames and I stood.

"You," he shouted, pointing at Welles. "You called me?"

"Yes," Welles said.

"You killed Kyle?"

"Yes," Welles said again.

"Why, you bastard, why?" McClory shouted, moving past us, almost to the porch where Welles stood.

"You know who Jerzy Kosinski was?" asked Welles, aiming the gun at McClory.

Ames had his shotgun out now, ready.

McClory hesitated, confused, and said, "Who?"

"Polish writer," said Welles. "Wrote *Being There*. In his suicide note, he wrote: 'I am going to put myself to sleep now for a bit longer than usual. Call the time Eternity.'"

He looked at me and said, "Don't let Janie see me."

With that Welles stood and lobbed the gun to McClory, who caught it in two hands, gripped it with his right and began firing, once, twice, three times. Welles staggered forward and tumbled over the railing onto the lawn.

Ames knocked the gun out of McClory's hands with the butt of his shotgun and I ran forward, flung open the screen door and rushed inside. I found Janie Welles in a tiny room past the living room whose walls were lined with books. She was sitting in a worn brown chair that might have been leather. Her eyes were fixed on a tennis match. She was eating an apple.

"There was noise," she said.

"Yes."

"Is my dad crying again?" she asked, without taking her eyes from the screen.

"No," I said.

"Good," she said. "He hasn't been happy since that boy spit on me. I told him it was okay, but he loves me."

"Yes," I said. "He loves you."

It was too soon to use the past tense.

"I'll be back in a few minutes. You sit right there."

"And watch SpongeBob?"

"Yes," I said.

I found the phone and dialed 911. Then I went back outside. Three people were coming out of a house across the street, but they weren't about to get too close to the scene.

"He's dead," said Ames, kneeling at Welles's body.

McClory was shaking as if he had Parkinson's or was coming down from a week-long drunk. I looked at Ames's shotgun.

"I called 911," I said.

He got up, nodded and moved slowly past Welles's body and around the house. While he was gone, I stood close enough to McClory to keep him from deciding to go for the gun that lay on the grass, the gun he had dropped, the gun with which he had just killed Welles.

"He's dead," McClory said flatly.

"He's dead," I confirmed.

"What time is it?" he asked.

I checked my watch and told him the time.

"I've got a patient I'm supposed to see at the hospital," he said, dazed. "I've got to call, tell them I can't make it."

"They'll understand," I said.

"I really killed him," he said, looking at Welles's body.

"Yes," I said.

"He gave me the gun," McClory said. "Why?"

I was sure he would figure it out later. It wasn't that hard.

Ames came back around the house minus the shotgun. I went back in the house and called Sally. I used her cell phone number and told her what had happened. I gave her the address.

"I've got a friend in Children's Protection in Manatee County," she said. "I'll call her."

"Thanks," I said.

"Lew? Are you all right?"

People were always asking me that question. The real answer was almost always no but I said, "Yes."

I was sure Sally didn't believe me.

"I'll be right there," she said.

Ames and I spent two hours with the Bradenton police, mostly talking to a detective named Charles St. Arthur, about forty, bulky, thick weight-lifter's neck, blue eyes behind his glasses. I wondered if he was taking steroids. He wore a white shirt with the cuffs rolled back.

Ames's explanation was simple. We came to see Welles on business. Before we got inside the house, McClory came, started shooting. He stuck to that. So did I except that I said the business we had come for was part of some queries I had been making on behalf of Nancy Root about her dead son. I said I had tracked down Welles, that he had called McClory, told him he had killed McClory's son, threw the gun to Mc-Clory and McClory had killed him before we could talk.

The answer didn't come close to pleasing Charles St. Arthur, but he had his shooter, two witnesses, and McClory's lawyer on the way. Ames and I were just paperwork he wanted to keep brief.

"We found a copy of Welles's will, insurance papers and a list of relatives in Nevada on the kitchen table," St. Arthur said, rolling his pen in his thick fingers. "Almost as if he wanted us to find them. He say anything about this?"

"No," I said.

"Know what it looks like to me?" St. Arthur said. "Our Professor Welles found a legal way to commit suicide and leave his daughter a pile of money."

It looked that way to me too. I suggested that he might want to talk to a Detective Michael Ransom in Sarasota, that the death of Kyle McClory was his case. St. James said he would.

Ames shook his head.

Sally and her friend had taken charge of Jane Welles. I called Sally on her cell phone when St. Arthur let us go.

"How is she?" I asked.

"We're keeping her busy," said Sally. "We reached Welles's cousin in Reno. She's coming. Should be here tomorrow to handle the funeral arrangements. We'll start the paperwork to get Jane placed in her custody. Lew, you want to come by the apartment tonight?"

"I don't think so," I said. "Maybe."

"Basil's roasted chicken," she said.

"I'll let you know. You might want to let Andrew Goines know what happened."

"I'll call his mother," Sally said.

I drove Ames back to the Texas. We didn't talk. We had nothing to say. I knew he would take his scooter the next day to retrieve his shotgun from wherever he had stowed it behind Welles's house.

"Beer?" he asked, getting out of the car.

"No," I said. "Not now. I might come back later."

He looked at me for several beats and shook his head no to let me know that I wouldn't be coming back, at least not that night.

I picked up two burgers and a large banana Blizzard at the DQ and went to my office, closing the door behind me, not turning on the lights. There was still light filtering through the blinds. I flicked on the air conditioner and sat at my desk. I had finished one burger when the phone rang. I considered not answering it. I considered it for sixteen rings.

It couldn't be Welles. He was dead. I realized that I would miss his calls, at least for a while. I wasn't sure why.

"Fonesca," I said, picking up the phone.

"This is Darrell's mother."

"Yes."

"I want to thank you," she said. "Darrell's been talking about what-all you did. I know he's making up more than half of it but whatever you did, he's looking forward to doing more of it. And he said something about a Dixie and computers. Wants me to go with him to see her. She really mean it?"

"She means it," I said.

"And you're gonna keep seeing Darrell?"

"I like Darrell," I said.

"Most don't," she said. "Next Saturday?"

"I'll be waiting," I said.

"Thank you again," she said. "Wait. He wants to talk to you."

I took another bite of burger and Darrell came on.

"You catch that guy?"

"Yes."

"And? What happened?"

"We'll talk about it next Saturday," I said.

"Old Ames, he shot him, right?"

"No. Next Saturday," I said. "Stay out of trouble."

I hung up before he could say more and the word came to me, the word I needed, the word that had been playing with me for almost two days. I was tired. I was more than tired. If I went to bed, dreams might come and I might lose the word.

"There was a farmer had a dog and Bingo was his name," I said rather than sang. *"B-I-N-G-O."*

I was pretty sure I knew who had died at the Seaside Assisted Living Facility. I was also pretty sure who the woman was who was trying to kill me.

I called Dixie's phone number. She was home. I told her what I needed. She said she had a date with a SaraSox first baseman, but that she had about forty-five minutes and could probably find what I needed through the Internet in less than half an hour.

There were still a few things about it I needed to know. They would have to wait till tomorrow. I finished eating and sat in the near dark waiting for Dixie's call. It took her less than half an hour.

I wrote the information she gave me in my notebook, thanked her and said I'd drop an envelope with a cash payment in the mail the next day.

I made another call, this one to the Seaside Assisted Living Facility, and asked one question.

When I got my answer, I hung up and unplugged the phone.

Ann Horowitz had said I kept the phone plugged in because even though I denied it, I wanted some connection with the outside world, the world of the living.

This night she was wrong.

18

EARLY THE NEXT MORNING, I parked in the Seaside lot next to a small white van with the words MICRON LABS written on its side in red letters. I was halfway toward the nursing station when Amos Trent, the hefty director of Seaside into whose office Ames and I had broken, stepped out of a doorway and blocked my path.

"I'm going to have to ask you to leave, Mr. Fonesca," he said.

"I've come to see Dorothy," I lied.

"I'm afraid she's resting now," he said. "We can't disturb her."

"I'll wait till she wakes up."

I tried to walk around him but he took a sidestep and was in front of me again.

"I think it would be better if you don't come here again.

In fact, if you do return, I'll have our lawyer seek a restraining order."

His voice was low. His breath was minty.

"Why?" I asked.

"Because residents and their families are now asking questions about the murder Dorothy dreamed up," he said. "People don't like to send their family members to an assisted living facility where someone may have been murdered."

"And if you found out that someone had been murdered?"

"It didn't happen."

"It did," I said.

He inched closer to me.

"If our residents and their families believed that," he said, "they would start an exodus from which it would be very difficult to recover. We're running a good facility here, but our profit margin is very low. So, if you are trying to blackmail us, not only is there no money to pay you, but I would be forced to report it to the police."

"Emmie is on duty," I said.

He looked puzzled.

"Emmie Jefferson?"

"You've got more than one Emmie?"

"What are you doing, Fonesca?"

A man in janitor blue denim jogged past us, they keys attached to his belt jangling.

"Whirlpool's down again," the man in blue said to Trent as he hurried by.

"See?" Trent said, turning back to me. "You know what it costs for parts for a whirlpool?"

"No," I said. "Emmie Jefferson."

"You want to talk to Miss Jefferson?"

"Yes. To her or a policeman named Viviase if I have to," I said.

"She's a night nurse," Trent said.

"But she's on this morning. I called."

The corridor was cool, but Trent was perspiring, not much but enough to dapple his upper lip.

"Let's say we put you on a retainer for a while," said Trent. "Two hundred a month for a year, to provide security. That's all we can afford. Might that be incentive to give up your delusion that someone was murdered here?"

"It's not a delusion," I said. "I talk to Emmie Jefferson or I talk to the police."

"You go public with this madness and I'll sue you," he said, his voice rippling with anger, his face pink.

"No, you won't," I said. "I don't own anything and you'd have to pay your lawyer."

He leaned very close now and whispered, "And what if I just beat the fucking shit out of you?"

"It's an option," I said. "But it wouldn't stop me."

Defeated, he took a step back and said, "Okay, five minutes with Emmie and then you are out of here. Let's go."

He turned his back on me and headed for the nursing station.

"Alone," I said.

He stopped and looked over his shoulder at me.

"I could just wait till she gets off of work and talk to her outside," I said.

"Five minutes," Trent said, facing me again, holding up the fingers of his right hand. "You talk to her, you leave and I never see you here again."

I knew that wasn't to be. He knew it too, but if it helped him save face in the hallway, it didn't cost me to keep my mouth closed.

Stuart M. Kaminsky

"Thanks," I said and walked past him to the nursing station. Emmie Jefferson was standing behind it talking to an old woman whose eyes barely reached the top of the counter. The old woman was wearing a black sweater with baggy sleeves.

"Mrs. Engleman," the nurse was saying, "there isn't any mail for you. I'm sorry."

"He told me he would write every day," the little woman said, reaching up to slap her palm on the counter.

"If a letter comes for you, I'll bring it to your room personally."

"You won't look inside and read it?" the little woman asked with suspicion.

"Cross my heart," Emmie Jefferson said, crossing her heart.

"A Bible promise would be better," the woman said.

"Swear on a Bible," the nurse said, holding back a sigh.

"Better if we had a real Bible you could put your hand right down on," Mrs. Engleman said.

"There's one in the library if you want to go get it."

"Maybe I'll do that," the old woman said, stepping back. "Maybe I'll just do that. I won't tolerate censorship."

"I understand," said Emmie Jefferson as Mrs. Engleman shuffled slowly away.

She hadn't seen me yet, but now she looked up, let out a massive sigh and put her right hand to her forehead.

"Mrs. Cgnozic is sleeping," she said.

"Really?"

"No, but that's what I've been told to say if you or that old cowboy show up. Trent sees you here and he'll throw a fit and probably call the cops."

"I just talked to Trent. He said he had no objection to my talking to you," I said. "Call his office."

She folded her arms and looked at me, waiting for me to ask whatever it was I was going to ask.

"The night Dorothy told you she saw someone murdered, your first night on the job, Vivian Pastor checked out."

"That's right," she said. "Her daughter-in-law checked her out. I asked her to wait till the morning. I don't know the paperwork, but she insisted, said her mother-in-law wanted out right then. I called Marie, the head nurse, woke her up. She said we've got no legal right to keep anyone here who doesn't want to be here. Marie told me where the forms were."

"You saw Vivian Pastor leave with her daughter-in-law?"

"Technically? No," she said. "I was down the hall in Mrs. Denton's room. She needed help getting to the bathroom. I saw Mrs. Pastor, the daughter-in-law, waiting for me at the desk. Told me she was checking her mother-in-law out for good."

"So you never saw Vivian Pastor?"

"Didn't say that," said Emmie Jefferson. "Daughter-in-law asked me to help her carry some of the woman's things out to the car. I thought she was plenty big enough to carry it out herself, but she pushed hard and offered me five dollars. So I helped, carried a lamp and a suitcase. Old woman was in the car. Just sitting there smiling. Skinny bag of bones, hands shaking."

"You'd never seen Vivian Pastor before?"

"That was my first time on the job. No, I hadn't seen her before. I told you. She wasn't dead. She was alive. That enough?"

"Yes," I said. "Thanks."

"What is going on?" she asked and then held up both hands and added, "Don't answer that. I don't think I want to know."

I got back to my car without running into Trent and

considered picking up Ames, but that would take time and I just wanted this over with.

Nothing had changed about the house on Orchid, but it felt different. There was no car in the driveway and the garage doors were down. When I knocked at the door, a plain woman of about forty wearing a wary smile, which showed clean but uneven teeth, answered it.

"Mrs. Pastor home?"

"Vivian is," she said with a distinct inland southern Florida accent.

"No, Alberta," I said.

"At work," said the woman.

"You take care of Vivian?"

"Yes, I do, but we don't call her Vivian. Her nickname is Gigi. Mrs. Pastor, Alberta, says she was given the name by one of her grandchildren and it stuck. That's what she wants to be called."

I looked over her shoulder into the dark living room. It was filled with cardboard boxes.

"How long have you been taking care of her?"

"Two, no, three days," she said. "Had a sheet of paper up at the Mennonite post office over in Pinecraft saying I was available for in-home care. Mrs. Pastor called and here I am. It's only for a day or two more. They're moving, you know."

"I'm a friend of the family," I said. "I've got some papers I need signed. You know where Mrs. Pastor works?"

"Sure," the woman said brightly. "Over on Clark right near I-75. You know where the new building just went up is? Medical offices and such-like?"

"Yes," I said.

"She has an office in there."

"Trapezoid," came the voice of the old woman inside the house.

The woman at the door said, "She's a hoot. Poor old thing. Comes up with the darndest things. Doesn't make much sense, though. Easy to take care of. Just feed her, remind her to use the bathroom and let her look at the TV or her ads."

"Thanks," I said.

"Sure you don't want to just pop in and say hi to Gigi? She likes company."

"Next time," I said.

I stopped to make a phone call and then took the Trail to Clark and across to the new two-story medical/office building. The last time I had seen it, the building had been swarming with workmen and the land around it was a tire-rutted mess of dirt and mud. Now it looked finished, professional and surrounded by something that looked a little like grass. Two palm trees propped up by wires were doing sentry duty on the lawn.

I pulled into the lot next to the building. Eleven or twelve cars were parked there. One had a caved-in right front fender and a broken headlight.

The lobby smelled Lysol fresh with a hint of recent pain in the background. There was a bank of names, nine of them, black on white plastic tabs mounted on the wall next to the elevator.

Alberta Pastor, massage therapist, was in Suite 203. There are no offices in Sarasota. Everything, even a cramped single room with a desk and space for another chair, was a suite. Calling your business a suite was worth a 10 percent markup on your bill.

There was a carpeted waiting room beyond the door to Suite 203. It was big enough for two wooden chairs, a small table with a wooden dish filled with Tootsie Rolls and wrapped root beer barrels. A neat pile of old *People* magazines sat next

Stuart M. Kaminsky

to the dish. An orchestra played a languid Muzak version of "Surrey with the Fringe on Top."

I could hear voices through the closed door of the room beyond the one I was in. I sat, selected a root beer barrel, unwrapped it and placed it in my mouth. I sat for twenty minutes learning about the latest clothes, sex partners, awards, problems and triumphs of people named Justin, Renée, Antoine, Mel, and Russell.

The outer door opened. A young blonde woman with a pink, healthy face, large breasts, long legs came in, looked at me and said, "You waiting for someone?"

"Mrs. Pastor," I said.

She looked at her wristwatch. It had a big round face with large numbers. She was wearing washed jeans and a white blouse.

"I think I've got the eleven o'clock," she said.

"Mrs. Pastor may be running a little late," I said.

"Emergency?" the young woman asked, sitting across from me.

"You could say that," I said. "Tootsie Roll?"

She nodded yes and I handed her one.

"Your back?" she asked.

"Haven't been gone," I said.

She laughed. She had a nice deep laugh.

"No," she said, "are you having trouble with your back?"

"No," I said.

"I am," she said, popping the small Tootsie Roll into her mouth. "Ski accident. Tahoe. Last week. Alberta's a wizard with her hands."

"Sorceress," I said. "Wizards are men."

"You are funny," she said.

"I'm not trying to be."

The inner door opened. A man in his sixties on crutches

came out, looked at us. He gave the girl a pained smile. He didn't seem to notice me.

Alberta Pastor, wearing a pair of white trousers and a white short-sleeved T-shirt, stood in the doorway and watched the man leave. Then she looked at the blonde woman and said, "I'm sorry, Christina. I've got to take care of Mr. Fonesca. Could you possibly come tomorrow? Nine? I'll give you a double session and only charge for one."

Christina checked her watch again and said, "I guess I can go to the bank and pick up some things I need on St. Armand's. Nine tomorrow?"

"Nine," said Alberta Pastor.

Christina gave me a thumbs-up and left. Alberta Pastor sat in the chair the young woman had been in and looked at me for the first time.

"I tried to find the Florida Assisted Living and Nursing Home Board of Review when you left my house," she said. "There is no such organization."

"I made it up," I said. "Forgot it when I was out your door. You looked my name up in the phone book."

"Not many Lewis Fonescas in the Sarasota/Bradenton phone book," she said.

"Only two in Chicago," I said. "The other one is my uncle."

"Interesting," she said. "What can I do for you?"

"Confess?"

She shook her head no.

"You tried to kill me," I said. "You're not much of a shot but you did manage to finish off a Dairy Queen Blizzard."

She looked at me calmly and said, "I thought you were someone from Seaside, someone planning to blackmail me. You're not. What are you, Fonesca?"

"I find people," I said.

"And who are you looking for?"

"Vivian Pastor," I said.

"My mother-in-law is at home."

"Mind if I take another root beer barrel?"

"Help yourself," she said.

I did.

"I know the woman in your house isn't your mother-in-law," I said. "Dorothy, one of the Seaside residents, said Vivian was a big woman who played four bingo cards at a time. The woman in your house is nearly a munchkin and I don't think she can tell a bingo card from a Dove bar."

"And?"

"If I bring someone from Seaside to see her," I said, "they'll know she isn't Vivian Pastor. That's what you were afraid of, why you wanted to kill me, why you're packing to leave town. Who is the old woman in your house?"

"My mother," she said. "Your turn."

"You killed your mother-in-law and now you're trying to convince the world that she's not dead. Emmie Jefferson was new at Seaside. First night. She didn't know what Vivian Pastor looked like, saw an old lady in the car with you and assumed with a little help from you that it was your mother-in-law. You were lucky a new nurse was on duty."

She was shaking her head no now.

"Not luck," she said. "Turnover at nursing homes and assisted living facilities is constant. I work in the physical therapy room at Seaside once a week. Let's say I waited till I found out a new nurse was going to be on duty."

"You planned it?"

She leaned forward and spoke softly. "Maybe."

She wanted to talk, wanted to be admired for what she had almost gotten away with.

"But you left your mother-in-law's door open enough

for Dorothy, who was taking a late-night walk, to see you killing her. You saw Dorothy."

Alberta held up her hands. The fingers were long, strong.

"You pushed Vivian's body out the window and climbed out after her. Then you closed the window and moved the body where it wouldn't be seen from the window if Emmie Jefferson came in the room and went to the window."

No answer.

"Dorothy went to the nursing station to report the murder," I said. "You waited till the doors were locked to the outside and you were sure no body had been discovered. Then you pressed the night button. Emmie Jefferson let you in. You pretended you were just coming in and you told Emmie Jefferson—"

"That I'd had Vivian out for the day, that she, my mother-in-law, wanted to leave Seaside immediately. She didn't know the procedure. I told her. Then, I asked her to help me carry Vivian's things out to my car."

"You wanted her to see an old woman in your car."

Alberta was silent.

"Then when Emmie Jefferson went back in, you moved the car right near the end of the building, picked up the body and put it in your trunk without anyone seeing you. Right?"

"Let's for the moment say it's possible."

I reached into my pocket and came up with the folded slipper I had found behind Seaside.

"Now all we have to do is find Cinderella," I said.

"Why would I want to kill Vivian?"

"I know why," I said.

"You can't," she said.

"The Internet is a wondrous thing, especially if you know a hacker," I said. "You are coholder with your mother-in-law of a joint checking account. Her social security checks are directly deposited, sixteen hundred dollars every month. She has an annuity your husband set up for her, twenty-three hundred dollars a month. That gets directly deposited too. Stocks, as of yesterday, worth about 313,000 dollars. You asked a month ago to sell it all and put it into an IRA rollover with quarterly deposits of fifty thousand dollars going into that checking account."

"And don't forget," she said, "with her out of Seaside, I don't have to pay them. There are a lot of perks, Mr. Fonesca, as long as the world thinks Vivian is still alive."

"Just takes the murder of an old woman to get them," I said.

"I haven't got time for any more games with you. I'm going to try to explain but you're not going to understand," she said. "David died broke. Vivian wouldn't help, well, no more than a few thousand here and there. We couldn't touch her money. David wouldn't. The old woman checked her accounts twice a week. David was the cosigner on everything till he died. Then Vivian was advised by Trent to put me on the accounts with her."

"Why?"

"Because I told Trent I'd see to it that a donation of one hundred thousand dollars went to Seaside when Vivian died or, if he preferred, to a charity of his choosing."

"Like the bank account of Amos Trent?"

"His choice," she said. "Anything else?"

"Where's Vivian Pastor's body?"

"Let's say there's a well-fed alligator or two in the lake at Myakka."

She checked her watch, stood up, locked the door, turned to me and said, "I think it should take about ten minutes to kill you but I'll give myself extra time. You're not very big. You'll fit in the closet in the other room. I'll give Jean Herndon her three o'clock session and close up for the day. Then I'll come back sometime after midnight and get you."

I was no match for Alberta Pastor. I needed a weapon. I didn't think a pile of magazines or a wooden candy dish would do.

"I'm really not a bad person."

"Hitler loved dogs and little children. Goebbels's children called Hitler Uncle Adolph."

"Vivian was the monster, not me. With more help from her, David wouldn't have had the stroke. She was eighty-seven years old, Fonesca, and mean as a drunken redneck. She would probably have lived another ten years."

"If you hadn't killed her."

"If I hadn't killed her, yes."

"I'm not a monster," I said, standing. "Why kill me?"

"You're an obstacle. I deserve something more than eight-hour days on my feet, kneading the bodies of people who tell me how they've hurt their shoulders at Vail or slipped a disc in Paris."

I could have thrown the candy dish at her. Tootsie Rolls and root beer barrels would crack against the walls and bounce on the floor, but it wouldn't stop her. I reached for the door to the inner room.

"No place to hide in there," she said, taking a step toward me. "No window. Just a massage table, a pile of towels, a locked cabinet and closet. If you like, you can shout for help, but no one can hear. The door behind me is very thick and nearly soundproof. I'm really sorry about this, really I am."

"That's it. Anything else to say? Like, 'You'll never get away with this,' or 'If I found you, someone else will' or even 'I told someone, maybe the police, where I was going and they'll be here any moment'?"

"All of the above."

Stuart M. Kaminsky

"I don't understand you, Fonesca," she said. "You don't look frightened."

"You do," I said.

She looked at her hands. They were shaking. Then she looked at me.

"I deserve something good," she said. "I've earned it."

It would be more dramatic to say her hands were around my throat and I was trying to get a punch in when the door exploded. But it wasn't like that. She was just standing there, hesitating.

The open door crashed against the wall, hitting Alberta Pastor's left shoulder and sending her into the wall next to me.

Ames stood in the doorway, shotgun in hand.

"You okay?" he asked.

"Yes," I said.

"You do some fool things," he said, his eyes and his gun leveled at Alberta.

She was holding her injured shoulder now. She was also crying.

"I'm not a monster," she sobbed.

19

FOUR HOURS LATER I knocked at Flo's door. She took a long time answering. When she did, she had the baby in her arms and the voice of Johnny Cash behind her telling me he kept his eyes wide open all the time and walked the line.

I could have used Cash's advice when I got up that morning.

"She's sleeping," Flo whispered. "Loves the man in black."

I stepped in and she closed the door.

"Adele?"

"In school. You look like a soaked coyote that's just dragged itself out of the Rio Grande."

Flo's knowledge of coyotes and the Rio Grande were acquired from movies, television and country music. She was a product of New York City, but a longtime citizen of popular country-and-western land.

"Ames is in jail," I said.

"What the hell did he do now?" she said, moving to the sofa in the living room.

I sat in the straight-backed armchair across from her.

"Want to hold her?" she asked, offering the baby.

"No," I said. "No thanks."

Looking at Catherine was all I could handle. I wanted no responsibility. I hadn't been doing very well with responsibility lately, particularly this day.

"He blew an office door open with a shotgun," I said.

"What the hell for?"

"To save my life," I said. "The gun is legal, owned by Ed at the Texas, but Ames has a record. He's not supposed to carry a gun."

"He saved your life?" Flo asked as Johnny Cash rasped out that he kept a close watch on his heart.

"Long story," I said.

"I like long stories," she said. "Just keep it interesting."

I told her what had happened, kept it as short as I could and then said, "When the police came to Alberta Pastor's office, she was crying. Very convincing. She insisted that the police arrest Ames and me. I told them that Alberta was a murderer. There were two of them, both too young to remember when Reagan was president. They took all three of us in. I asked for Ed Viviase. Alberta Pastor asked for her lawyer. I asked for Tycinker."

"Sounds like a goddamn mess," said Flo.

The baby stirred as the song ended. Flo rocked her gently. Johnny walked into a ring of fire and Catherine was still again.

"Alberta said Ames and I were trying to blackmail her about a story we made up about killing her mother-in-law. When she refused to give in to us, we threatened her."

"What about the missing mother-in-law?" asked Flo.

"She said her mother-in-law checked herself out of the Seaside and insisted on being driven to the Tampa airport, where she said she was getting as far away from Sarasota as she could, that she was going to stay with friends. Alberta says her mother-in-law didn't say where she was going."

"But she lied to you about her mother being her mother-in-law," said Flo.

"She says she never said it, that I was making it up on the spot."

"What about the nurse, Emmie Jefferson?" asked Flo, leaning forward.

"They talked to her, showed her a picture of Vivian Pastor. She said it wasn't the woman she had seen in Alberta's car the night of the murder, but Alberta Pastor had never said Gigi was her mother-in-law."

"What's Alberta Pastor say now?"

"She insists that the police conduct a nationwide search for her mother-in-law to prove her story. I told Viviase that Alberta had fed her mother-in-law in pieces to the gators in Myakka Lake."

"How many gators in the lake?" asked Flo. "A few thousand?"

"Right, the police would just have to cut open a few thousand gators looking for body parts," I said.

"You went in ass first and she almost tore it off," said Flo, smoothing down the baby's fine yellow hair.

"I underestimated her," I said.

"Where is she now?"

"Probably at her lawyer's office filing a civil suit against me and Ames."

"They let you go?"

"Viviase believed me," I said. "Told me I should have come to him with what I had instead of going to Alberta's office."

Stuart M. Kaminsky

"He was right, Lewis."

"He was right."

"What's the word? Hubris. That's it, right?" she asked.

"Walked into a ring of fire," I said. "Brought Ames with me. We got burned."

"And you want me to buy you asbestos suits or did you just feel the need to tell your tale to someone who'd listen to you and pat you on the cheek and say, 'Poor boy'?"

"I'll settle for you coming up with Ames's bail."

"Good," she said, standing up. "I'll get Catherine dressed and we'll go down and get the Lone Ranger out of the jail. One condition."

"What's that?"

"Stop feeling sorry for yourself and nail the bitch. Deal?"

"Deal," I said.

When we got to the lockup on Ringling Boulevard, Viviase met us and ran the maze to get Ames out. He also told me that there was a restraining order against Ames and me. We couldn't get within sight of Alberta Pastor.

Ames needed a shave. Catherine was awake and made it clear she wanted to be fed. I wanted someone to tell me to pack up and get out of town.

"Fonesca," Viviase said, his face pink, his red tie loose. "You are in serious need of a shrink."

"I've got one," I said.

"Double your sessions," he said. "You were an investigator for the Cook County states attorney. You had to know what could happen when you went into Pastor's office. What'd you think? She'd just break down, confess, say she was sorry, take a plea with the district attorney?"

He was right.

"She killed her husband's mother," said Ames.

"And she's going to pay for it, right?" said Viviase with

a sigh. "You have any idea of how many murderers are driving around the city drinking coffee at Starbucks, deciding if their next car is going to be a Lexus or a . . . the hell with it. You two."

He pointed at Ames and me.

"You two come with me and you, Mrs. Zink, the baby's hungry," Viviase said.

"I'll get her home," Flo said.

"You do that," he said.

"I'll call you later, Flo," I said. "Thanks."

"Let's go," Viviase said when Flo went through the door.

"Where?"

"To talk to a witness who might be able to save your very pathetic carcass," he said, leading the way through a thick steel door. "But don't count on it."

"Who?" asked Ames.

"Georgia Cubbins," he said.

We turned a corner, walked down a narrow corridor of polished white concrete. Viviase stopped at a door, reached for it.

"McKinney, you wait here," he said.

"Who's Georgia Cubbins?" I asked.

"Alberta Pastor's mother," he said. "Gigi."

"But she—" I started as he opened the door.

"I told you not to count on it," he said.

We were in a small dark room without furniture. In front of us was a glass partition, a two-way mirror. Beyond the window seated at a table was the old woman I had last seen at the Pastor house concentrating on newspaper ads and coupons in a state that could be called out-of-it. A very thin young woman in her early thirties wearing a white blouse and dark skirt sat across from Gigi Cubbins, who was drinking from a white porcelain mug. She held the mug in both

Stuart M. Kaminsky

hands and nodded, smiling at something the young woman, who had a pad of yellow, lined legal paper in front of her and a pen in her hand, said.

"Alberta Pastor's lawyer is out looking for a judge, the chief of police, the governor or the president of the United States to get her mother out of here," Viviase said. "If we're lucky, we've got about half an hour."

He pushed a button on the wall and we could hear what was being said inside the room beyond.

The young woman held up two fingers and said, "Mrs. Cubbins, how many fingers am I holding up?"

The old woman's eyes widened and she said, "You mean you don't know how many fingers you're holding up?"

"Yes, I know."

"So do I," Georgia Cubbins said.

"How many?" asked the young woman patiently.

"Two."

"Good."

"What is?"

The young woman reached over and patted Gigi's wrinkled hand.

"Do you know your husband's name?"

"He's dead," Gigi said.

"Yes, but do you know what his name is?"

"Was," Gigi said, putting down her cup and looking puzzled. "Is it still his name if he's dead?"

"Yes," the young woman said.

"Good."

"What was his name?"

"Samuel."

"Good and—"

"Walter."

"Was it Samuel or Walter?" the young woman asked.

DENIAL

"Samuel Walter Cubbins," Gigi said with a smile.

"And your son-in-law?"

"Dead too. Almost everyone is."

"His name?"

"My . . . ?"

"Your daughter's husband."

"David."

"Your daughter's name?"

"Turnkey."

"Her name is Turnkey?"

"It's what I call her. Her name is Albert, no, Alberta."

"Good."

"It's good that her name is Alberta? Wasn't my idea. My husband's mother was named Alberta. I never liked the name."

"Okay," the young woman said.

"Did I pass?" asked Gigi.

"Yes. Do you mind if a policeman asks you a few questions?"

"Not silly ones like 'What's your name?'"

"I don't think so."

The young woman got up and said, "It was nice to meet you, Mrs. Cubbins."

Viviase opened the door to the room beyond the two-way mirror and the woman stepped out.

"What do you think?" he asked.

She looked at me, pursed her lips and shrugged.

"Dementia's there," she said, "but I think she likes to play games. She also doesn't like her daughter."

Viviase entered the room beyond the window. There was a crackle on the speaker when Viviase said brightly, "Good evening, Mrs. Cubbins."

The old woman looked up at him in confusion. I saw no

Stuart M. Kaminsky

hope beyond the sheet of glass. I looked at Ames, who stood at near military attention, his eyes fixed on the old woman.

Viviase sat at the table. A uniformed woman stood against the wall.

"Do you mind if I turn on the tape recorder?" he asked, taking a small, silver recorder out of his jacket pocket and putting it on the table.

Georgia Cubbins looked at the recorder.

"It's okay, Gigi," said Viviase gently. "I can call you Gigi?"

"Oh yes," she said. "You know, Walgreen's has a two-for-one special on aspirin, the hundred-tablet size."

"I didn't know that," Viviase said.

"You'll need a coupon."

Viviase pressed the record button, sat back and said, "How's your coffee?"

"Tea," Georgia Cubbins corrected. "With pretend sugar."

"Right," said Viviase. "May I ask you some questions?"

"Questions?"

"About your daughter," he said.

"Alberta," said the old woman. "Her name is Alberta."

"Yes, Alberta. And about Vivian Pastor."

"Oh, Vivian is dead," said the woman. "So is David. He's my son-in-law."

"Dead?"

"Oh yes. David is *d-e-d*."

"And Vivian Pastor?"

"Dead. Alberta cut her up into little pieces and we went to the lake and she threw the pieces to the alligators."

Georgia Cubbins was smiling.

"We stopped on the way home for coffee and apple pie. I don't remember where, but the waitresses had those little white hats, like the Jews, only white and not black."

"They were Amish," Viviase said.

"That's their business," Gigi said.

Georgia Cubbins might be well on the way to total dementia, but no one but her daughter could have spoken to her about cutting up Vivian Pastor and feeding her to the gators.

Viviase reached forward and turned off the recorder.

"You know you can see through water," Georgia Cubbins said. "If it's clean water."

"That's interesting," said Viviase, rising and putting the tape recorder in his pocket. "Officer Willett will get you more tea if you'd like."

"With pretend sugar," she said seriously.

"Pretend sugar," Viviase said, touching the old woman's shoulder.

Viviase came out of the room and closed the door.

"Too damned easy," he said.

"I think she wanted to tell someone," the young woman next to me said. "Just waiting for the first one to ask her."

"Not much of a witness, is she?" asked Viviase.

The young woman shrugged.

"I'm taking this to the district attorney," he said. "I think we've got cause for keeping Mrs. Cubbins in protective custody. There's reason to believe her life might be in danger if we returned her to the custody of her daughter."

"She's not a good witness," I said.

"Understatement, Fonesca," he said. "She is one hell of an awful witness, but she's enough to keep the investigation open, to put a hold on Vivian Pastor's social security checks, checking accounts, annuity payments. It's a start."

Ames was waiting for me outside the room. I told him we had another stop to make.

Amos Trent didn't have to intercept us at the Seaside this

time. He was in his office working late. I knocked at his door and he looked up.

"What?" he asked.

"I think the police are going to be calling you," I said.

"Why?"

"I think the police may be about to arrest Alberta Pastor for the murder of her mother-in-law," I said.

Trent said, "No," and closed his eyes. When he opened them, Ames and I were still there.

"Might want to apologize to Dorothy," said Ames.

"No," he said. "I mean yes. Everything I touch turns to shit. This is my fourth job in three years, my fourth job. I've got an MBA but . . . I'm a haunted man."

He looked at us for sympathy. I knew what it was to be haunted. He would have to deal with his own ghosts.

Dorothy Cgnozic was sitting in the armchair in her room watching a rerun of a rerun of *Hollywood Squares*. She was wearing a pink robe. The room was dark except for the glowing screen. It took her a beat or two to recognize us. She reached over her shoulder and turned on the lamp on the table by her bed.

"Tell me something good," she said. "I need something good."

"The woman who you saw murdered was Vivian Pastor," I said. "Her daughter-in-law killed her."

Dorothy pushed a button on her remote and the screen of her television went black.

"The people here know?" she asked.

"We just told Amos Trent," I said.

"I think maybe Mr. Trent's going to be looking for another job," said Ames.

"That wasn't what I wanted," she said. "I just wanted to be believed. I'm sorry about Vivian. I can't say I particularly liked her, but I would prefer her not to have been murdered."

"Want to know what's going to happen to Mrs. Pastor?" I asked.

"No," she said. "I'm content to leave that to the police and her God."

She stood, opened a drawer in the table on which the lamp was standing and came up with a box and a manuscript of the book she had shown us before. She opened the box and the three of us had a chocolate-covered cherry.

"Will a check be all right?" she said.

"Fine."

She handed the manuscript to Ames, fished out a checkbook, asked me how much she owed. I told her a hundred dollars would do it. After she had written the check and handed it to me, Ames held the manuscript out to her.

"No," she said. "It's for you. You remember my husband's work. It should be with someone who appreciated him."

"Thank you," Ames said and shook the hand she offered.

"One condition," she said.

Ames waited.

"You visit me once in a while," she said. "If it's not too much to ask."

"I'm looking forward to it," said Ames.

"I'll walk you out," she said. "I've got people to tell and vindication to savor."

I had another stop to make. It could have waited till the next day but I wasn't sure there would be a next day and I didn't want to think about what I was going to say.

I called the number Nancy Root had given me. Yolanda answered.

"Fonesca," I said.

"I know," she said. "You want to come over right now and pick up your check."

Stuart M. Kaminsky

"I want to talk to your mother," I said.

"Some other time," she said.

Then Nancy Root came on the line.

"Mr. Fonesca, I've been trying to call you. Can you come over now?"

I told her I could and she gave me directions to her apartment. When we got there, Ames waited in the car while I pushed a button and was buzzed in through the thick glass doors.

The lobby was large and lifeless. The lights were night dim. I had the feeling that the couches and chairs had seldom been sat in and the artificial flowers had never been touched.

Nancy Root met me at the open door. She was wearing jeans and an oversize white sweater. I took off my cap. She said nothing, stood back and let me pass. In the small entryway was a bank of posters of plays she had been in, *Man and Superman, Antigone, You Can't Take It with You, Othello*.

"This way," she said.

I followed her into a living room with a night view of lights on the bridge to St. Armand's and Longboat Key. Yolanda sat in a large, white armchair big enough for her to tuck her bare feet under her. She was hugging a pillow. She watched me as if I might be about to grab the family jewels and make a run for it.

Nancy Root nervously rolled up her sleeves. For the next ten minutes the sleeves kept creeping down and she tugged them up again. She pointed to the couch with its back to the window and sat in a chair just like the one Yolanda was in.

I sat.

"I thought you might have a show tonight," I said.

"Sometimes," said Nancy Root, "the show does not have to go on. In this case, however, the understudy is an Asolo Conservatory student who is very good, too young for the role, but, then again, I'm a little too old for it. I haven't offered you a drink."

"No thanks," I said.

Yolanda was glaring at me. I saw the glitter of her tongue ring when she opened her mouth.

"I know who killed Kyle," Nancy said. "I know all about what Richard did. I'm glad the man is dead. I'm glad there won't be a trial, delays, testimony, excuses, deals. The only thing wrong with the scenario is that I don't know why he killed my son. Why would a college teacher purposely run down a fourteen-year-old boy?"

Choices. Tell her the truth, that a man who prided himself on his understanding of morality, of right and wrong, had turned into a vengeance-seeking animal because his Down's syndrome daughter had been spat upon? That her son had stopped in the street and taunted his pursuer with an upraised finger, defied him because Kyle Root was frightened and angry and fourteen years old and had never thought about death? Tell her to ask Andrew Goines, her son's friend who could have been the one John Welles had chosen to follow, to kill?

"Was he drunk, high?" Yolanda said. "Was he insane?"

Her face was tight. Her eyes met mine. She was trying to tell me something. I thought I knew what it was.

"I don't know," I lied. "He didn't get a chance to tell me. I think he was going to talk about it but your ex-husband showed up. Welles had a gun. . . ."

I shrugged.

Nancy Root sank back in her chair once again, adjusting the sleeves of her sweater. She folded her hands and put the white knuckles of her thumbs to her lips.

I looked at Yolanda. I couldn't swear to it but I thought she gave me a barely existent nod of approval.

Stuart M. Kaminsky

"Okay," said Nancy, suddenly standing. "I'll get your check."

She hurried out of the room.

"Andy told me," Yolanda said.

"Told you?"

"Told me about what he and Kyle did," she said.

I looked toward where Nancy Root had exited.

"She'll take a few minutes," Yolanda said. "She's crying. I know Kyle. Knew him. She just thinks she does. If that dead guy backed him into a corner, Kyle would just tell him to screw himself or give him the finger."

Something must have shown on my face. Yolanda smiled, but there wasn't any satisfaction in the smile.

"Got it, right?" she asked.

I didn't say anything. Nancy came back in, check in hand, eyes red. She handed me the check.

"Yola's moving back in with me," she said. "We need each other."

Yolanda didn't deny the mutual need, but I didn't see any sign of it on her part.

"That's right," she said.

Nancy Root walked with me out to the elevator, adjusting her sleeves one more time as the bell dinged and the elevator doors opened. I got in.

"Thank you," she said and as the doors closed, she added, "The hardest part is not knowing."

It was almost ten. Ames and I drove to the Texas, had a beer and burger and looked at the manuscript of *Two Many Words*. Part One, *Too Many Words*, was about fifty pages long, each one with a crude drawing and no words. The drawings were of birds, people, pieces of luggage piled in an airport waiting area, a clock, a pencil, tables, a rabbit that resembled Bugs Bunny. Part Two, *To Many Words*, was also about fifty pages long, neatly handwritten in black ink, probably the longest single sentence ever written.

> I began my search for the sunlight as I came out of the womb, my search for sunlight and God, and found sunlight pretty quickly, and darkness too, but I have the feeling that someday I'll go back into that womb and find that God had been there waiting for me the whole while and he'll say, Where the hell have you been, and I'll say, Looking for you, and he'll say, What the hell for, to which I will tell him that I wanted to know why I had been plucked timely from the warm darkness and sent out to grow old, feel pain and doubt, love and be loved, laugh and be laughed at, doubt and be doubted, and old God will answer saying I had just answered my own question

And words kept coming, but I stopped reading over Ames's shoulder. I left him sitting there and knew that he would keep reading to the last word. I wondered if there would be a period after the last word. I meant to ask Ames in the morning.

Back in my office, it took about ten minutes before the phone rang. It was Viviase.

"Alberta Pastor is gone," he said. "Packed up, got in her car, ran. Her lawyer says he doesn't know where she went. She's got no money but whatever she had on her and a Visa credit card. We'll track her down. Looks like we'll drop the charges against you and McKinney, except for the illegal weapon. Given the situation, the district attorney is willing to accept a fifty-dollar fine, an apology and the promise that Mr. McKinney's love affair with firearms will not be hands-on."

"Thanks," I said.

"I thought about telling you to stay out of trouble," he said. "But that won't happen, will it?"

"It finds me," I said.

"Maybe you welcome it."

"You sound like Ann," I said.

"Ann?"

"My therapist," I said.

We hung up and I did a dangerous thing. I should have washed, gotten into my pajamas and watched a Thin Man movie, but I sat at the desk, looked at the painting of the dark jungle on the wall, had trouble finding the spot of color and thought.

I thought about a dead philosopher and a smiling parentless girl with Down's syndrome. I thought about a father who had lost his only son and had helped the boy's killer commit suicide. I thought of a mother whom I had faced and told about what had happened to her dead son. I thought about an old woman whose mind was slowly slipping away and I tried not to wonder what would happen to her. I thought about my dead wife and my dead life. I thought about them till I fell asleep at the desk with my head on my arms.

I wanted nothing but to be left alone, maybe for a day, a week, a month, a year, forever.

THE LAST CHAPTER

THAT IS THE STORY I told Ann Horowitz. Not exactly in those words, but essentially that was it.

It took us through lunch. She called and had a pizza delivered, half double onion for me, half spinach for her. During my telling she had to use my phone to reschedule three appointments.

She assured me that none of the appointments was within years of approaching emergency status.

"You have forty dollars?" she asked.

"Yes."

"We've been here four sessions," she said. "I won't charge you for a house call."

"I didn't call you and this isn't a house," I said.

"Sarcasm?"

"No," I said.

"I was hoping for sarcasm. You are a tough case, Lewis. Are you sure you aren't Catholic?"

"I'm sure."

"You think it would work out if Georgia Cubbins moved into Seaside and shared a room with Dorothy Cgnozic?"

"No," I said.

"How about if Jane Welles moved in with Adele and Flo?"

"No," I said.

"Do you think either of those suggestions was serious?"

"No."

"Why?"

"You're too smart."

"Thank you," she said. "It's getting late. I still have to get back to the apartment, put on my bathing suit and do my twenty laps. If I miss my laps I get grumpy. Have you ever seen me grumpy?"

"No."

"I'll have to let you see that side of me sometime," she said.

"I'll look forward to it."

"So, let's get to the heart of darkness," she said. "Why do you do what you do?"

"Serve papers?"

"Yes, and help people in need find other people they think they need," she said.

"I serve papers to make enough money to live. I find people because I can't stop people from finding me."

"Because they sense in you a person who will empathize, will find, will give them closure?"

"Maybe."

"You could make money other ways than serving papers, finding people."

"I'm good at it."

"Professor Welles could have shot you. Alberta Pastor could have strangled you."

"I know," I said. "I'm suicidal, but I don't want to commit suicide. I want someone to do it for me."

"Like Welles?"

"No," I said.

"No," she said. "Here comes the profound part, the part where I really earn my money. You feel guilty about your wife's death. You've convinced yourself at one level that you deserve to die, but you know you don't want to die and that makes you feel guilty."

"This sounds like the end of *Psycho*," I said. "Where the psychiatrist gives a pompous explanation of why Norman Bates isn't a transvestite."

"Interesting choice for comparison," Ann said.

"In the end Norman Bates is sitting alone in his cell, smiling, determined never to speak again," I said.

"I remember," she said. "But I've got a solution for you, well, at least a possible solution. You are helping other people search because something is keeping you from searching for the person who might give you some relief. Who am I talking about? Who, with your skills, could you be looking for?"

Silence. Silence. Silence. Except for the cars whooshing down 301 beyond my window.

"Lewis, a swimming pool of uncertain temperature beckons."

"The one who killed my wife," I said.

"Why didn't you, with your skills, stay in Chicago and find that person instead of driving more than a thousand miles to hide behind a Dairy Queen?"

"She was gone. Finding who did it wouldn't bring her back," I said. "We've talked about this."

"No, Lewis," she said. "I am old, nearly ancient, but my

memory is trained and I take very good notes. If you've talked to anyone about it, it is Lewis Fonesca."

"So?"

"You have clung with great tenacity to your grief," she said.

"Finding the person who killed my wife . . ."

"Catherine."

"Catherine," I said. "Finding the person who killed Catherine might help me give up my grief?"

"You tell me," she said.

"I don't know. Even if I did try, where would I be if I failed?"

"It is a no-lose situation," she said. "You find the person and that part ends. You fail to find the person and you know that you tried. Your life of quiet desperation will always be waiting for you in these two rooms, at least until they demolish the building."

Ann got up. I opened my wallet and handed her two twenty-dollar bills, which she tucked into the outer pocket of her briefcase.

There was a knock at the door. Ann looked at me. I nodded my head yes to let her know it was all right to answer it.

Sally was standing there.

"Lew," she said. "Thought you'd like to know that Jane Welles is going with her aunt to Reno tomorrow."

Ann touched Sally's shoulder and left the office. Sally stood in the doorway waiting.

"How would you like to go to Flo's for a barbecue dinner tonight? The kids, Adele, Ames?"

"No," I said.

"Good," said Sally. "Because there is no dinner. What there is, is a pair of tickets to a movie at Burns Court. You can't say no. I already bought the tickets."

"I don't go out to movies," I said.

"You were going to take Darrell."

"I would have found a way out."

"Life is full of new and crazy adventures, Lewis," she said. "Look, I just got off of a fourteen-hour day. My feet hurt. I can't stop seeing the face of a ten-year-old girl I think is being abused by her stepfather and I need a movie. Help me out here. Don't make me work for it."

"Let's go see a movie," I said.

"Good. You were a real hit with Darrell."

Sally smiled as I folded the empty pizza box and shoved it in the wastebasket. I tried to smile back.

"Made a decision," I said.

"Tell me about it on the way," she said. "The movie starts in fifteen minutes."

"It'll just take a few seconds," I said. "I'm going to find the person who killed my wife."

"Which means you're not going to lock yourself in your office in the morning?"

"No," I said. "I'm not going to lock myself in my office. No."

Stuart M. Kaminsky